Miss Wetherham's Wedding

The Brides of Mayfair
Book Three

LINORE ROSE BURKARD

LILLIPUT PRESS
OHIO

MISS WETHERHAM'S WEDDING
Copyright © 2021 by Linore Rose Burkard
Published by LILLIPUT PRESS
OHIO 45068

Publishers Cataloging-in-Publication Data
Name: Burkard, Linore Rose, author
Title: miss wetherham's wedding / by Linore Rose Burkard
Description: 1st edition
Summary: A widowed matchmaker in Regency England must help a handsome man win his bride but falls in love with him herself.

Identifiers: Library of Congress Control Number: 2021905208

ISBN: 978-1-7333111-9-9 (print) / ISBN: 978-1-7333111-8-2 (ebk)
Subjects: 1. Fiction—Romance, Historical, Regency 2.Fiction—Romance, Clean and Sweet

Printed in the United States of America

What Readers Are Saying About
Miss Wetherham's Wedding

5 STARS

"**Lushly romantic,** especially the epilog. **Linore Rose Burkard is the queen of Regency Romance.** I will have to read and enjoy this one again!"
DeAnna Julie Dodson

5 STARS

"**Absolutely delightful** from the first page to the last. And by LAST, I mean the VERY, VERY, end to the outtakes!"
Sarah Sarber, Blogger

5 STARS

"**Regency fiction at its best. Romance and intrigue** (lead) the reader into through a tangled web to a very satisfying ending."
Janice Dick, Author, *Out of the Storm*

5 STARS

"**Fun, engaging story, a devilish hero you have to love**, and a corkscrew plot that makes you wonder if there's a way out! Highly recommended."
Teresa Slack, Author, *Willow Wood Brides*

5 STARS

"**Misunderstandings and machinations abound** in this delightful Regency Romance! Just the sort of fun book I needed at this time. Highly recommend."
Brittany Searfoss

A Note from the Author

for readers who are also writers

Please be aware from the outset that I write in omniscient POV. That is, in 3rd person, but unlike limited 3rd person, I can move freely between characters. This allows me to write a scene more like a movie camera, capturing the inner life of more than one character in quick succession. Experience tells me that many writers of today are not up to snuff with what omniscient POV is. This is not their fault; many writing instructors are equally ill-informed, calling every use of omniscient POV "head hopping." Oh, dear.

Please be advised: "Head hopping" in its pejorative sense occurs when a reader cannot tell whose head they're supposed to be in. Head hopping is confusing; it is omniscient POV done poorly.

My readers always know whose head they're in. You may not be accustomed to this point of view in storytelling, so consider this fair warning! Please don't leave me a bad review because you are unfamiliar with the technique.

Also, please note that I have used British spellings in keeping with the British setting.

Now that we've got that settled, I hope you enjoy the story!

--Linore Rose Burkard

Special Back of the Book

Bonus Content

Never Before Released: OUTTAKES

and

A SHORT GLOSSARY OF REGENCY TERMS

Love doesn't just sit there like a stone; it has to be made, like bread, remade all the time, made new.

—*URSULA K.LEGUIN*

Prologue

Lettie clung to dear Steven for a long, sweet kiss, though they stood right in the doorway of their Georgian brick home on Russell Square, for today he was leaving. The sky was inky black, the road empty of carriages and foot traffic. Dawn wouldn't arrive for an hour. Earlier, in their bedchamber, she'd savoured each second of their union, the feel of his lean body against hers, the meeting of heart, mind, and soul that happened during the mystery of joining as man and wife.

Steven Wetherham, her husband of two years, was embarking by ship on a long, perilous voyage to the coast of Africa. Once the schooner left its London dock, he would be gone from her for eight months or more, depending upon how the business went. He was sailing to visit their diamond mine.

"Dearest, must you go?" she asked for the hundredth time, resting her head against his firm chest.

At first a lucrative endeavour, the previous two years had seen the mine's storehouse of gems drying up. They'd moved from fashionable Curzon Street to the outskirts of Mayfair to economise, but continued to invest in the mine, sending teams to discover new veins, hoping to revive it. But it gave up nothing, while, with an endless appetite, swallowing their savings.

"You know I must, darling," Steven murmured into her ear. His warm breath spread like a familiar blanket over her heart. "Other mines have seemed to run dry but then been wonderfully productive. It only took the right man to determine where to blast. With all the research I've done, we are sure to find a new vein. I feel it in my bones!"

Lettie was to remain in London, but not entirely alone. Cousins Horace and Harriette Cantrell, and Horace's wife Amelia, were in town for the Season. Harriette was a spinster.

Ignoring the presence of the butler and one footman, Steven and Lettie kissed once more, a last, lingering, desperate attempt to maintain their oneness. When their lips parted, he dropped his hands to her arms and said earnestly, "Move into the light. Let me memorise your face, your lovely face and eyes and hair."

"You haven't forgot my miniature portrait?"

"No; but it does you no justice." He paused, studying her as with the eyes of a painter, taking in every detail. Steven adored her champagne blonde hair, high cheekbones, full lips, and determined chin. "Promise me," he said gravely.

"Anything, dearest!"

"Promise me. If anything should happen—"

Lettie frowned. "Do not even conceive of such a thing!"

"We'll be rounding the Horn, as you know. Many ships capsize there."

"You'll get through. You have a marvellous captain, and his ship, *Fair Haven*, has made dozens of safe journeys, you told me yourself."

"Promise anyway."

"Promise what?"

"If something happens. When you fall in love again with someone else—"

"Dearest!"

"Promise you will only love a good man, a trusted man, and

that it will not be the same way you love me. Our love must always be special."

Lettie stared, unable to speak, her mind a torment.

"Say it, dearest. That you will only consider good men, and never have again what we have had."

A tear spilled from one of her eyes. "But I needn't make such a promise at all!"

Steven's eyes were a storm of sorrow. "Say it anyway, darling, please!"

She sniffed, and her voice broke with emotion as she choked out the words, "No love shall ever be…could ever be to me as our love!" Her heart ached at the words just as if she had lost him, as if saying such words made it certain. "But I maintain, I shall never love another!"

She'd tried to stay strong this morning of their farewell. It was the first real parting since they'd wed. She'd determined not to let him see her cry, for a tear-stained countenance, and red nose and eyes, was not the image she wished to send him off with. Especially her nose. When Lettie cried, her nose turned red. It must not be his last glimpse of her.

But it was no use. When he kissed her cheek one last time, tears were kissed away. He whispered, "Thank you, dearest. I love you always." He touched a finger gently to her nose. "From your darling red nose to the tips of your feet. My heart is yours for as long as God gives me breath."

With eyes full of both excitement and sorrow, he took his hat and cane from Dudley, their butler, and, blowing her yet another kiss, turned toward the carriage in the street. His heels clicked on the pavement as he hurried to step up into the compartment. Lettie waved her handkerchief and smiled through tears at him as the carriage wheels rumbled off. Then she dabbed at more tears, which continued falling.

She must not despair. Steven would be back. Why, there were ships rounding the Horn every day. And he hadn't gone off to war, as many another lady's husband had done. He wasn't about to join a militia against the Corsican. She had no good cause for alarm.

As she plodded back to their bedchamber—a place which now seemed desolate without him—she knew she'd have her hands full trying to keep the worries at bay. Happily, she had pin money and would bespeak a new gown. Steven had made sure to leave her with pin money. It wasn't at all the same as her allowance when the diamonds were plentiful, but it would do. And once the mine began producing again, things would return to normal and they'd move back to Curzon Street. Besides, it was the start of the Season. She'd stay busy by accompanying the Cantrells to entertainments, concerts, and balls. Mayhap she would help some neglected girl find a husband. Lettie had a knack for making matches. Her only failure was Cousin Harriette, a determined spinster.

Yes, London was full of diversions; and time, Lettie was sure, would pass swiftly, bringing dear Steven home again and into her arms.

Chapter One

Nicholas Dellacort, in a beautifully tailored jacket with fitted knee-breeches, white stockings and black shoes, joined his friend Mr. Stewart Trafford watching a throng of dancers at Almack's. Trafford turned at his arrival, saw the instantly recognizable thick dark hair and profile with its Roman nose, and cried, "Nick! Gad, didn't expect to see you here. Mr. Dellacort at Almack's—a singular night for the society columns, I warrant."

Nick raised a brow but said nothing.

"Thought you'd be with that lovely apparition known as Miss Sophia Alden," continued Trafford.

Nick's lips hardened. "The apparition is enjoying the attentions of that tulip Elston, Earl Brest, as we speak; and with the full approval of her deuced parents."

"But her papa welcomed you! He let it out that he fancied you as his future son-in-law after a certain happy event shall occur."

"I never made an offer." He flicked a miniscule speck off his immaculate jacket of jet-black superfine.

"And now you're sorry for it?"

"I'm sorry the marquess discovered new revenue attached to the estate his son is to inherit and dangled it before the Aldens. Suddenly Sophia's papa was distinctly less friendly to me, and more to him." He grimaced. "He turned me out, if you must know."

Trafford's eyes bulged. "Turned out the incomparable Dellacort? Lud, that Elston must be swimming in lard!" But a smile played at the edges of his lips, and he shook his head with mock sympathy. "Tsk, tsk. Never thought I'd see the day when your coattails were turned, by Jove!"

"Try not to relish it overmuch," was the acid reply. "I've a plan to turn the tables."

"Miss Alden must be more alluring than I recall," said Mr. Trafford. "I've never seen you battle for love's sake."

"Of course not," Dellacort murmured. "I much prefer to let our softer sex battle over me."

"What is your plan? How will you convince Miss Alden to look away from Midas when all is gold there?"

Dellacort turned to his friend with a sagacious smile. "That's the beauty of it. I shan't have to. The trick is to turn Elston's head, not hers. He's not in love, just under the hatches with the marquess until he finds a wife; which means that another pretty face more amiable than Sophia's should do. But there's no time to spare. If the Aldens press for a hasty wedding, the whole muddle will have thickened beyond repair."

"So that's why you're here. Dellacort at Almack's is rarer than a brace of pheasants in Hyde Park! You wish to find an unsuspecting chit to foist off on the earl!"

"Is there a better place to find a girl eager for a husband? I warrant there are fair damsels here, graduates from the 'school of amiability,' who have mastered the art of pleasing just such a man. And what young woman would shun the chance to become a future marchioness?"

"How will you make your intentions clear? Every mama here will be equally amenable to making a match for her daughter with you, as you well know."

Nick sighed. "I'll risk that; until I can arrange an introduction to Elston."

"Arranging an introduction is nothing; but managing to get the heir to take your bait—that may take some trickery."

Nick's lips curled. "I've been told Elston is denser than a Yorkshire pudding; he's got no wit and can't hope to equal Miss Alden. All we need is a fair conjurer with a dowry, an eager girl who is certain to turn his head."

"Long enough for you to descend upon the Aldens, make your offer, and win the hand of the beauty, is that it?"

Dellacort looked out at the long, high-ceilinged room, his eyes far away. "I suppose. I hadn't decided if I wished to offer for her. Elston's arrival removed the possibility."

Trafford eyed his friend with amusement. "I think there is more of male pride to be restored than a love relationship."

"Either way," replied Dellacort. "I must win."

"In that case, sir, as your friend, I am at your service." He looked out at the ballroom with fresh interest. "Surely there must be unclaimed beauties in abundance here. And of the best families."

Nick joined him in surveying the roomful of white gowned figures of all statures and girths, many of them seemingly fresh from the schoolroom.

"How does Miss Gotham strike you?" Stewart motioned with his head toward a shy looking creature staring timidly out at the room.

"Cheeks red as apples," replied Dellacort. "High nerves; she'd swoon at the introduction."

"Very well. Here's Miss Westerville. Quite pretty, I think."

Dellacort surveyed the lady in question. She was of average height and build, with unremarkable brown hair, and a common face. "I recollect her; it's her second season, meaning she isn't as pretty as all that."

Stewart continued searching the room. "Ah! There is the famous Miss Grenville. She makes every hostess happy with her witty conversation."

"Wit can be entertaining," returned Dellacort smoothly, "but not enough to disguise a face like a flattened biscuit!" He turned and gave Stewart a reproving look. "I'm looking for beauty, Stewart, to stand up against Miss Alden, recall."

Stewart nodded with proper remorse. "Of course."

Two young women walked past, keeping their eyes rigidly ahead. Before Stewart could speak, Dellacort said, "One, too long in the face, and the other, shadowed eyes."

Stewart pursed his lips. "Come, Nick, we don't need a Helen of Troy; a pretty enough face will do very well indeed; and if we pair it with a fortune corresponding to Elston's, he'll call it a heaven-made match."

"Fortunes that correspond to Elston's are not everywhere to be found, not even at Almack's," returned Dellacort.

Three more young women were dismissed by Nick with equal ease. "That one? Timid as a dormouse." Another, "What are you thinking? Too old by far. Surely past twenty-five. And when Stewart referred to a passing bright-eyed girl as a delicate swan, his friend retorted, "long-necked as one, I own!"

"Here's a pretty-tempered girl," said Stewart beneath his breath as an attractive brunette came their way. "They call her Miss Prim for her exceedingly proper manners. A future marquess would appreciate formality in his wife."

"To be known as Miss Prim in this society," replied Dellacort, "when most all women are proper by habit indicates a severe lack of good humour. Elston must want some spirit in his wife. Miss Alden is full spirited, I assure you."

Now there is a pretty woman," offered Stewart, who was growing exasperated with his friend. He nodded at Miss Chippendale whose hair was piled high and ornamented with strings of pearls cascading in shining rows along ebony hair. Dellacort surveyed her a moment and then snorted, "Never ceases to prattle, that one. She'd terrify the earl. We wish to enrapture him, not send him running."

"You are severe upon the softer sex!" Stewart admonished. "We'll never find the lady you want, for it must be Miss Alden herself. I begin to think there is no paragon of femininity who can approach her."

But suddenly Dellacort's eyes were fastened across the room upon a slim, flaxen-haired young woman coming from another room, trailed by two ladies and a renowned bore known as Mr. Nitts, who seemed determined to claim her attention. While he prattled and motioned with his arms, she barely acknowledged him but was smiling as though endeavouring not to laugh. She had an appealing, bright smile. She took a seat against a far wall, the two other women at her sides, and Mr. Nitts, still talking, stood before them.

"Who is that chit in the centre with the winsome smile?" he asked. "And why did you not suggest her? She may be the handsomest woman in this room, if I mistake me not, though she is in need of fashion advice; but she has an appearance of intelligence."

Mr. Trafford turned to look. "Miss Wetherham. Won't do—an ace of spades. Her husband died when he was endeavouring to explore a diamond mine they'd invested their fortune in."

"A widow? Then she is no 'miss,' but a 'missus.'"

"The ladies call her Miss Wetherham; say it's more genteel." He paused. "And she needs all the gentility she can get. It just came out—" He lowered his voice as if imparting a morsel of great secrecy. "She charges a fee for her matchmaking. It's bound to get around, and, when it does, you know as well as I that she won't be welcome in these hallowed halls again."

Stewart gazed thoughtfully at the lady in question. He paused. "Those are her relations with her, Harriette Cantrell and her sister-in-law Amelia."

Nick surveyed Miss Wetherham's vivacious, attractive face. "The husband died three years ago? And still a widow?"

Stewart had a ready answer. "She's the type says she'll never remarry; won't risk another heartbreak."

Dellacort raised a brow. "He had the decency to leave her well off, I trust?"

Trafford leaned in again as if to impart another secret. "We all thought so. The diamond mine, you know. But apparently it an't producing. He left her out at the seams. The ladies say she alters her gowns from previous seasons." Stewart sighed pityingly. "She's nought but a Cambridge fortune, now. A smile to light a room, but she'd be in the duns if not for her knack for arranging marriages. She takes on girls who are, let us say, difficult to place."

Dellacort's look was thoughtful. "Arranges marriages, you say? The very thing we are endeavouring to do, and you had no thought of giving me notice of her?"

"Well, it's how she butters her bread, but to remain respectable it must come off as the veriest lark. Finances are strictly under the table. You cannot simply approach her and make a proposition." He sighed. "Poor thing. She'll be barred from crossing the threshold of this institution, I needn't remind you, if she don't carry out her business henceforth with the strictest delicacy."

Dellacort turned and gave Trafford a curious look. "You are well versed in this lady's affairs."

Trafford shrugged, but cleared his throat. "No more than in a common way, I assure you. You know I attend the best scandal broths."

Dellacort turned to regard Miss Wetherham again. He saw a handsome woman gowned in sweet white cambric with a lace fichu tucked into the bust for modesty; she had nothing of a sepulchral look of mourning. Rather than endeavouring not to laugh, as he had found her earlier, she now shook with mirth, sharing a smile with her cousin beside her, a brilliant smile. Her head turned and their eyes met. The smile vanished, she bit her lip and looked away.

Nick turned to Trafford, "I must conscript her in my cause. She can find the match to lure Elston from my prize."

Mr. Trafford hesitated. "Well, you cannot conscript her here. And she don't accept just anyone, you know. It's one reason she's still considered good *ton*—the ladies need her. But even eager mamas who wish to see their daughters wed must win her trust first. I suspect the case will be no different for you," he added.

"Then I must court that trust without delay," he said with sudden energy. He cast a wizened eye upon Trafford. "Introduce her to me."

Stewart let out a breath. "There you go. Assuming superiority. I dare say, Nick, the lady will prefer if you are introduced to her."

Something in Dellacort's eyes twinkled, and he crossed his arms. "Is that so? I begin to think I must know her. Make any introduction, as you please."

Stewart looked from Dellacort to Miss Wetherham. "You'll be on good behaviour?"

"Of course! We need her favour."

"There's a look in your eyes I've seen before," he returned, not in a happy tone. "Do not think of giving her a comeuppance. She'll do nothing for you if you stand upon points."

"I wouldn't dream of it!" he replied, so heartily that Stewart was not mollified in the least.

"So be it," he said, turning toward Miss Wetherham's direction. "If you raise the lady's wrath instead of her approbation, recollect, it's your future bride that will accompany the earl to church."

"I cannot forget it," replied Dellacort, while his eyes continued to size up the widow he was suddenly eager to know.

She had a sweet face and smile from afar, but as they approached, and her gaze swung their way, he saw bright, very green eyes holding a challenging, almost mocking look.

It wasn't often Mr. Dellacort drew any such reaction in a female. He felt a small thrill of anticipation. To meet a lady with backbone at Almack's was decidedly rare, unless one took into account the patronesses who ran the place. Even this woman, he feared, was ten to one a bluff. She would soon collapse into the obsequious attitude or tedious timidity he usually received from the opposite sex. While not as wealthy as the earl's family, Dellacort had an income of £10,000 per year—nothing to snivel at.

A woman staying afloat by matchmaking would not, could not, pose a challenge to equal the merit in that.

Chapter Two

Mr. Trafford had no trouble at all in begging an introduction, during which Nick bowed graciously and Miss Wetherham met Nick's eyes with uncommon courage. Indeed, with a mischievous sparkle in those green orbs she said, "I know, of course, the name of your friend, Mr. Trafford. All ladies are warned of his existence before ever they step foot inside a ballroom."

Harriette Cantrell, Miss Wetherham's cousin, a worried-looking creature, turned alarmed eyes to her. Mr. Nitts raised his head and stared at Miss Wetherham. But Nick, with a smile curving the edges of his mouth said, "Warned against me? Do not say I am given out as an ogre!"

"An ogre? Dear me, no." Lettie's eyes flashed mischievously. "Only a merciless flirt and a rake," she said airily, as if she had remarked upon the weather.

Mr. Trafford put a finger to his lips to hide a sputter of laughter, then bit his lip and glanced at his friend.

"Lettie!" hissed Harriette. "Recollect yourself!" Harriette was only a few years older than Lettie but saw herself as advanced in age and wiser, despite having never married. To her relief, far from having his hackles raised, Mr. Dellacort was giving Lettie a look of appreciation.

"How refreshing that I am spoken of at all," he said, meeting Miss Wetherham's gaze with lively eyes.

Lettie returned his look calmly as she added, "But certainly it must be said to your credit that you pay no mind to a lady's fortune or lack of it." She paused for a beat and then added, "I understand you are as happy to ruin a pauper as easily as an heiress."

Mr. Trafford's brows were raised as high as they could go, while he glanced uncertainly at Nick. Why was Miss Wetherham purposely insulting Nick? Did she comprehend his standing in society, and that the right word from him, considering the gossip going about, could cast aspersion upon her character such that Almack's might never be open to her again?

Mrs. Amelia Cantrell said laughingly, "How do you do, Mr. Dellacort? Pray, ignore Lettie; my cousin always takes the side of injured females."

"Real or imaginary, I take it?" he asked dryly.

Lettie huffed, as if to say, 'Nonsense!"

Harriette cut in. "She is nothing but—but—saucy!" She gave her cousin as she finished this mollification, a wide-eyed look of warning.

The description seemed only to amuse the lady in question, for she tittered, "Oh, yes! I am nothing if not *saucy*, sir. Peculiarly so. If peculiar seasoning is not to your taste, then I beg Mr. Trafford will take you elsewhere." She looked about the room with feigned interest. Almack's was renowned for launching upper class debutantes into society, many fresh from the schoolroom who were shy and awkward. "We have an excess of timid debutantes here, I daresay. But I expect this will suit"—she looked at him pointedly. "Or else why are you here?"

Mrs. Cantrell rubbed her lips together, her eyes filled with the same surprised amusement as Nick's. The others seemed to hold their collective breath to see his reaction, sure that

Miss Wetherham had made a shipwreck of the meeting. Harriette went so far as to grip Letitia's arm and hiss, "Lettie! You've gone mad!"

But Nick, crossing his arms, said to her, "Fear not, ma'am; I assure you, I find Miss Wetherham's remarks revitalizing! Though I must object on one account; she gives me too much credit."

"Too much?" Lettie asked. "How so?"

"You said I am happy to ruin a pauper as well as an heiress. I maintain, I have never been guilty of ruining a woman."

Miss Wetherham pursed her lips and gave a calculating look. "As a man, you are ill-suited to judge what a female suffers. You suppose there is only one manner of being ruined, when to a woman, if her heart is broken, she considers it destruction enough."

"Destruction? Ruin?" Nick turned and gave Stewart a look of amusement. "I believe she confuses me with Bonaparte!"

Miss Wetherham was forced to smile at that. Dimples appeared when she did, around full lips. Before she could answer, Harriette said, "Sir, I am sure my cousin *has* confused you...with, er, some other gentleman. I never heard any such thing regarding your character. No man should make an offer he is not eager for, whether it is lowering to the lady or not," she said, turning another wide-eyed stare upon her recalcitrant cousin as if Lettie had grown two heads. Miss Wetherham merely smiled.

"If I am known to you as such a blackguard, Miss Wetherham, I wonder at your allowing the introduction. But since you have," Nick continued quickly, "you must afford me an opportunity to refute the charges."

Miss Wetherham raised a delicate brow.

Nick continued, "As much as I relish the notion of a fearful reputation, I am forced to admit," he said with a keen eye upon her, "that although I am not as innocent as your cousin suggests, neither am I as reprehensible as you would have me."

Miss Wetherham raised her chin at him. "I welcome any defense, I assure you," she said without conviction. "But if you do not seek a bride, you should not spend time at Almack's raising hopes."

Leaning in and meeting her eyes, Nick asked, "Have I raised your hopes, Miss Wetherham?" Her eyes blazed at him, but before she could offer a retort, Mr. Cantrell at that moment, joined them. He nodded at the gentlemen, and then turned to his wife. "My dear. Lady Farnworth looks for you."

"Heaven save us from Lady Farnworth!" said Amelia. "Must I see her now? I am enjoying Letitia, who is in rare form this evening, I assure you."

Lettie, smiling, slapped her cousin's arm lightly with her fan.

"You are, dearest, but you are not this prickly as a rule," she added, turning her eyes up to Nick. "Mr. Dellacort should be aware of this."

"Lettie, in rare form?" said Mr. Cantrell, with an alarmed glance at his cousin. "In that case, I ought to drag her away also!"

"Don't be absurd," Lettie said comfortably, and then bit her lip to keep from laughing. Secretly, she knew Amelia was right. Her flippancy was unusual—she blamed it on Nicholas

Dellacort. He was suave, good looking, rich, and known to avoid marriage—a deadly combination to women, in her estimation. Her aim was to be repellant.

Harriette cast a worried glance at Dellacort. All her relations were misbehaving, in her opinion.

Horace Cantrell cleared his throat nervously. Horace was perpetually anxious on one account or other. Tonight, it was due to Lady Farnsworth. "Her Ladyship," he announced, "is a great eccentric, and insists upon discussing this instant, since my wife and I are here, a small matter about berry bushes growing at the edges of both our estates."

Harriette blushed. With an uneasy glance at the company she muttered. "Discussing berries and bushes at Almack's! Is it not vulgar?"

Lettie looked away to hide a smile.

Amelia cried, "As I have said a thousand times, cannot our stewards settle the matter?"

Horace gave a breath of a laugh. "It began with her telling us our berries were not properly netted against blackbirds, don't you know; but now, what, she insists the fruit on *both* sides of the bushes belong to *her* estate."

"How inordinately greedy!" said Dellacort with such feeling that Lettie, sure he was mocking, had to repress the laugh that flew to her lips. Amelia, too, gave him a look of appreciation. Harriette, however, welcomed what she took for sympathy.

Looking in an injured fashion to Dellacort, her lips hardened as she exclaimed, "She insists she will have *all* of them this year!"

Before Mr. Dellacort could make another reply, Miss Wetherham, unable to suppress a chuckle, cried, "Oh, give her the berries, my dears! She'll send you a jar of jam and a fat goose for Christmas."

"We have geese enough of our own," returned Harriette with aspersion. She turned to her brother. "Allow *me* to speak with her ladyship," she said, archly. "I am certain I could bring her to reason if you allow me the opportunity."

"She wishes to speak with Amelia," he said.

Undeterred, Harriette rose. "Come, dear," she said to sister-in-law. "We must not allow her to take all!"

Mrs. Cantrell rose with a smile at Lettie. "I am summoned." She curtseyed to the gentlemen. Harriette made her curtseys but stopped to whisper in Miss Wetherham's ear. "Guard your tongue! Mr. Dellacort has much influence, and you are in need of—well, you know, families to avail of your services." She paused. "Not to mention, a husband of your own!"

Miss Wetherham said aloud, "Thank you, dearest, fear not."

The gentlemen bowed politely, after which Nick nodded towards a now vacant seat beside Lettie. "May I?"

Lettie looked startled but quickly conquered her expression. "If you wish." He took the seat and gave Mr. Nitts, the bore, such a reproving look that it sufficed to evoke a hasty bow and mumbled regrets followed by his immediate departure. With Mr. Trafford he was more direct. "Make yourself scarce, will you, Stewart? I've need to speak with Miss Wetherham."

Trafford raised a brow at his friend and shook his head frowningly. He'd warned Nick not to try and do business with

Miss Wetherham tonight but was certain this was his aim. Nick regarded him unrepentantly and motioned with his head to be off. Trafford shook his head again but bowed politely to Miss Wetherham and moved off.

Lettie watched Mr. Trafford leave and felt a ripple of trepidation, an undertow tugging a warning at her, to be on her guard. Most men would have been insulted enough to bow themselves off by now, but Dellacort was sticking around and wished to speak to her? She had no wish to prolong the meeting. Everything she'd said of him she believed to be true, and thus his good looks and wealth only made him perilous. Insincerity in anyone was anathema to Lettie, but in Dellacort, known for trifling with women, it was dangerous. As a widow, she was practically without protection. She had only the Cantrells between herself and the world, between independence and indigence, honour and dishonour. If a dishonourable man sought to trifle with her, timid cousin Horace was her only champion. Likewise, if she failed to generate enough income, he was her sole fallback.

Her cousins encouraged Lettie to remarry, of course, and would welcome any suitor of good standing. Dellacort had standing in buckets but nothing would convince her he aspired to be a suitor. And the Cantrells had just abandoned her to his company—they would not frighten him off. Fortunately, since her husband's passing three years earlier, Lettie had been forced to grow accomplished at doing it herself.

He turned a pair of penetrating green-grey eyes upon her. "I comprehend you are not interested in mere chatter; you prefer to cut to the quick, is that right?"

Her earlier barbs deserved such an appraisal. "I am capable of enjoying a great deal of senseless banter, sir, since you ask. I am fortified by senseless banter, I assure you." She blinked at him innocently. A sincere man, she would have treated kindly and given all due respect. But a confirmed flirt? Especially one that had the smooth tongue and wit of a Dellacort, as well as looks to send a tender female heart swooning? No, she had no heart for a flirtation, not with him or anyone. Nor the time. Her evenings in society were sadly not for personal enjoyment as much as keeping an eye out for young women "on the shelf." Those who were on their second or third season and still hadn't found a husband. Those whose mamas might pay a handsome fee if Lettie found them a good match.

Dellacort was not a possibility as a client, nor a suitor. Why had she consented when he asked to sit beside her?

His mouth curved with mirth, but he said, "Fortified by mere banter? I have only just met you, but if I mistake me not, you are also bored by it. And since I am not in the least interested in empty formalities or meaningless conversation, I beg your permission to forego it."

"To what purpose, sir?" she asked, keeping her expression carefully unmoved.

He paused. "I have business with you. But first, may I ask why it is you have not remarried, *Mrs.* Wetherham?"

Startled green eyes tinged with caution turned to him. "That is not your concern."

"An unwed woman with no certain means must be in want of security?"

She stared at him as her cheeks paled. Were her reduced circumstances common knowledge? The thought horrified her. "And does *that* concern you, sir? Is that polite conversation, Mr. Dellacort?" She gazed at him indignantly, but as though assessing him for the first time.

"I was greeted with accusations against my character only a minute ago. Was that polite conversation, ma'am?"

She took a breath and looked away. Yes, she fully deserved that—but she sniffed and asked, "Why did you seek the introduction? You might have insulted me from afar more easily than to my face."

"I meant no insult. I merely took the liberty of being forthright, as you were with me." She felt her cheeks flush. She wondered if he was always this adept at finding weak spots in people. While she struggled with how to answer, he continued, "A widow without certain means *must* be in want of security, and I am prepared," he said firmly, "to offer a substantial sum in return for a certain service you may do me."

Nick had no idea why he was making himself odious to her, knew his manner of approach could only be found monstrous, but was compelled to continue. He must win his cause.

Now sparks flashed from widened green eyes. In a lowered voice she hissed, "What manner of service do you believe I offer, sir? Depend upon it, you are misinformed!" She glanced anxiously about, then added hotly, "How dare you imply such a thing! That I—"

Nick held up a hand. "You mistake me. I wish to make a proposition with regard to finding a wife for a certain gentleman of my acquaintance."

The ire in Miss Wetherham's eyes ebbed, but high colour in her cheeks remained. "I fail to see what this can have to do with me."

Undeterred, he said, "Pray, do not be coy; I am acquainted with the service you provide for girls in need of husbands. I am here to provide you a husband; all you needs must do is provide the girl."

She turned to him with stark curiosity. "Are *you* the gentleman in need of a wife?"

Nick let out a breath of exasperation. "My dear woman, if I were in want of a wife, I would not, believe me, require aid to obtain her!" In point of fact, this was precisely why Nick required her help—to remove his competition from Miss Alden—but he was not prepared to view it in that light, and especially not at this juncture of the conversation.

She regarded him with lively eyes. "I am inclined to agree with you there, though I regret to admit it."

Something in his eyes flickered, and he stifled a smile.

"Why does this gentleman friend of yours not find a wife for himself?"

"He thinks he has. I wish him to find another."

She gave him a look of dawning recognition, her chin and brows high. "Ahh, I see. It is a case of jealousy, then."

He smirked. "You might say that."

She shook her head. "This is very irregular." She looked around at the room with trepidation on her face. "And very ill-conceived in you to speak to me of it now!"

Nick came to his feet. "For that, I beg your pardon. If you will grant me the honour of calling upon you, we can speak on it in closer surroundings."

She hesitated, looking away. He wished to hire her! Had her service become so well known that even Dellacort, who did not often grace society with his presence, would approach her so cavalierly? If he was aware of her business, would not all of society shortly follow suit? She was on dangerous ground. "I fear, sir, that you mistake the matter. While I have been known to match girls with husbands, it is merely for a lark. A token of friendship. I seem to have a knack for knowing who will suit who..." Her voice trailed off. Everything in his eyes told her he knew this to be utter drivel.

In a soft tone, he said, "I will pay twice the going rate, whatever it is, if you assist my cause."

She swallowed and looked up at him, her face flushed. For a startling moment, Nick thought she looked quite adorable in her confusion. But he must stick to his purpose.

"For your information, Mr. Dellacort," she said, as another fine blush rose on her cheeks, "I am set up with a reasonable income, though it is no business of yours, and I do not engage in propositions concerning any payment whatsoever." She gave him a belligerent stare. "Do you take me for a *cit*? I am not in *trade*, sir!"

He surveyed her a moment, and then spoke gently. "I understand you. Of course you are not. I only mean that I treat my friends very well; and any friend who would help in this matter, I should be very grateful to, and wish to reward handsomely." His eyes pierced hers. "More grateful than you might imagine, I expect."

The tension in her face diminished. He was in earnest. He needed her help. Slowly she answered, "I have a very good imagination."

His lips curved into a smile. "I will call upon you tomorrow, then."

She hesitated. Finally, in a low tone she said, "Do you know where to find me?" A defeated tone, it seemed. A surprising pang of regret hit Nick. He'd wished to secure her help at any price, but not at the expense of her pride. But there was nothing to be done for it for now.

After confirming that she lived on Russel Street, and inquiring as to the manner of fanlight on her door (so that he might easily be assured of finding the right house), Mr. Dellacort moved off in long strides. He had a purposeful air, quite different than the studied nonchalance of the town bloods trying to look modish.

Lettie could have kicked herself. She'd as much as admitted to being in business by agreeing to let him call upon her the following day. She watched his tall frame as he headed toward the exit but was stopped before he could escape by Princess Esterhazy, one of Almack's patronesses. The princess said something, turned and gestured at the dance floor, and then at a circle of young women—wallflowers. But Dellacort shook his head and said something, made a polite bow and left. The princess had hoped to call upon his gallantry, Lettie was sure, but Dellacort hadn't risen to the need. The wallflowers would have been ecstatic—or ready to swoon—had he agreed to stand up with one.

She'd never been asked to find a wife by a gentleman on behalf of another gentleman, especially for one who already considered that he'd found one. But Dellacort said he'd pay twice the "going rate." What he did not understand, what Lettie wished was not true, was that a "going rate" did not exist. Indeed, the uncertainty of receiving compensation for her trouble regarding matchmaking was an ongoing bane. Demanding payment was out of the question—it would brand her a businesswoman. It was a delicate business, getting members of the upper class to part with their blunt.

Some families, fortunately, were generously grateful for her help, sending all manner of gifts, from fattened geese and fowl to covering her lease for months at a time. But others pretended ignorance of Lettie's expectations, declaring themselves only too aware that a gentlewoman could not, by any means, be persuaded or induced to accept payment. The very idea was vulgar! This left her income upon precarious legs. It was precisely, she thought bitterly, as Dellacort had said. *An unmarried woman without certain means must be in want of security.* It was too true, maddeningly true. But how monstrous for him to have stated it so plain. She wished she had told him he was incorrigible, that his manners were appalling. In fact, the more she thought on it, the more convinced she was that dealings with him could only mean trouble.

She recalled the intense gaze, the directness of his address, the knowing eyes. There was something unsettling in it. And he was bound to be difficult; his cutting remarks were well known. For the next few minutes, she pondered it; and far from feeling hopeful that a prospect was coming her way, she felt only burdened. She decided that she must refuse the business. She would be no worse off than she had been and would not have to be on her guard with a man who made her uneasy.

But a small voice told her that she ought, at least, to hear his offer. The whole world knew he was fabulously rich, and jealousy could drive a man to do unreasonable things with his money. Perhaps securing her help would be the unreasonable thing—she could charge him beforehand, charge an exorbitant amount. He already understood her business—he'd made that unpardonably clear! —leaving no point in pretending it away. And he had the means to pay a high sum. Perhaps, after all, this was a boon from heaven. If she asked enough from him, it could keep her through the winter and well beyond it.

A small fear surfaced: what if he, knowing her wish to be discreet, refused a fair compensation? She could hardly complain or spread it about that he'd cheated her. No, her position of need was entirely in his favour. Ah, the uncertainty of it all was lowering! If she knew him better, that his word could be trusted—then she might feel optimistic. In the meantime, she could only hope for the best, but Dellacort did not seem the sort of man one should put hopes upon.

In general, Lettie did not allow the cares of life to get the best of her. It would distress dear Steven, had he lived to see the struggle she faced to make ends meet. The shock of his accidental demise was quickly followed by an additional one: that no more diamonds had been found. The same African mine that at first had produced such promise, and upon which Steven had pledged all their holdings—was now defunct. The first shock had sent tremors into every inch of Lettie's heart, soul, and mind. Indeed, she was shattered to the core. Steven, gone! They'd only been married two years. A release of noxious gases in a tunnel, a "pipe" in mine lingo, during his last exploration had stolen not only their hopes, but his life, and that of two servants who perished with him.

It was sorrow upon sorrow for Lettie, for she'd quickly sunk from a life of comfort to shabby gentility. But she was wondrously good at matchmaking, and she turned to it for sustenance. It provided, however, only an unsteady and insufficient income. She augmented this by selling her jewellery, including her diamonds. But now she had only one valuable bauble left, and she'd vowed not to part with it. A necklace with a flawless, emerald shaped diamond, cut with exquisite attention to its brilliance.

At the same time, if business did not pick up soon, she'd be so deep in the duns that only a departure from town to a less costly place would answer. She enjoyed the country, but leaving London meant losing further opportunities of earning income, for here was where upper-class ladies came to seek husbands. Not for nothing was the London season known as the "marriage mart."

With such worries on her brow, soon Miss Wetherham found herself alerting the Cantrells that she wished to go home. Her cousins were all curiosity—was she unwell? Did she have the headache? Harriette asked if she should accompany her cousin home to play nursemaid? ("Heavens, no!" Lettie had exclaimed. Harriette would give her twice the headache.) The carriage was called.

Lettie hated to be the cause of their leaving, but cousin Horace assured her that a night at Almack's once a season was enough of a trial to his mind; and why he had agreed to accompany the ladies, he was sure he'd never understand. Also, if they did not depart soon, he might *die* of a stupor; and didn't Brummell look peaked this evening?

At the entrance, she realised they were leaving almost on Mr. Dellacort's heels, and she stopped to survey the street and ensure that he was not in front awaiting his coach. Only when she saw the area was clear of Mr. Nicholas Dellacort did she venture from the establishment and climb into the Cantrells's carriage.

Chapter Three

Miss Wetherham's morning routine the following day began an hour earlier than usual and followed a night of tossing and turning.

She'd admonished Betsey, her lady's maid, the prior evening to ensure she awoke no later than nine, for she had much to do before a certain gentleman called. Betsey put Lettie's hair in papers for proper curls upon waking, and a morning gown of shaded, striped black silk with small sprigs of gold embroidery, was chosen and carefully flat-ironed. Crape and satin figured prominently in Lettie's attire because both were available in blacks and dark greys, her preferred colours, as befitted, she felt, her widowhood. Her only aberration from this habit was when she appeared at Almack's, as the patronesses did not allow "widow's weeds."

The striped silk was her finest. She'd worn it on the day of Lord Nelson's funeral in January of the year past, and again in January this year when Pitt, the Prime Minister, poor man, died so unexpectedly.

Why she should take extra concern with her appearance, she did not stop to examine. If it crept upon her that she had an unusual desire to look her best, she was certain it signified only the distressing nature of the business. To her mind, only a well-dressed woman was prepared to face a formidable challenge, and Nick Dellacort had already proven himself to be that. The memory of his piercing, unnerving eyes was of itself sufficient to justify her toilette.

That she could think of precious little *except* that Mr. Dellacort was to call, she also attributed to anxiety regarding the business. That the man understood it, that he knew its importance to her welfare and comfort should have made it easier, since there was no need for pretence. But it filled her with dread. She would certainly have to behave better to him today. Perhaps she ought to apologise for attacking his character directly upon their introduction.

And if the business went well? She might pay off debts; perhaps even revive her dream of having a nest egg, some small savings for the future. Steven had put every last penny of their savings into the mine, and no amount of matchmaking had been sufficient to restore it. Try to save as she might, creditors steadily eroded her efforts. The sad truth was that Lettie was nearly destitute. She had long dreamed of saving enough so that one day she might leave London and live off the interest of her funds. The stark memory of her mother, a woman in comfortable circumstances until the death of Lettie's father, could never be erased from her thoughts. Her elegant mother had been reduced in her later years to near poverty, a fate Lettie would have shared but for the generosity of the Cantrells. If she remarried, her circumstances might improve; but every thought of dear Steven's passing sent her heart into such misery that she could not bear the thought of ever loving another. Love meant pain.

Cousin Horace's father should have helped Lettie's mother, but had not. Her uncle's lack of generosity still made Lettie shudder, but only strengthened her resolve to ensure her own welfare, now and for the future. If the day came when she saved enough to live independently, she would no longer have to arrange marriages. On that day, she could secure a modest cottage near the sea and be done forever with having to balance her reputation with her need for income. But it was becoming precariously clear that her dream of independence only grew more faint, like a scene disappearing from the window of a carriage, perhaps never to come into view again. But she *must* believe in it. It gave her hope.

And until it came to pass, she must stay in Town, for every Season drew flocks of debutantes searching for the husband of their dreams. Many of these newcomers did not require help in finding that man. But the ones who failed to attract an offer came back the following year, and sometimes the year after that. Those on their second year were often anxious to enlist her help. Third year unmarried girls were considered spinsters, "on the shelf," all but unmarriageable. These were desperate for Miss Wetherham to take their case; poor Miss Wetherham who was an unfortunate widow but experienced in life and knew which girl would appeal to which gentleman, and vice versa.

Lettie had a good string of successes behind her. No sooner did a girl suspect she was on her way to being shelved but would clamour to her mama to avail her of Miss Wetherham's peculiar talent at finding husbands. They came to her drawing room humbly. Unfortunately, this humility did not always translate to willingness to part with their blunt. For every family that bestowed gratitude (in the form of cash if Miss Wetherham was lucky), there were two families who did not. Far too often Lettie's most difficult job was not in finding the marriageable men, but in tactfully suggesting gifts of gratitude could best be expressed for a poor widow in pounds sterling. "Strictly as a token of affection, of course," she would say. "There is no cost for my help, as I am assuredly not in trade!"

At this remark, the ladies in the room, herself included, would laugh heartily at the ridiculous notion of Miss Wetherham being in trade. How utterly disrespectable it would be to conceive of such a thing! But by the end of the interview, Lettie preferred to have an assurance of a certain amount to be paid upon the success of the endeavour. As soon as an acceptable gentleman made his offer to the anxious young woman seeking a match, the "gift" was due.

But Lettie could never stipulate the amount. In some lucky cases, the young woman would insist upon a sum higher than what Miss Wetherham would dared have asked. She believed they saw it as a measure of their worth—a dowry of sorts. If Miss Wetherham had received such a generous amount simply for arranging the match, why, what a catch that miss must be. Such was how some young ladies seemed to feel. And that was perfectly amiable and right to Lettie's mind.

But Dellacort was no needy mama seeking to wed off a daughter. To be meeting with him on behalf of a fellow man, to be spoken to with such indelicacy right within the venerable walls of Almack's—it was worrisome. And if she was unable to fulfill his request? A man of such consequence and with such a temperament could ruin her with a word.

With a gasp, Miss Wetherham saw that this indeed could be her fate. She searched her brain for a young woman suitable to his case but came up empty. She reviewed the eligible girls who had come to her this Season, but all had already been paired off with gentlemen. Why had she not thought of this sooner? If he had approached her five weeks earlier, she would have had at least three young misses to propose for the purpose. (Assuming the gentleman in need was respectable, of course. Miss Wetherham would never match a girl with an unworthy man.)

But alas, she had done her task only too well. All the unmarried young women put before her this Season were now in courtships. If only Miss Wetherham hadn't started the wheels rolling in other directions with such a great degree of success, she might have had someone to offer for Dellacort's consideration. But she had no one. What did he mean by coming to her so late in the Season? What kind of matchmaker would she be if she hadn't by now already manoeuvered her girls into courtships with eligible men?

These facts, coupled with his insolence, made her regret that he had approached her. She had no reason to suppose him agreeable or forgiving. Not even trustworthy. Mamas with unmarried daughters were grateful when Miss Wetherham secured a match for them, so much so that they wouldn't *think* of betraying her, of whispering in the wrong ear that her service did not come without a price. At least, not intentionally. But Dellacort was not discreet. Had he not displayed his utter contempt for discretion when he had the temerity to speak of paying her—as if she were a common tradeswoman—in Almack's? Had the conversation been overheard, it would have been all sixes and sevens for her. No, no, her reputation could not have survived. And if she were to cease getting invitations to tonnish events, dinner parties, soirees, and balls—how could she continue using her fortunate talent? In order to make matches in the best circles, one had to be welcome in them. There would be no nest egg to retire to the country with, if her reputation went to pieces.

As Betsey put the finishing touches upon Miss Wetherham's hair with a ribbon that matched her gown, with sudden alacrity, it came upon Lettie, what she must do. She ought not to have agreed to receive Mr. Dellacort. But since he would come, she must simply feign ignorance of the prior night's discussion. She did not relish a pretence but saw no other way out of the situation. Dellacort's deep pockets were tempting, oh, very tempting! But they could not counter the weight of a tattered reputation. And, although she was seasoned at handling most men with aplomb and easy accord—widows were not treated as the delicate flowers that debutantes were—Dellacort was different. He was not a patient man. He would be out of countenance when she told him she could not help. He might be disparaging of her in company, purposely "slip" her means of subsistence. She *must* refuse to deal with him, refuse to even acknowledge the gist of their discussion. He'd have to find his friend—whoever it was—a bride without her help.

Her resentment and suspicions of him grew as she continued to think on the matter, and she hardly knew time passed. Breakfast was hastily consumed, the newspapers scarcely given their usual scrutiny, the week's menu hardly gone over with cook, (including a remonstration to use *only* Mrs. Rundell's book on domestic cookery, as it alone instructed on methods of economy), and herself no sooner ready to change into afternoon dress when suddenly Mr. Dudley, her butler and man of all work—her sole male servant, save for a boy—announced his arrival.

Lettie's pulse quickened. She reminded herself that no transaction had passed between them, no monies had changed hands. She was safe from accusations and she would stay safe by sending him on his way. She held her body erect as she entered the first parlour and stopped as Mr. Dellacort, tall and sanguine, turned to behold her. He bowed politely.

He made a fine figure of a man, and for some reason Lettie resented this. Very few men, since dear Steven's passing, could turn her head, and she liked it that way. One broken heart was enough for a lifetime, thank you. She was fully prepared to survive as a widow to the end of her days.

But it would have been easier to fob off a slovenly fellow, even a peer, had he come looking less dignified and gentlemanlike. And yet Dellacort only wore what was customary and fashionable for gentlemen; close-fitting pantaloons with a watch fob and black boots; an embroidered waistcoat and white cambric shirt peeking out of a beautifully fitted topcoat; and a white stock circling his neck with a pointed standing collar Yet no duke could have looked better tailored.

She gave a small curtsey and took a seat, motioning for him to sit across from her. "Please, have a seat, sir."

"How do you do today, ma'am?" he asked, making Miss Wetherham stare at him speechlessly a moment. After last night's rather shocking encounter, she had not expected common chit chat from him. "Oh—er—well enough, I thank you." She studied him curiously. He seemed to be on the verge of a grin, a thing which she found disagreeable. Was he mocking her? Well, she must make quick work of this.

"May I ask the reason for your call?" she inquired in a polite tone. She looked at him innocently.

His eyes narrowed, thoughts flitting across them. In a moment he recovered and said, "Do you mean to say that you cannot recollect the reason for my being here?"

Miss Wetherham had a moment's pang of conscience; she did, of course recollect perfectly why he'd come. And she hated dissembling of any kind. Only desperation could move her to purposely proceed in this course—but proceed she must. He *had* to believe it had been a misunderstanding. He must not leave her home with incriminating evidence against her, with the thought that she was in trade! "Sir, you astonish me; surely you did not conceive for a moment that I was speaking in earnest last evening." She pursed her lips and frowned, pretending to think hard upon the matter. "Indeed, I had not the least thought that you would truly appear today in my drawing room!"

He stared at her a moment, cleared his throat, and levelled an earnest gaze upon her. "Why, I believed we had an understanding." His eyes were piercing; his tone so soft as to be caressing. "We are to begin a courtship, are we not?"

Miss Wetherham allowed one brow to crack out of place. His words startled her for only a second; *they*, begin a *courtship*? But she realised he was referring to starting a courtship for someone else—the friend he was purportedly trying to help. Even this she must nip in the bud. "I beg your pardon, but I believe you mistake the matter. I have no such recollection. My memory is frightful, I allow, but even so—."

Dellacort's mouth wavered but then a look of decision crossed his eyes. He shot up from his chair and stood before her in so quick a movement that Lettie was too stunned to move or even finish her sentence. To her utter dismay, he took her by the arms and lifted her from her chair. She gasped.

With his eyes only an inch from hers, he said, "I am crushed that you could forget. Do you not recollect—this?" And in the next second his mouth came down upon hers. Miss Wetherham, for some inexplicable reason, allowed the kiss. Nick tightened his arms about her and drew her up against him, while she, utterly beside herself in shock, did nothing at all. Her mouth, of its own accord, seemed to return the kiss! Before dear Steven's passing, she had been a married woman, a happily married woman, and her mouth knew, even if she did not at this moment agree with it, that when a man kissed you, you kissed him back. Dellacort's mouth was warm and welcoming.

But suddenly the image of dear Steven transposed itself on her brain. A frowning image. She returned to her senses—she was kissing a virtual stranger, not Steven! This was Dellacort!

What was she doing?

In a rush of mortification, she pushed him away and hurried behind the chair, staring at him in sheer disbelief. "I— I—am beyond speechless!" She looked toward the door. "GO! Go at once! And never return!"

"But Lettie, dearest Lettie," he said, moving a step toward her.

Her eyes widened even more as she backed away further and pointed at the door. "How dare you behave so ill to me! What abuse is this? How dare you!"

"But last night," he said, looking deeply into her eyes.

"You know perfectly well nothing happened last night to—to—account for this!"

He stifled a smile, but with laughing eyes said, "Why did you pretend to forget what actually did transpire last night?"

Her mouth, opened to vent yet more outrage, shut suddenly. "That is of no consequence; I may choose to forget a conversation if I wish!'

"But you didn't forget. You only pretended to. Why?"

She glowered at him and took a heaving deep breath. "I may *choose* to pretend to forget a conversation if I wish! I owe you no explanation!"

"And I merely chose to pretend to remember one. We're even, then. Do you still feel wronged?"

She gasped. "You are a rogue, Mr. Dellacort!"

He almost smiled. "I'm afraid I can be; your misbehaviour in 'forgetting' was the only inducement I needed to misbehave myself." Here he bowed. "I beg your pardon. Now, can we get on with the real reason for my call? Which you are well aware of?"

She stared. He was all businesslike, his eyes veiled and impassive, as if he had not only a moment ago kissed her passionately. Her heart was still pounding, but he was as cool as if he made a habit of kissing women he'd only just met. What kind of man was this? Raising her head, she said, "That is not possible. Before you arrived, I had decided that we can have no business with one another; indeed, after this meeting, I am beyond certain we never can!" She took a deep breath to regain her composure. "Besides which, I am afraid you misunderstood my, er, past involvement with matchmaking. It is only the veriest lark, I assure you, a mere pastime…"

"Pray, Miss Wetherham, do not attempt to bamboozle me. I understand your role perfectly. I spent the morning making calls, and I now know precisely which marriages you may credit to your account, and exactly how you were compensated—or not—for your trouble for each one."

The storm in Miss Wetherham's gaze only deepened. "That is of no consequence! I have nothing but loathing for you; you must agree that we can have no business between us." Sudden tears were pools that shimmered like morning dew at the rims of her wide green eyes. She swallowed and continued, "I have done you no harm! Indeed, I cannot see why you should wish to ruin me—"

"My dear woman, I have no such ambition. I thought I made myself clear. I only seek your help."

She stared at him. Perhaps she had worried over much. Perhaps he was not a threat. But she shook her head and said miserably, "You are too late. Every girl given to my charge this year has already been paired with an eligible match. I am sorry, but now you see why you can have no further business here." She took a breath. "Shall I ring a servant to see you out?"

He said, "I know of an unmarried woman who will answer perfectly."

She seemed surprised. "In that case, why do you not approach her? I fail to see why you need my help."

He motioned for her to resume her seat, for Lettie was still cowering behind an overstuffed, claw-footed chair. "Please."

"I will stay here, sir."

His pressed his lips to stifle a chuckle, but said, "Why do I not approach her myself?" He paused and gave her an inscrutable look. "I am in the process of doing so, this very moment."

She blinked. "I beg your pardon?" What did he mean by that? How could he be 'in the process of doing so' from her drawing room? *She* was no prospect for marriage.

"The man I must find a wife for is Lord Elston, Earl Brest. As you may know, he is the son of the Marquess of Warthenshire."

She vaguely recalled Lord Elston. He wore colourful cravats that lent an air of dandyism to his dress, but before she could object that earls were hardly in need of help to secure wives, he continued, "His father has settled upon Miss Sophia Alden; whose parents, I should add, are content to welcome and pursue the match."

Again, she blinked. "I do not understand. The match is set and expected, and both families are happy to have it so. What is the problem?"

"The problem is Miss Alden. She is not in love with Elston."

Miss Wetherham gave a breath of a laugh. "That is seldom considered an impediment to marriage for the upper class. And how does it concern you?"

"Not only does Miss Alden harbour no affection for Elston, but there is another man she loves very well."

Miss Wetherham's mouth fell open for a second and shut. "You mean yourself. She's in love with you?"

He nodded. "I believe so."

She began pacing and, putting her slim hands together in thought, steepled them at her chin. He watched. She turned to him, dropping her hands. "And you, I presume, are in love with Miss Alden?"

"Let us just say the family was completely in favour of the match."

"And Lord Elston moved in and stole your prize?" Her eyes held a look of amusement.

"Let us say, he did."

She came around and took the seat which faced him. She sighed and said, "Alas, sir, I am not in the habit of dissuading people from a course that is already in motion, and which has the happy approval of both families."

"It does not have my approval."

"It does not need your approval." Before he could offer a retort she hurriedly added, "Perhaps the man in need of a bride is you yourself, Mr. Dellacort, and not the earl. You are perhaps unused to being rejected—"

"Madam, the matter is not one of rejection! The Marquess's family is ancient; he has a larger fortune and a title. The Aldens are set upon securing the highest income for their daughter, but the earl is a lily-liver and a bore. I cannot wish him upon Sophia, title or no."

"Yet, in a manner of speaking—in terms of marriageableness—he is the better man," she said innocently.

A gleam in his eyes and the slight curve of his lips told her he did not miss the jab. "Miss Alden goes along with it only to spite me. I was too slow with my suit, I gather."

"And you believe, if you approach her again, that she will accept you? Will not her family oppose it?"

"If Elston is an alternative, they will. So he must needs look elsewhere, first."

Understanding dawned on her expression. "So—let me understand you—you are asking me to find another woman for Lord Elston, to make him turn away from Miss Alden?"

"That's it."

"But if an agreement has already been signed—"

"It has not."

She regarded him a moment. He certainly was closely involved with Miss Alden to know even this. But she said, "The case is still difficult. I normally place girls with men who are *looking* for a bride," she said, utterly abandoning the idea of pretending away her matchmaking business. "Lord Elston has already found one." Before he could reply she added, "And what if Miss Alden is not in love with you? Have you secured her heart in the matter?"

"Do not concern yourself with that. I know Sophia better than she knows herself."

She stared, considering. "Well, this changes nothing concerning me; as I said, there are no eligible women of my acquaintance who—"

"You forget, I know of one." His piercing eyes held a challenge.

"And who would that be?"

His head went back as he regarded her with almost a smile. "It is you, Miss Wetherham. You will offer yourself to Elston. Do not object; you will thank me one day, for you will become the future marchioness in place of Miss Alden.

Chapter Four

Lettie felt she had endured enough. She folded her hands firmly on her lap. "That is utterly out of the question."

Mr. Dellacort calmly produced a snuffbox and flicked it open. "Do you not wish to marry a future marquess?" He took the smallest pinch, sniffed it with seeming satisfaction, and shut the box.

Lettie replied calmly, "I have no plans to marry again at all."

"Foolish of you. Marriage can ease your present circumstances and secure your future comfort."

She took a deep breath. Her own heart had echoed this sentiment on more than one occasion. She'd had two offers of marriage and turned them down. At times, she'd wondered at the wisdom in doing so, but the problem was that Lettie could never marry without affection. She said, "Even if the earl were to look my way, there are many reasons why such a match is not to be thought upon! You have only just informed me that Lord Elston is a lily-liver and a bore! You would not wish him upon Miss Alden. But, knowing nothing about me, you presume to believe that I should be agreeable to a match with such a man."

He nodded, surveying her placidly. "I do believe it, and I'll tell you why."

Something about his calm manner filled her with dread. He sat forward and she found herself shrinking back into her seat.

"I happen to know that you are three months behind in your lease; that the last two young women you arranged matches for paid you with fowl, tea, and other commodities— but gave nothing to satisfy a single creditor. I know that your family, the Cantrells, are also in dire circumstances."

Letties gasped, for she had no knowledge of this. "That's not true!"

"Oh, it is, Miss Wetherham. Your cousin lost a fortune only last week on 'Change; has he not mentioned it? I shouldn't be surprised if this is their last Season in town until he can recover the losses, if he can at all. Miss Harriette Cantrell is already their burden; if they have to take in another poor relation as well—"

Lettie felt sick. She had indeed been comforted in the knowledge that the Cantrells would support her if it ever came to that. Her cousins had suffered a previous loss at the same time Lettie had, for they were the second largest shareholders in the diamond mine. They had weathered that storm better than Lettie, for they had a landed estate and other holdings. But if this was true, and they were now in dire straits also— what recourse did she have?

"Consider, Miss Wetherham. I am offering you an opportunity to help us both. Miss Alden will live in clover whether she marries Elston or not; but you will continue in genteel poverty unless you marry well; you will be a constant worry to the Cantrells. With the earl you will never have another financial concern. As a countess and future marchioness, you will enjoy every dignity. Elston will get an intelligent woman who may even elevate his social graces—I grant you could do it. Everyone gets to live happily ever after."

Lettie's face was troubled, revealing doubts. She said, "You are not thinking clearly. I am a nobody—an earl can pick whomever he pleases from the best families. As you yourself pointed out, my circumstances are hardly even respectable. He will not deign to consider me. And a widow! My word, his family will laugh me to scorn."

"Prince George married a widow; it's almost become the fashion."

"An illegal marriage that did not stand!" she interjected, shaking her head.

"The Pope sanctified the union; and the prince has reconciled with Mrs.Fitzherbert, recall."

"While married to Princess Caroline! He's a profligate!"

He moved on. "As for being a nobody, you are a nobody who owns the greater share of a diamond mine."

"A worthless mine!" she cried bitterly.

"The earl needn't know that. And who is to say the mine does not have undiscovered value? Miss Alden's family is not an ancient one; her chief attraction is beauty and a large dowry. If that mine is found to have value—or said to have it—you have every bit as much appeal as Miss Alden."

Ignoring the fact that Dellacort had as much as called her beautiful, she could think only of dear Steven's untimely death and asked sadly, "Found to have value? There is too much danger to pursue the possibility, and I shan't give false hope of its being productive when it isn't."

"Mines such as yours have been known to offer new and valuable gems if they are explored sufficiently. Is your venture open pit mining or tunnelling?"

Large, troubled eyes met his. "Tis hard rock tunnelling. My husband *died* pursuing 'new and valuable gems,' and he found none! He *died* trying, I tell you! The mine is worthless!" She blinked back tears.

"I beg your pardon for mentioning it," he said quickly, and instantly produced a handkerchief from a waistcoat pocket which he offered her.

Miss Wetherham took it, thanked him, and dabbed her eyes. In a low tone she said, "My solicitors recommended we close the mine after Steven's accident, and the shareholders agreed. I was entirely in favour of it. No one has touched it for these three years."

Gently he said, "You own the controlling number of shares. You could open it again."

She stared at him in surprise. Mr. Dellacort had managed to discover even this? "How do you know all this?"

"Inquiries, Miss Wetherham. Mere inquiries."

Lettie had no idea how he could have discovered so much since only last night. His methods of inquiry, she thought, must be powerful indeed. Had she suspected that her cousin, Harriette, was the source of the lion's share of his knowledge, her estimation of his powers would have gone down a notch; or that her relation had glibly confided that she hoped her dear Lettie would cease this matchmaking nonsense and find herself a husband instead.

Dellacort continued, "Elston need only know of your majority shares in the enterprise and it will suffice to interest him."

"Majority shares that are worthless since the mine is defunct. And you speak as if opening a diamond mine is a small thing. There are enormous costs involved and terrible amounts of manual labour." Her voice shuddered with emotion. "And—and—unspeakable danger!"

He studied her. In a gentle voice he said, "Tell me what happened."

Lettie looked away, summoning her memories. In a low tone, staring at nothing, she said, "The mine was discovered through a volcanic fissure; a tunnel, you see, that brought tons and tons of rock to the surface, some embedded with diamond." She paused. "By digging up the area around the tunnel, and using explosives, the mine produced even more. But it dried up. Steven was only supposed to take a cursory look and then direct the hired men where to keep looking, where to blast." She sniffed. A shaky sigh escaped her. "He went down into one of the tunnels—pipes they call them— and natural gases, noxious vapours, escaped from the wall of rock. It killed him, and all the men with him."

She turned pain-filled eyes to his. "So you see, in addition to the immense cost of exploring, there is the human cost. I cannot afford the one, and I *will* not countenance the other."

Dellacort said, "I understand you. Fortunately, Elston can well afford to hire any labour necessary to revive the mine if he wishes. But I warrant he is more interested in securing an attractive and amiable bride than in adding to what is already an enormous fortune and estate."

She bit her lip, considering this. In a low tone, she said, "I suppose there are ladies enough who would delight at this opportunity to attract an earl to the altar. But I, sir, am not one of them."

"You need this."

His eyes, deep and intense, the kind that seemed always to be harbouring a hundred thoughts at once, bored into hers. Thick brows, a well-proportioned face and strong nose accompanied them. Why was it, she wondered, that the veriest devils in society always bore the most angelic faces? With pursed lips she said, "I own, that presently my circumstances are not the most fortuitous, but there is the little Season to come, when more young women are apt to need my help—my fortunes will improve, I warrant."

"Come, come. You have earned a reputation as a matchmaker because you excel at it, but your circumstances bear no indication of success." He glanced around the parlour. She followed his gaze and saw it with his eyes, the unmistakable air of neglect—Lettie could afford only one chamber maid—so that even the good quality furniture and curtains, remainders from the good days, looked somehow shabby. If he had called in the evening, he'd have seen that some of her candles were of tallow, not the better beeswax the upper class used. Those, she saved for entertaining, which most often amounted to having the Cantrells over for a light supper.

He said, "This will continue to be the case for you; it will *always* be the case. When people know they are not obliged to recompense you handsomely, they will not." He levelled a hard stare at her. "You know this to be true."

His words struck an ache in her heart, for she knew it indeed. She swallowed, trying valiantly not to let the effect of his words, the truth of them, appear in her expression.

"As I said last night, I am prepared to offer a sum that will make it well worth your time. Let us say, in light of your objections, a *guaranteed* sum, regardless of whether you succeed in the business or not—so long as I am satisfied you gave your best effort."

She looked at him for a long moment. To have a "guaranteed sum" was something she had not encountered before. She lowered her head and stared at the carpet. "What is this guaranteed sum?"

"Name it," he said instantly.

A flicker of excitement rose in Lettie's breast—she'd never been able to name the sum for her help! But it faded with equal speed. The *beau monde* was not known for paying its bills promptly if at all; and they sought bargains as much as the poorest of the land. If she named a truly wonderful amount, would he not walk away? Then she remembered that she *wanted* him to walk away. In fact, it was the very way to be rid of him. She thought of an exorbitant sum.

Her heart hammered crazily as she raised her eyes to his. Surely he would take a disgust of her for this. He would, he must, walk away. She hoped it would not seem so audacious as to raise his ire overmuch. He might spread the incident abroad and ruin her reputation. She had accused him of ruining women, believing he'd left a string of broken hearts in his path. Such a man might not think twice about ruining her, though it was her name at stake, not her heart. *But she must not squander this opportunity! He'd said she could name the sum.*

"A thousand pounds." While her pulse pounded in her ears, his eyes sparkled. He thought upon it for a few seconds—

excruciating seconds—and then smiled. *Smiled!*

"Done."

She gasped and stared at him in surprise.

"And now let us discuss the terms. Though it is guaranteed, you will receive only half in advance, and the other half upon completion of the agreement."

"You said whether I was to succeed or fail in it."

"Yes, but I must see you make a proper effort." She blushed under his steady gaze, unnerving as ever. He continued, "And for that sum, I *will* watch to ensure that you do."

She said, looking away, "I have never taken on the case for a gentleman in need. I have only sought to help ladies find suitors."

"And yet you do marry off girls to gentlemen, I presume?"

Her lips pursed and she returned her gaze to his. "You are most discerning, sir," she said in a tone so dry it made him laugh.

"Come," he said, "We must begin again. I shall apologize for my boorish approach and for my earlier indiscretion, if you will allow that your behaviour was equally uncalled for."

She sniffed but made no move to accept the olive leaf. "If you can call that shocking kiss a mere 'indiscretion,' my behaviour, in comparison, was nothing at all. I only wished to make it clear—so you would know from the outset—that I am not one of the fawning women who court your favour; nor would I become one of the distressed creatures you flirt with and then abandon."

His eyes filled with mirth. "You are severe upon me, Miss Wetherham. I encourage you to stop listening to scandal broths, however." He paused. In a softer tone he said, "It is not my habit to distress women of my acquaintance, whatever you have heard to the contrary."

She eyed him dubiously. "Not your habit? But can you deny this? That you failed, this very Season, after giving many indications of honourable intentions, to make an offer for the hand of a woman you supposedly cared for? I do not wonder that Miss Alden welcomed another suit if you treated her as this other lady!" Suddenly she stopped, realizing that what she had heard about Dellacort must concern Miss Alden herself—it was the very thing he had already acknowledged, his slowness to offer for her.

"You fascinate me more and more," he said. "You must have Miss Alden in mind."

She swallowed—there was no other lady. "Well, I suppose I do. Unless you have sunk the hearts of multiple young women recently who waited upon you with hopes."

He stifled a grin. "Are you acquainted with Sophia?"

She looked away. "No. But talk does circulate."

His look became businesslike. "I will inform my solicitor of the arrangement. It would be wise to safeguard the entire thousand pounds when you receive it, and call it your dowry along with the mine, for Elston's sake."

Lettie's face clouded and a blush rose on her fine cheeks. "I have creditors to satisfy. I can only put some aside. The worthless mine will have to do."

"What do your bills amount to?" he asked, as if he had every right to know. And for some reason, some inexplicable reason, she told. Slowly she said, "I believe, in all, two hundred and twelve pounds." The number horrified her. Living expenses were shockingly liable to pile up.

He took out a notepad and scribbled something in pencil. "Have them sent to me. Or gather them while I wait." He handed her the note with his direction on Berkeley Square.

Woodenly she took the slip of paper. Was it seemly that she should send her bills to him? Why would he wish to pay her expenses in addition to the one thousand pounds? Particularly when he was in love with another woman? The whole business suddenly felt repugnant to Lettie, as did all talk of money, of paying bills, of creditors. All matters she normally did an admirable job of *not* thinking about. Yet some weight about her heart was lifting. The dread of facing creditors, of having to coerce yet more patience from them or admit defeat and throw herself upon the mercy of the Cantrells—which no longer was to be thought of in light of their current difficulties—those dreads were lightening. Only one thing, it seemed to her, still stood in the way.

"You are above generous, Mr. Dellacort; but even if I have a thousand pound dowry, it is hardly a sum that will turn the head of an earl!"

He gave a little smile. "What will turn his head is you. The thousand pounds and the mine will soften the blow to the Marquess."

Her pretty face puckered in thought, but finally she shook her head. "I fear this cannot answer." Her eyes became pleading. "I *cannot*—I cannot pursue a man for such reasons!" He surveyed her silently for a moment. "I admire your sensibility in the matter. Let us do this: I shall escort you to meet His Lordship. You may feel differently after speaking to the man yourself. Not everyone considers him a bore as I do; I find most people trying, if you must know." A smile played at the edges of his mouth. "You may find him agreeable. You may even find that you suit."

She gave a sighing breath. "If he is honourable, he will hardly grant me the attentions necessary to discover whether we would suit or not. He will more likely ignore me, Mr. Dellacort."

Nick brushed off his waistcoat and met her eyes. In a voice that seemed softer than anything he'd said previously, he murmured, "No man could ignore you, Miss Wetherham."

She blinked, trying to discern how he meant that to be understood. It sounded suspiciously like a compliment. And then his voice was its usual, businesslike tone. "I will send my solicitor this afternoon with half of the agreed upon amount—five hundred pounds. And I will come for you tomorrow evening at eight-thirty."

Alarm filled Lettie's breast. "I must think further on this! Nothing you have said convinces me you are *not* an utter scoundrel whom I should not deal with."

He seemed amused. "I do not require your trust. Perhaps the money will reassure you."

"Money cannot excuse all. When I consider your behaviour to me earlier, I –I loathe you." What she loathed most of all was her shocking, instant, visceral reaction to him, but of course she said nothing of this.

"I understand," he said, nonplussed, as if nothing she might say or accuse him of could possibly cut up his peace. "If you play your part well, you will not have to suffer my company long."

"What if I do not find Lord Elston agreeable? I recollect he is almost a dandy."

He waved a hand in the air. "No, no, that's coming it too strong. He is…a mild eccentric, you might say."

"If he is very disagreeable, I will not pursue the matter further."

"In that event you will have earned five hundred pounds for very little effort. You have nothing to lose, and much to be gained." He came to his feet. "By the by, who are your solicitors?"

"The Morgan Firm, on Mount Street."

"Until tomorrow night, then." He gave a polite bow and turned to leave, but at the door he stopped and, turning back, said, "Pray, do not wear black."

Chapter Five

As Nick sat behind a ponderous mahogany desk in his study writing instructions to his solicitor, he explained, in a calm, drawling voice, to Stewart, sitting across from him, why he was forwarding five hundred pounds to Miss Wetherham. The monies would be delivered in conjunction with a business agreement she must sign in order to receive the funds; and said agreement would ensure her cooperation in what he called "the Elston-Alden" case.

What he did not mention was that the instructions included his authorization to purchase as many shares of a certain diamond mine in East Africa as could be had. After sending a footman to deliver the note speedily by special messenger, he looked up and saw Stewart shaking his head.

Stewart was more of a hanger-on than a confidant of Nick's, but he had grasped enough of Dellacort's character over the years to recognize an anomaly. "I can hardly credit this," he said. "You *must* be in love with Miss Alden. Either that, or you've fallen for the widow. I've never known you to be eager to put yourself out like this. Especially to the tune of five hundred pounds!"

"A thousand pounds," Nick corrected him, rising from his seat. "In fact, twelve hundred and twelve altogether! And that's just the start of it. Come, let's share a drink on it, shall we?"

"Twelve hundred!" Stewart's voice was as fraught with horror as if he'd learned Bonaparte had crossed the Channel.

He followed his host along the corridor to a wainscoted drawing room with an enormous portrait above the mantel, shaking his head. "And what do you mean, that's just the start of it?"

Nick said, "Diamonds. I plan to buy shares in that mine."

"The Wetherham's Venture? The one that killed her husband?"

"The same."

Stewart's frown turned into a little knowing smile which he wore while Nick instructed a footman regarding the drinks, and which remained upon his face while a maid scurried to get a fire going. He knew at once that if Nick was purchasing shares in the mine, everyone had been wrong about it. Contrary to the story spread about by the widow, it must hold value. Nick was no pea brain. Stewart made a mental note to get his man of business on it as soon as possible.

Inside the handsomely furnished room in the Greek Revival style of neatness and proportions, Stewart settled into a plush wing chair with satisfaction. Nick sat nearby in an identical seat. Both faced the fire, and, after receiving drinks from Eggers, the butler, sipped in contented silence. Until Stewart let out a breath of a laugh. "Will you not explain yourself? My head is like to burst with conjectures, but I'll merely trouble to tell you two that rise to the top. First, you aren't careless with the blunt, so why should you go in so deep unless you *are* determined to marry Miss Alden—or second, are enamored of the widow? Even you wouldn't put out so much for a simple matter of restoring your pride."

"Restoring one's pride is never a simple matter. And a man might well put forth more than twelve hundred to do it." He paused. "Think of the gaming table—if it eases your mind, I've lost more than this sum in a single night at Brooks's."

A ripple of doubt crossed Stewart's face. "Still strikes me as havey-cavey, your being so generous to Miss Wetherham—unless it is Sophia only that you thought of."

Nick took a slow sip from his glass, staring into the fire. "It wasn't for Sophia."

Stewart's brows shot up. "The widow, then?"

"Why must it be for either of them? Perhaps 'twas just to have my way. I make no pretence of noble motives. Miss Wetherham was reluctant to take the case, so I did what was necessary."

"She would have taken it for half that; even a quarter or less, I've no doubt. Come, come, there's more to it."

Nick took a deep breath. "She would not have; she distrusts me exceedingly. Or, if she would have, consider it charity, philanthropy, call it a moment of hen-heartedness for a pretty face, or call me a gudgeon, I care not. Whatever you like, 'tis done. And whether or not the business goes as I wish, I've done a good turn for a widow. Now I've some insurance against Judgment Day, think you?"

Stewart's mouth fell open. "Judgment Day? Philanthropy? Why—you're—you're in love, Nick!"

Dellacort turned with a grimace. "Now who's the gudgeon?" Looking back at the fire he added, calmly, "I believe I am incapable of love, actually. Particularly the kind of love that makes a man want a wedding. This business with Sophia merely strengthens my conviction on this, for, despite the spectre of losing her, I am no closer to walking the aisle with her than I was before. My only aim was to restore our acquaintance to what it was."

"And to boot Elston out of the way."

Nick raised his glass and met Stewart's eyes. "Make no mistake, the marquess meant to displace me when he came of a sudden and dazzled the Aldens with his son and the title. His family has blocked my path before; they won't get away with it this time." He took a large swig of the drink.

Stewart was silent, staring at Nick thoughtfully. "By Jove! It was the marquess that bought that land adjacent to your estate; the land you had begun proceedings to purchase. He knew your interest, doubled his offer, and closed the sale secretly before you could say Jack Robinson."

Nick nodded. "Half the tenants on that property are employed in my fields. And that land is better situated than mine; would've doubled our crop yield. He stole it from me, quite simply." He took another sip of his drink. "He has come against me numerous times at the gaming table, which, I'm happy to say, rarely ended in his favour."

"Which means that my first conjecture was correct. This is about restoring your pride more than gaining Miss Alden."

"Frame it however you like. But Sophia will thank me for turning Elston away; and Miss Wetherham will thank me when she is a countess and later a marchioness. 'Tis seldom a man gets to settle an old score while scattering good deeds in his path. I could not have asked for a more propitious opportunity."

"The Aldens won't like it."

"To the devil with the Aldens. Sophia's papa was quick to consign me to that fate when Elston came along." He shook his head. "Even that lily liver shall do well, for he will be spared life with Sophia—she is quite merciless."

A log sputtered and fell, sending off a shower of little sparks that fell harmlessly to the floor. "She'll want an offer from you at the end of it, depend upon it," said Trafford.

Nick nodded. "She has long wanted that." With a sigh he added, "The only soul *not* to be rewarded handsomely from this endeavour is mine, if you think on it."

Stewart echoed his friend's sigh and sank further into the cushion. "You'll have some satisfaction when the Aldens beg you to renew your offer."

"I never made one," Nick said.

Stewart cried, "And why should you! I confess, I did not like the prospect of losing you to matrimonial obscurity. I've seen it before—the most confirmed bachelor, the best company, an all-around good blood, supposes himself in love, makes an offer and soon is nowhere to be seen. He forsakes his club, his fellows, all his gentlemanly pursuits and disappears to a remote country estate to sire offspring. No, I'm not sorry if you are content to have things just as they were. Leave the parson's mousetrap to another man."

"My thought exactly," said Nick comfortably.

"How will she take it—Miss Alden? When she learns that after you've upset her apple cart with his lordship, you have no intention of filling his place."

Nick's lips came together. "She only welcomed him to punish me. I daresay, she is aching with regret; waiting in suspense for me to rescue her, no doubt."

Trafford had to smile. "You call it a rescue? Getting rid of the title she might have married, and putting no alternative in its place, for you shan't make an offer yourself?"

"I have no plan on doing so at present." He turned to eye his friend evenly. "But every man must see to an heir sooner or later." He turned back to the fire. "As for the earl, as I said, she will not rue his loss. He will bore her to Bedlam. She will be happy enough for us to return to our former relationship."

"Then why bring in Miss Wetherham at all? Why put yourself out a thousand pounds and more if Sophia will welcome you back with open arms?"

"Because her parents will not, unless the earl is out of the picture. Without him, I am the hero for their daughter. But if they have a choice between us—they've already made it. A title wins the day."

Stewart nodded. "And so Miss Wetherham is tasked with turning his head?"

"She has looks to rival Miss Alden's and has only to be more pleasing and amiable to Elston than Sophia—which, I assure you, shall be easily accomplished. Sophia, you and I know—" he hesitated and a smile curled his lips—"is a shrew."

Stewart sighed. "She is, by Jove! I thought you didn't know it."

"Of course I know it."

"Why do you dangle after her? Let her go to Earl Brest with your best wishes. You can do better, Nick."

Nick nodded, gazing into the fire. "Perhaps I like a shrew."

Chapter Six

The following evening at precisely eight-thirty, Nick Dellacort called upon Miss Wetherham. He wore exquisite evening wear and looked quite as handsome as she'd ever seen a man look. For herself, she appeared in the entrance hall with high colour in her cheeks, close curls framing her face, and a Greek style, embroidered band on her head. In place of her usual black or grey, she wore a dark green silk gown with puffed sleeves that accented the green of her eyes, while a stand-up lace collar and square neckline showed off the single diamond necklace to perfection, the last diamond from her jewel chest. An over-gown of silk with metallic embroidered borders and three-quarter length gloves completed the outfit.

"Thank you, Miss Wetherham," he said with a polite bow and an appraising eye. "Charming."

She looked up curiously. "Are you not thanking me too soon? Before we have accomplished aught?"

"It is for your appearance that I expressed gratitude," he said, as he took a tippet from the hands of Mr. Dudley, Lettie's butler, and put it about her shoulders.

"Your thanks belong to Mrs. Cantrell, then," she said honestly. "For I have leased out her wardrobe!" In what Lettie later considered a godsend, her cousin had stopped by the previous day after Mr. Dellacort's departure, marching into the house followed by two footmen, one carrying bandboxes and the second an armload of gowns. To Lettie's wide-eyed stare, Mrs. Cantrell said, "We are both in a muddle, dearest, but I have thought of a way to help one of us—*you*. As for me and Horace, well, that is another story."

What ensued over tea and conversation was the discovery that Horace and Amelia were indeed in narrow straits due to a disastrous trade on 'Change, just as Mr. Dellacort had said. Their little mountain of savings had had its head lopped off in the business; indeed, the greater part of their fortune had vanished, leaving only a veritable anthill.

With a heartfelt sigh Amelia said, "We will close up the town house when the Season ends, let go of the major part of our staff, and thereafter, hide at Barth Hall in the country until—God willing—Horace is able to turn things around."

Lettie was horrified and expressed her sympathy with tears at the edge of her eyes, extending a hand to touch Amelia's. "How odious this must be for you both!"

"Do not cry, Lettie! I am determined not to shed tears over this, for it cannot be helped."

Lettie smiled sadly. Sniffing, she added, "How very strong you are. But to conceive of you having to pinch and economize! I am accustomed to doing so, but—poor Amelia and Horace!"

Her cousin smiled. "Recollect, we have Harriette to school us. My sister in law is well-versed in such things, for she has always sought to keep her expenses as low as possible. She has already drawn up a plan, laying out what expenditures are unavoidable, and those which, sadly, we must refrain from." She took a sip of tea, considering. "We will survive." She looked brightly at her cousin. "Harriette tells me we had an interesting visitor yesterday. I, unfortunately, was out when he called."

Lettie met her eyes and knew instantly. "Mr. Dellacort!"

Amelia smiled. "Himself. Asking all about you."

Lettie rolled her eyes. "No wonder he knew so much. Harriet needn't have told him everything!"

Her cousin eyed her with amusement. "You know how she is. She must have poured out her miseries and every concern on her heart, in which case he is now undoubtedly in possession of the details of our misfortune as well as yours."

"Yes, he is aware of it all," Lettie said with a sigh, recalling her conversation with him.

Amelia said, "I gave her a combing when she told me, but she insisted she had to make your situation clear so that Mr. Dellacort would not *think* of taking advantage of a poor widow." With a raised brow she asked, "I daresay she left him predisposed to be above generous?"

Lettie laughed. "The vixen! But I cannot deny he was generous." But then her face fell, and she sighed. "If he had not approached me, I might have gone on living with the *illusion* that I could get by. I was sure my circumstances were not nearly as bleak as he made them out; but now I am constrained to feign an interest in the earl, who will think me a tuft hunter! And I am sure he moves only in the highest circles, which my wardrobe cannot accommodate."

Lettie had hardly purchased any new apparel since she'd gone through the proceeds from selling her last good piece of jewellery, a diamond brooch. Even her modiste, one of "the faithful" according to Betsey, (since she extended long credit) had lost patience and would no longer allow Lettie to bespeak so much as a sash without payment up front. And more mortifying yet, was how Wirgman Dressmakers on Hanover Street treated her. They took any client ahead of her, making her wait insufferably long to be served, and thereby notifying anyone present that Miss Wetherham's account was behind.

This season, Lettie'd been making do with alterations to keep her wardrobe modish. Her eyes landed on the pile of gowns, draped neatly over the brow of a sofa.

Amelia followed her gaze and smiled. "Which brings us to why I brought my gowns."

"Are you having them altered?" Lettie asked.

Amelia's eyes lit. "Part of our new economy is to stay home more of an evening, for which reason I shan't be needing so many. As I hoped to find that you and Mr. Dellacort came to some agreement, I brought them for your use. Your wardrobe will not be a concern!"

Lettie's breath caught in her throat. She had expected to stay in mourning clothes for many years and had not minded the thought. Even somber colours came in beautiful fabrics and styles; but the sight of the colorful, costly gowns made her rise with excitement from her chair to inspect them.

She held up one after another, sighing at their loveliness. When she reached an especially elegant gown of pale pink satin heavily embroidered with silk, she was speechless. It had a train from the Empire waist, and both the puffed sleeves and neckline were edged with French lace in the elegant fashion of Empress Josephine. She turned to her cousin. "You cannot mean for me to wear this one. It is too fine! You must keep it for yourself."

Amelia smiled. "I do mean for you to wear it. We want you looking your best for Dellacort, do we not?"

"For Dellacort?" The memory of that stolen kiss shot instantly to mind and Lettie's cheeks flushed. But she said, "I shall make no effort for *his* pleasure, though for the sake of our agreement, I must." She returned the gown gingerly to its place, considering how the Cantrells had always been generous to her, even offering to pay her lease at times when they knew her to be low in the pocket. And now, Amelia was giving her use of an expensive wardrobe when she was herself financially out at the seams. If only she could help them in return, especially now in their time of need.

"Dearest," she said, turning back to her cousin, "Mr. Dellacort has already advanced me half of what I asked for. Allow me to lease these gowns, or I must turn them away."

Amelia waved a hand at her. "Stuff and nonsense! We are relations. I am happy to grant you the use of them, for, as I said, our social outings will be thin for now." With a pointed look and pursed lips, she said, "I do not need them."

"But you are in need. I insist."

Amelia sighed. "We are short this month, I own; but Horace will comb me over if I take a ha'penny from *you*."

"Tell him I've come into a good sum. Tell him I can afford it."

Amelia regarded her with large eyes. "Did you get a substantial amount from Dellacort? I daresay it would be no hardship for him."

Lettie smiled sheepishly, nodding, and told her tale. How she'd not wished to deal with the man and so had suggested an outrageous sum, only, to her great surprise, he granted it.

Amelia's eyes bulged. "That is indeed most kind in him!" She rubbed her chin. "He must be dreadfully in love with Miss Alden." Her eyes rose suddenly to search Lettie's. "Unless…I wonder, dearest, if he seems interested…in you?"

"Nothing like that. He needed to ensure my cooperation. It speaks only of how much he values Miss Alden."

Amelia said nothing while she thought it over. "Well; your cousin won't object to my receiving a very small sum. Only a few pounds, Lettie."

That settled, Lettie smiled, rang a bellpull and then resumed her seat. When Mary, her sole parlourmaid appeared, she said, "Bring the gowns to Betsey, who will take care of them properly."

"Aye, mum," the servant said with a quick bob of a curtsey. She took the armload with a face as serious as if she held gold newly spun by Rumpelstiltskin and left the room. Lettie watched as the pile of textile finery vanished, and then turned to Amelia. "You are very kind, dearest; this is a bargain on my part. I will wear your gowns proudly. But I am not concerned, as you suggested, about looking my best for Mr. Dellacort."

Amelia pursed her lips and gave a sideways shrewd glance. "Of course not. I only meant for his circle of affectatious friends." But her eyes were lively with mirth when Lettie met her gaze.

"You mock me. I can assure you, he is in love with Miss Alden, and wants only my help in a professional sense. And even if that were not so, I should not set my cap at him for anything in the world. He is a known flirt, you must allow."

"Even known flirts must marry one day."

"And so he may Miss Alden, with my best wishes."

The mirth in Amelia's eyes subsided, but she said, "He may believe himself in love. But spending time with you shall cure him of that affliction. Miss Alden is nothing next to you. Oh, a beauty, yes, but only half as sweet as a sour lemon."

Lettie giggled, but said, "I consider them well matched then, for he is none too sweet himself, and I have an eye for a good match, recollect."

Amelia said, "Be that as it may, Harriet came away with the impression that he was most curious about you."

"Of course; as a business prospect." Lettie said archly.

The cousins parted after Lettie had pressed some bank notes into Amelia's hand, and said their goodbyes with many affectionate gestures.

"I will call again soon," Amelia said with a mischievous grin. "I must know how you fare tomorrow night."

"Say nothing to Harriet, if you please!" cried Lettie, knowing her older cousin would wish to know everything also, but might not keep any revelations to herself.

Amelia pressed a finger to her lips. "Not a word. God bless you!" And with a smile, she was gone.

So it was with great deliberation and a shiver of nervous anticipation that Lettie chose to wear the green silk. The beauty of the gown helped allay one part of her fears, for even Dellacort, a man careful in his dress, could not take issue with it. Not knowing their destination, she hadn't chosen the best gown, for she might have need of it another time for a more pompous occasion. Dellacort wasn't a regular member of the prince's set, but what if he took her to Carlton House? The green silk was fine enough to face an earl; and the low décolletage was daring for Lettie.

But every thought of the earl struck a sad note in her heart. What would Steven think if he could see and know what she was about? He would be shocked to learn that she must lure a man away from an unsuspecting woman. What had she got herself into?

Suddenly her deal with Mr. Dellacort took on a different hue and she saw it in its most bare, its saddest, complexion. She was to set her cap at a man purely because he had stolen Dellacort's bride. It was a role of deception! She detested the thought of it. Yet Mr. Dellacort had made painfully clear how precarious her situation was. Her struggle to make ends meet would continue indefinitely. *It will always be that way*, he'd said. And she could not argue, for it *had* been that way since dear Steven's passing. Their last savings had financed his doomed trip. Dellacort's five hundred pounds, coupled with the payment of her current debts, gave her no choice in the matter. Like it or not, she must do her part, no, her *best,* in his cause.

She'd accepted the deal. There was no turning back.

While she waited for his arrival, suddenly a small way of escape appeared. She could do her honest best to interest the earl without a thought of it leading to a heartless marriage. All she must do is make him waver long enough for Mr. Dellacort to move in and reclaim his lady. This was more practical a path in any case, since despite all Nick said, a man with a title, in line for a higher one, would never consider her proper wife material. She could not change that. But she could earn the second payment by showing every appearance of *trying* to.

While the last minutes ticked past for his arrival, she went over and over it in her mind, casting her part in the drama in the best possible light. It would allow her to live in comfort for perhaps two years. Her world would change from staving off desperation to enjoying some delights. It would restore a lost love to Dellacort, and, according to him, Miss Alden to her true love. It would prevent the earl from marrying a woman who was not agreeable and did not like him. Slowly she began to feel easier and easier about it. She might even, she supposed, make a friend in the earl, and find him agreeable. She did not require brilliance in a man. Amiability, good manners, kindness—these counted for more than a fat bank account. (All things Nicholas Dellacort lacked!)

With optimistic thoughts such as these, then, Lettie met Mr. Dellacort, not only a feminine vision in green, but with a convivial expression in her greeting that he had not as yet experienced; both were reasons why he had thanked her upon his arrival.

When they were seated in his spacious coach and four, she asked, "What is our destination?"

"The theatre. Did I not mention it?"

Her face lit for a second before she caught herself. She did not wish him to know how splendid she thought this, for she seldom attended the opera or ballet of late, as both cost money. She would not buy the cheapest tickets for fear of being spotted in the gallery with the working class. She and Steven had used to own a box, like most upper class.

When she had quelled her excitement, she asked, "Sadler's Wells or Haymarket, I suppose? I believe Covent Garden and Drury Lane are closed until Autumn."

"Haymarket. I hope you won't find Greek tragedy too tiresome?"

"I shan't." She paused. "Do you mean to introduce me to Lord Elston this evening?"

"Miss Alden will spot us in my box. That will do it. She'll bring him round at the soonest possible moment." He leaned toward her. "Recollect that your sole ambition is to make yourself as agreeable to Elston as possible."

Her eyes sparked at him. "I cannot be *that* obvious. If I were to behave as though I meant to please him at all costs, he will immediately take me for a tuft hunter."

"He may, but if he has a brain in his head, he'll know by now that Miss Alden is no different, for she cannot feign affection where there is none. You will be the more agreeable fortune hunter."

Lettie sat back and eyed him disconsolately.

"Yes?"

"I detest being thought of in that character."

Mr. Dellacort surveyed her, not unkindly. "Better to be thought a fortune hunter than to starve." At that, she only looked tragical, so he added, "I doubt Elston will ever conceive of such a thought. By all reports, he is a kitten. Indeed, his gentleness is what makes him supremely unfit for Sophia. She'll make mincemeat of him. If you make a match with the earl, I warrant you will spare him much grief."

Lettie took that in, but after thinking it over said, "Considering the tenor of our conversations since we met, why do you suppose I shall be more agreeable than she? I have reassured you often that I loathe you."

A glimmer of mirth appeared in the dark eyes across from her. "In my estimation, you are more cautious than caustic.

Your barbs are laced with self-preservation, not perversity or disagreeableness."

Uneasiness passed through Lettie's breast as she recognized how very true his words were. Mr. Dellacort seemed an excellent judge of character. How well he understood her! It was rather unnerving that he knew this much of her upon so brief an acquaintance.

"I assure you," he continued, "that is the difference between you and Miss Alden. She injures where there is no need, with no provocation. It is her nature."

She fell silent, thinking it over. Finally, approaching it from another angle she asked, "And what of your reputation? It will seem as though the lady in your company (me, that is) favours another man over you. Will that not distress you? When you have already lost Miss Alden to this man?"

He scowled. "I have not lost Miss Alden's affections, recollect. And as for what other people think or believe, I care nothing. You would do well to have the same mind."

Chapter Seven

When they arrived at Haymarket, Lettie upon Dellacort's arm, they were stopped often for greetings. Looks of amazement, polite notice by peers, more deference than she'd ever before received, surprised Lettie. Appearing with Dellacort apparently carried societal clout. Distracted by her mission that evening, the business with the earl, she'd almost forgot she'd generate interest being seen as a lady friend of his.

Society was used to seeing Miss Wetherham without a male companion and expected her to stay that way. To not only have one now, but for it to be the mysterious Dellacort! She understood their surprise. With a pang of conscience, she enjoyed it, though it was a hoax. Soon enough they would find out that Dellacort's real love interest was Miss Alden, not the widow Miss Wetherham. But she seemed to hold her head just a little higher than usual as she accompanied Nick to his box.

When they reached it, Lettie had a long, sad moment while she gazed at the galleries of bejewelled, sparkling patrons, for there was the box she and Steven had used to subscribe to for the Season. A couple whom she did not recognize were seated in it. But she could not be sad for long. The company held too much interest, and the general air of excitement before the parting of the curtains was a thing she could not be impervious to.

Nick moved two plush velvet chairs so they were just at the balustrade and offered the first to Lettie. Seated beside him, she nodded as he pointed out notable personages. In the royal box, though it was curtained, was the Prince of Wales with Mrs. Fitzherbert, he assured her. "Poor lady!" murmured Lettie, thinking of the shameful treatment she'd endured at the prince's hands.

In a box further from the stage, there, he said, was Miss Sophia Alden and Lord Elston. Even at this distance, she could tell Miss Alden was a dark-haired beauty. Lord Elston was more difficult to make out, as his hair and figure melted into the background, his features half hidden by Sophia, who was sitting forward much as they were, leaning out and looking over the company. But a gleam of yellow seemed to shine out—his cravat! Yellow, at the opera.

"Be sure to wear your brilliant smile, Miss Wetherham," Dellacort said, "when she looks our way. If ever a woman can be said to have a smile worth envying, 'tis you."

Lettie glanced at him in surprise. People did compliment her smile, a thing she credited to her habit of tooth brushing. She was an avid tooth brusher, having that in common, she was told, with Brummel. But a compliment from Mr. Dellacort always felt unexpected. As they watched, Miss Alden's gaze came their way. Sophia froze, staring at them. Lettie smiled at Mr. Dellacort as if he'd just granted her an audience with the Queen.

Nick said, "There; 'tis done. She'll be here at the intermission."

"Will she consider me her foe?"

"Does that concern you?"

"Why should it not? You have described her as formidable. She will darken my name among the *ton*."

"When you are seen to flirt with the earl, she will withdraw her claws, I've no doubt."

"Seen to be flirting! Good heavens. How shall I ever live this down? And you evidently do not understand women," Lettie continued. "She may not care for him, but to allow another woman to intrude upon her domain is another thing."

He gave a breath of a laugh. "Fear not. I shall keep her occupied."

Miss Wetherham nodded, but trepidation rose in her breast. She'd met many a peer in society, but never with the idea of trying to snare one's romantic interest. She was not used to pretence, not accustomed to planning out her behaviour to achieve a certain goal, certainly not in order to gain a man's affections. She had a dismal foreboding she would be an utter failure with the earl. Too late, she wished heartily that she'd never agreed to the scheme.

When the curtains parted, her attention went to the stage, and she watched with growing delight. Soon she was utterly engrossed and forgot all other cares. Lettie was accomplished at pushing away unpleasant thoughts. When in debt, she managed to not even think of it until she had means to pay— unless creditors came knocking and forced her brain to acknowledge it.

But the intermission brought her back to her present situation as surely as a tide returning to shore. Nick's box was suddenly a-flurry with guests who had not earlier greeted them, as well as hopeful fruit sellers, and messengers carrying notes. Nick pocketed the notes after a quick glance at each, and then Nick made short work of the others, including Stewart, who bowed graciously for Miss Wetherham with a friendly eye. Mr. Trafford had always been polite and admiring, and she returned a sincere smile before Nick sent him away.

And then Miss Alden arrived with a gentleman whom must be Lord Elston. Nick rose and bowed. "My lord; Miss Alden," he said, taking her hand and caressing it with a kiss. She stared at him, her lips pursed. "We have seen precious little of you, sir, of late," she said cooly. Ignoring that, but still holding her hand, Nick turned to the earl.

"May I present Miss Wetherham to you, my lord? She is a valuable acquaintance."

"Valuable?" asked Miss Alden, staring at Lettie with cold curiosity as if she were a display at the latest Scientific Exhibition.

"One I hold dear, I assure you," Nick said. He turned and cast a smile at Lettie. She stifled the objection that flew to her lips. *Valuable acquaintance? One he held dear? Because he'd paid well for her help, no doubt!* But even more flustering was his smile—he'd never smiled fully at her before, and Nicholas Dellacort, whatever else one might say of him, had an endearing, charming smile. It was almost boyish and so unlike him, it seemed to belie his very character. It could not, of course; yet to cast such a look at her nearly tumbled her off her mission. She must concentrate on the task at hand. Lord Elston. She turned to the guests. Miss Alden surveyed her icily, but his lordship smiled.

"How do you do, Miss Wetherham?" The earl had dark, heavy hair, a round, slightly pudgy face, not unhandsome; full lips, and a dusky complexion. His most distinguishing feature beside the aforementioned unmistakably yellow cravat, was a pair of round spectacles that seemed to diminish light brown eyes surveying her benignly. Overall, it was a mild countenance, his voice, gentle, and Lettie liked him at once, despite the disconcerting neckcloth.

She nodded from her chair. "I am very well, my lord, I thank you. How does Your Lordship?" He smiled politely. "Well, indeed, thank you." And with that, Nick drew Sophia to sit beside him in a second row of chairs in the box, and the two sat together, knees facing each other. Lord Elston watched, but found Miss Wetherham smiling sweetly at him when he chanced to glance back at her.

She nodded at the chair beside her that Nick had vacated. "Have a seat, my lord," she said, encouragingly. His lordship hesitated, but with another wistful glance at Sophia, took the proffered chair. She smiled encouragingly. The earl met her eyes and then, glancing at her necklace, said, "You wear a very pretty necklace this evening."

Lettie saw her opportunity and dove in. "The diamonds are from the mine owned by my late husband."

"My condolences, ma'am. You are a widow, then, at so young an age?"

They continued to talk, and Lettie was able to share how dear Steven had died, carefully inserting the fact of her owning the controlling shares of the mine. She found herself assuring him she had every intention of exploring it further for new veins, and suddenly her heart was lodged in her throat. She'd never intended to explore it further! Dellacort had poisoned her mind with the thought that it might yet contain untold riches. But she stifled her conscience, for he was older and wiser and no doubt perfectly right. Then she admitted to the earl that the mine was closed at present due to safety concerns, though Steven was convinced more diamonds could be found if one searched. Still, a sense of dishonesty sent a flush to her cheeks.

"If your necklace is any indication, the mine must hold great value."

"It was wonderfully productive at first," she replied. Fingering the necklace, she said, "Steven had this set at Rundell's. They did admirable work, would you not say?" She held it up to let him admire it, hoping to further impress him with the quality of the jewel. He leaned over to look and seemed very intent. Lettie felt a small triumph. He had an eye for good diamonds, it seemed, and this would make him consider the mine's value.

The earl took the necklace in one hand, running a thumb across the stone. Another ray of triumph shot through Lettie, until at almost the same moment she realised his gaze must take in the white rounded tops of her bust, just beneath the necklace and visible in the lowcut bodice of the fashionable gown. She made a mental note to never be without a shawl or fichu in the future! He said, "Very pretty, Miss Wetherham," and with a smile, dropped the necklace. "I beg your pardon," he said, with another smile.

She turned away, blushing.

Leaning toward her, he asked, "How do you find the production? Do you come often?"

She was grateful to move on to a safer topic. She shook her head. "I have scarcely been here this season."

Nick's voice broke in. "Miss Wetherham is too unselfish to insist upon coming, for she is nursemaid for her cousin-in-law, Mrs. Cantrell, who has not been well this year."

Lettie's colour deepened yet more.

"'Tis very good of you, Miss Wetherham," said the earl.

"Not—not at all. I—I am happy to assist my poor cousin." She turned and gave Nick a look of indignation, for now she had been forced to another lie. Amelia was not ill, and Lettie was not her nursemaid. He only grinned.

"Is she in danger?" Lord Elston asked, pulling her gaze and attention back. "A young lady in our employ in Lincolnshire, only a fortnight ago, perished suddenly after suffering from a mere ague."

"A young woman, you say? Dreadful! I am sorry for it. My cousin is in no such danger, I assure you." She swallowed and searched her brain for a way to change the subject. Mr. Dellacort had smoothed over her real reason for not attending, which was a lack of finances, probably because to admit to financial distress in this crowd was to invite scorn. But he'd made Amelia out to be unwell.

"To miss the performing arts is regrettable," Lord Elston murmured with sympathetic eyes. "But there must be some amusements Mrs. Cantrell approves of and can partake of?"

Lettie smiled. "The Cantrells are known for their card parties."

"And is that your preferred amusement?" he asked politely.

Lettie was charmed. Surely an earl could care less which amusements she preferred, but he spoke earnestly. He really was mild-mannered as Dellacort said. Smiling she said, "I enjoy playing at cards as much as anyone, I own, so long as we do not play for stakes."

"No stakes?" he asked, smiling. "Does that not remove the chief diversion in it?"

"Not at all," she said. "You might find, my lord, that removing the financial incentive relieves a burden while *augmenting* diversion. One's mind is much easier when there is no loss to be feared other than the joy of winning against one's opponents."

"We must hold a card party so I can test your theory," he said. Before she could form a reply, a voice from the stage "begged to inform the illustrious company that the production was about to resume." Lord Elston came to his feet and waited for Miss Alden, who just then let out a clear, fluid laugh. In the next moment, after quick fare-thee-wells, they had gone, and Nick returned to sit beside her.

"And how does Lord Elston strike you?" he asked, as servants slowly snuffed out the lights. Lettie hesitated. The scene flashed in her mind of the earl holding her necklace and seeing beneath it. But that had been accidental. "I believe he is agreeable."

"You hesitated. You have doubts."

Lettie turned to him. "Mr. Dellacort, must you pay *so* close attention to *everything* I say and the *way* I say it? Cannot you take my words at face value?"

He chuckled. "How adorable you are. I shall endeavour to take your words at face value."

She could not see his expression. She did not know whether she'd been served a turn of sarcasm but thought it likely. Perhaps she ought not to have scolded him. Without another word, she turned to face the stage, ready to lose herself in the performance. But his voice cut through the robust orchestral effusions reaching their ears from below.

"Accepting your words at face value, I assume it will be no hardship for you to draw him away from Sophia, then?"

"It *is* a hardship, sir, because it is deceptive on my part. But not on his account. He is not disagreeable. But if His Lordship cares for Miss Alden—"

"He cannot care overmuch; Miss Alden is happy to ignore him, as you saw just now."

"That is no indication of how she might behave generally toward him. Tonight, she was reacquainted with an old friend—you. Her behaviour, in that light, is forgivable."

"Her behaviour, in any circumstance, would be the same."

The actors were on stage now, and Lettie turned her attention to them. She meant to enjoy this one night of pleasure, even if it was only on account of what she suspected more and more amounted to near devilry. If Mr. Dellacort loved Miss Alden, why did he not plead his case with her and win her hand cleanly?

Afterwards, while the audience awaited the inevitable pantomime that always followed the main event, Miss Alden and Lord Elston returned to their box. Another couple trailed in behind them and greeted Nick, who introduced Lettie.

"We're leaving now, but I insist you join us," said Sophia. "We'll have a late supper at the marquess's mansion." She spoke as if only to Nick.

"We mean both of you, of course," said Lord Elston, moving forward to meet Lettie's eye. Miss Alden pressed her lips together, looking back at Nick after taking only a short, cold, glance at Lettie.

"Do join us," the earl repeated, with quiet earnestness, belatedly moving his gaze to

include Nick.

Dellacort said, "With pleasure. Park Place, if I do not mistake me?"

"That's it," said Lord Elston.

Afterwards, as they wound their way through late-night traffic, usual for London during the season, Nick gave Lettie an appreciative nod. "It seems our friend is eager for your company. Well done."

Chapter Eight

Lettie had been to several town mansions and was accustomed to the trappings and grandeur of the upper class. The Marquesse's mansion was one of the grandest in her memory, however, gated at the street, and then colonnaded in front. Large flambeaux cast shadows on them as they approached the door, opened by a footman.

Inside the marbled entrance hall, a footman was assigned to their care. He led them through a cross corridor and then up a marble, cantilevered staircase. From there, they traversed a wide, carpeted corridor, rich with décor, and lined with portraits guarded by blank-eyed busts on pedestals and interspersed with ornate pilasters. The servant's bright candelabrum lit their way, as well as domed oil lamps spaced evenly along the walls of the corridor.

They were approaching a set of double doors from which emanated the sound of laughter when Mr Dellacort said, touching her hand upon his sleeve, "Give your brilliant smile when he looks your way."

She took in a breath. "Very well."

The doors opened to a high-ceilinged, magnificent neo-classical reception room with rich, formal drapes gracing three floor-length bow windows, elegant furniture and detailed plasterwork. Beautiful carpets and a crackling fire in a sizable fireplace warmed the space for the many guests sitting at card tables, playing cards, drinking, and jesting.

"I thought we were to join a *small* party," hissed Lettie.

"As did I." He stopped and searched the room.

"Who are these people?" she asked, surveying the crowd, which strangely, did not seem at all familiar.

"The marchioness is friendly to men of letters and the arts. Tonight's actors are likely here, as well as some notable musicians and artists."

Just then a short and balding man, well-dressed, and about fifty, holding two glasses, stopped before them. "Dellacort," he said heavily, with a tone conveying no pleasure in the meeting.

"My lord," said Nick, in a clipped tone.

"My son left instructions for ye," he said with distaste. "Though I've no good idea why he should require *your* presence ahead of his wedding."

"Has a date been set?" Nick asked, not eagerly, but as if to be polite.

"End of the month," he answered, waving one of the glasses a little. He turned and signalled to a footman, who came quickly. "Show them to the library." But he glanced at Lettie and said, "And who is this with you, eh? I hope this lady's presence signifies that you've moved on from Miss Alden, sir?"

"Allow me to present Miss Wetherham."

Lettie curtsied politely. "My lord."

"Miss—Wetherham? Never heard of it."

"Miss Wetherham owns a diamond mine, sir. In East Africa."

The marquess lowered his head to see Lettie better above spectacles which rested rather precariously at the bottom of a short, red nose. He had bushy brows and weak eyes. "A diamond mine, eh?" He turned to Nick. "Yes, yes, I heard something of diamonds, recently. You *would* make a splendid rebound, Dellacort," he said snidely. To Lettie he said, "A pleasure, I'm sure." He nodded at the footman and moved off, raising the two glasses high to keep them above the crowd.

"So that is Lord Elston's father."

"The same."

"I wonder what he meant. He said he'd lately heard something of diamonds!" She looked up at Mr. Dellacort with surprise.

"I haven't a clue. But it was propitious we should run into him. Now he knows of your mine; it will help pacify him when Elston puts you forward."

Lettie frowned, stopped, and pressed on his arm. "You know very well the mine is worthless! I told you about that."

"I know no such thing. I know only that your husband"— he raised his hands innocently— "God rest his soul, was not successful in finding its riches. That is not the same as proving it holds none. The verdict is out in that regard."

She huffed, as they moved on. "It *may* be worthless."

"And you *may* be a very wealthy woman."

They were shown through double doors into a large, round room, lined with books. Two windows with velvet drapery and cushioned reading benches beckoned, while at the far end, two settees sat facing a blazing, welcoming fire. There were desks and tables and more stuffed chairs, and one long table laid with linen, crystal, covered dishes, and silver cutlery, all of which seemed to sparkle in the light of an elabourate candelabrum.

"There you are!" said Miss Alden from her seat on one of the settees. The earl, sitting beside her, clambered to his feet.

"Glad you could join us," he said. "Miss Alden has only just told me how she longs to know Miss Wetherham."

Lettie looked in surprise at the lady, who regarded her coldly.

"Come," Sophia said. "We'll talk while we fill our plates."

The gentlemen stood talking before the hearth while Lettie and Miss Alden went to the spread on the table. A footman stepped forward from the shadows and handed them each a dish. As Lettie chose from cold meats and delicacies before them, Miss Alden, quite close at her side, said, "Miss Wetherham, I understand you do quite well, making yourself useful to society? Your chief occupation being the pairing of matches."

Lettie turned to her, recognizing a subtle threat in those words. Miss Alden was *that* close to saying Lettie was in trade. "It is my hobby, I confess," she said coolly.

Miss Alden smiled. "Only a hobby?" She looked down at Lettie's green silk. "And yet it garners you a pretty penny, if I am not mistaken?"

Lettie's heart raced. With false bravado she replied, "You *are* mistaken." She leveled a look at Miss Alden as if she were cork brained. It wasn't polite, but she sensed intuitively that she must meet venom with venom, for only this, she was certain, could ward off further attacks by such a one as Sophia Alden. Miss Alden, it seemed, welcomed a fight, much like Dellacort, and neither of them, she sensed, would allow an opponent to back off gracefully unless they stood up to the challenge undaunted.

Miss Alden merely smiled. "Am I, indeed?" She regarded Lettie challengingly but the look of aggression in her eyes went down a notch. "Tell me, if you had to pair me with a gentleman, who in our upper class would you pick?"

Lettie thought briefly of the eligible men in society but discarded the search. "That is no challenge. You are a match for only one man I know of in the sense of temperament, general agreeability—or should I say, disagreeability? —and, I suppose, wit."

Miss Alden huffed. "Yes?"

"But you know who it is. Mr. Dellacort, of course." She turned back to the array of dishes.

"You came upon his arm. Would you cut him loose, throw him to the wind so easily then?"

She turned only her head to Miss Alden. "We are merely acquaintances, ma'am."

Sophia's brows rose. "Ah. I am glad to hear it. But you are *not* gifted at matchmaking. As you must know, the earl and I are betrothed."

"You asked for the man I should match you with, not for the one you are betrothed to. I told you who, in my estimation, you would best make a match with." Lettie turned to finish filling her plate. "They are often not the same at all, are they?"

She did not look to see Miss Alden's reaction, and walked off to take a seat on a settee. Miss Alden, thankfully, chose a seat on the adjacent one, signalling their conversation was over. Nick returned with his plate before the earl and quickly sat near Miss Alden. The earl returned, took a quick look at Nick and Sophia, and then sat not far from Lettie.

A scene very like that in the theatre subscription box ensued, during which Nick and Sophia talked and laughed loudly, while the earl did his best to attend to Lettie. She felt she never had his full attention, and now and then they were both guilty of falling silent in order to listen to the conversation of the others. He was not at all impolite, but after fifteen minutes Lettie felt sure to the bone that he would never turn to her from Miss Alden. He rose twice, once to return their empty plates, after which he dismissed the footman. And once to order glasses of sherry.

"Elston, why do you not show us the house?" Sophia asked suddenly.

"Of course," he said easily. "One day it will be ours." Holding up his glass he said, "But first. Bottoms up." He nodded at them all, and they obediently emptied their glasses. Lettie rarely drank alcohol and closed her eyes as she did, not relishing the taste of the beverage. When she opened her eyes, she saw Nick watching her in amusement, his mouth turned up.

The earl hurried to offer Sophia his arm, so Nick escorted Lettie. As they trailed behind the couple, he asked, "Do I need to speak to Sophia? Did she bark at you?"

"Not so much." She glanced at the lady in question, who happened to look behind her at that moment to peer at them. Cold antipathy filled her gaze, but Lettie's heart pitied her. After a moment she said, "She is not so very formidable."

Nick looked at her appreciatively. "Perhaps because you are as obstinate and determined as she?"

"Me?" Lettie smiled. "Determination, I admit to, unashamedly. But why obstinacy?"

"Is it not obstinacy to shun the thought of marrying again, although it would ensure your future comfort, not to mention easing your present circumstances?"

She gave him a wide-eyed look. "My desire to avoid marriage has nothing whatever to do with future comfort or present discomfort."

"Precisely. Foolish girl. Entirely obstinate."

Her eyes flashed. "*You* have no reason to comb me for it. I am complying with all you have asked. I risk my own heart and..." she looked towards Lord Elston. "And that of His Lordship." Looking back at Nick she added, "That is, if his heart can be said to be at risk. I believe he has it entirely settled upon Miss Alden."

"You need to up your game, Lettie."

"What do you mean?"

"Polite conversation is all fine and well; but you must *flirt* with the man."

She blushed. "How very vulgar you are."

He chuckled. "No more than when I sent you five hundred pounds. Now, I will draw Sophia away shortly. You will have opportunity to be more than polite."

She said nothing, expecting dread to overtake her, but only a sudden dizziness did. She felt strange; she pressed upon Nick's arm. "Are you unwell?" he asked, coming to a halt.

"I feel I'm on the Thames in a boat. I think it must be the sherry," she said, fanning herself due to a sudden shot of heat rushing through her. "I am not accustomed to it."

He patted her hand. "You'll be fine. It won't last."

Sophia turned just then and cut in. "What are you discussing with such sober faces? Pray, let us know it. We are in want of a good discussion, are we not, Elston?"

Nick said, "We were discussing the benefits of matrimony to single women."

"Indeed?" Sophia asked, with raised brows. "I hope you are enlightening Mr. Dellacort, then, Miss Wetherham, for I own he is greatly ignorant in that regard."

Lettie laughed aloud, and then covered her mouth with one hand. The dratted sherry!

"Ignorant, is that what you suppose?" asked Nick, looking at Sophia with the little smirk he often wore.

Sophia met his gaze with challenging eyes. "Is not your aversion to marriage well known, sir? Indeed, I know it better than anyone," she said with a humorless laugh. "You are sadly in need of understanding how tying the knot is beneficial, not only to the lady who weds you, but to yourself." She glanced at the earl and said, "His Lordship understands it, I daresay."

How long and deep would she play her game, Lettie wondered? And how openly she was revealing her feelings for Nick! She thought it must be hurtful to the earl and felt sorry for him. And Lettie hadn't been doing her part very well at all. She'd been engaged to turn his head, but how to charm Lord Elston in such a setting?

"Matrimony is God's design for procreation, for lifelong companionship, and blessing," the earl was saying in a tone as confident as any vicar.

"And you have our blessing," returned Nick, meeting Miss Alden's glaring countenance with unruffled composure. He moved Lettie along, for they had been standing in the wide corridor. "What room is this?" he asked, stopping again before the next doorway.

"The Yellow Saloon," said the earl, going for the door handle. "Shall you like to see it?"

Sophia said, "Elston, the house is cold, and there'll be no fire, nor even a lamp lit. I have thought better of my request. Let us do the tour another time, when 'tis day."

"Of course," he said. "Whatever you like."

Nick moved swiftly and tucked Sophia's hand upon his arm and turned back the way they'd come. The earl watched them go, his lips set in a line. He met Lettie's eyes. She smiled. "I'm sorry," she said.

"For what?" he asked, offering his arm.

"For disappointing you. When you could have Miss Alden upon your arm, you are left with me." She giggled. The sherry was still having its effect.

He studied her with a rueful but gentle look. "I daresay, worse things could befall a man."

She laughed. "I earnestly hope so!"

"I beg your pardon. What I mean to say, Miss Wetherham, is that walking with you is no punishment, I assure you."

She nodded. "Thank you." Nick and Sophia were moving quickly and were almost out of sight. Nick's words crossed Lettie's mind. *You must flirt with the man!* She swallowed, and said, "I warrant, my lord, a lady could do far worse than to be in your company also." There, that was flirting, wasn't it?

He looked down at her, for he was taller by a foot, his eyes questioning. She stared up at him; understanding slowly dawned in his eyes. He glanced ahead at the empty corridor and then back at her. Yes, he'd understood. A part of her shrank back in instant self-disgust, but at least she could now report this much back to Dellacort. The earl said, "Thank you,

Miss Wetherham. Tell me, what is your relationship with Mr. Dellacort?"

She swallowed. "We are acquaintances. That is all."

They were passing a magnificent portrait of a man in medieval armour holding his helmet against his side. "Is this an ancestor of yours?"

The earl glanced at the painting and stopped walking. "He is the first Earl Brest. I am the sixth, you know." He turned to her. "'Tis only a courtesy title now."

His tone seemed heavy, so she tried to divert the conversation. "What a weight of armour he carries!"

He nodded but sighed. "We must all bear the weight of our armour in this life, eh?"

Her heart stirred for him. He did not seem the lily liver or the bore Dellacort had called him. "You are very burdened. What is the weight you carry, my lord? If I may ask?" Later, she would be astonished at her impudence to ask such a thing. But he looked down at her and she saw only gratitude behind the spectacles.

"Ah, Miss Wetherham," he said. "You are very discerning. If only...certain other people would ask me that." But he moved them on, and they spoke no more until they were back at the library. From the doorway, they could see the backs of Nick and Sophia's heads, side by side on the settee.

The earl gave her an inscrutable look. "Forgive me for this," he said. He went up to the others briskly. "I daresay you must escort Miss Wetherham home, Dellacort. She has the headache."

Lettie hid her surprise, and merely nodded when Nick looked at her. He came to his feet and said, "At once." To Lettie, he said, "I am sorry for you."

"I am sorry to cut your evening short."

"Not at all," he said politely. They said their goodbyes, during which Nick kissed Sophia's hand. She shot Lettie a look of triumph. The earl wished Lettie goodnight, saying he hoped a night's rest would relieve her suffering completely.

As soon as she and Nick gained the corridor he said in a heated whisper, "The headache? Is that what you call flirting?"

She glowered up at him. "I said nothing of it. I was astonished Lord Elston made that claim. I believe he invented it not knowing it to be true, as I do, in fact, have the headache. But he evidently thought it time to be rid of us. And I can scarcely blame him, as you are determined to insult him."

"Insult him?"

"By claiming Sophia at every opportunity. You could not be more obvious about it." They were still speaking in heated tones as they waited for his carriage.

"I hope I am obvious. He needs to see what any stripling in short coats would recognize, that Sophia cares nothing for him."

She met his gaze with a challenge in her eyes. "Oh? Or does he need to see she cares only for you? Is that not what you wish him to see?"

He bit back a retort and then said, "What I wish him to see is *you*; you are available and he, by proxy, is also. He should not consider himself tied to a woman who loves him not." He paused to help her into the carriage, motioning away the footman who came to do so. Seated across from her he continued, "*You* are the one we should be discussing. Did you take advantage of your time alone with him? What did you do?"

"I did exactly as you asked." Wide-eyed, she confessed. "I *flirted*."

His mouth twitched.

"Do not laugh. I detest myself. I am sure that is why I do have the headache."

"What did you do and how did he react?"

She pursed her lips. "Our agreement did not include that I must repeat to you my exact words to the man." She paused, eyeing him resentfully. "The thing is, he was not offended. But as you saw, he could not get rid of us soon enough. I never complained of the headache."

Nick sat back and studied her. He looked out the window. When they drew up to her home on Russell Square, he said, "We need only give him time. I believe he will be more welcoming to you when next we see him.

Chapter Nine

Amelia and Harriette called the next day. Amelia would have preferred to come without her sister in law, but Harriette could not abide the thought of Amelia making a morning call without her, especially when it concerned Lettie. She might miss an opportunity of schooling her indiscreet cousin to improve her behaviour. It was Harriette's cross to bear, the suffocating knowledge that she always knew better what anyone else supposed they knew; and her duty to share it.

Lettie knew Amelia was curious about what happened with Lord Elston but could not ask due to Harriette's presence. Harriette was all curiosity about Mr. Dellacort. What was his business with Lettie? Was he seeking a wife? Why had he called and asked Harriette for Lettie's history? He seemed a proper gentleman when she spoke to him; was he gentlemanlike and polite to Lettie? Did Lettie consider herself in love with the man?

Lettie gave truncated replies to the effect that, as for being in love, it was the furthest thing from her thoughts. But yes, he was seeking a wife, and she had agreed to help him find her. At this, Harriette's eyes lit as though she had fallen upon the greatest news since the invention of the printing press.

"Who does he consider for a wife?" she asked with undisguised interest and a hand over her heart.

"Sophia Alden," said Lettie.

Harriette's face slumped. "Oh. A tiresome, odious, creature. Very handsome, I suppose, as far as handsome goes;

but surely Mr. Dellacort wants an amiable bride!" She waited for an answer. Lettie said, "I assure you, he wants Miss Alden."

The three of them sat in silence then, contemplating why a robust, intelligent, and good-looking man like Mr. Dellacort, who was rich and could have anyone, should want a pampered shrew for a wife.

"Lettie," said Harriette thoughtfully, after considering the matter, "What if you were to endeavour to turn Mr. Dellacort's head *your* way? Only conceive of your improved circumstances."

Amelia smiled and surveyed Lettie with a sparkling eye.

"Banish the thought!" Lettie cried.

"His landed estate in Derbyshire is said to be a marvel of architecture. And he is quite the virile man!" Harriette exclaimed with astonishing sobriety, as if it should settle the matter.

Amelia tittered, looking at Harriette with surprise.

Lettie blushed. She said, "He may be rich and …and…virile, and own an impressive landed estate…" Here she paused, thinking of how rich and virile and impressive he was. She took a breath and finished, "But he is a rogue, make no mistake. And vastly in love with Miss Alden, and that is just as well. Dear Steven would turn in his grave were I to conceive of marriage to such a man!"

Harriette sniffed and nodded. "I suppose you have the right of it. Your dear departed husband was a saint; we all know it. And we miss dear Steven, of course; but how many men like Dellacort will cross your path? How many eligible men," she asked, with pursed lips, "must come forward before you see the propriety in marrying again?" Her eyes flashed. "Pray, recall, that you have now rejected two suitors who were well able to keep you in comfort!"

Harriette's crusade to push Lettie to marry had been ratcheting up of late, likely due to the reversal of fortune suffered by her brother. She worried lest Lettie come to depend upon the Cantrells for support when they already had a perfectly good poor relation—herself—and could little afford another.

"My dear Harriette," said Lettie. "I do not see *you* rushing to the altar! I have offered my help as a matchmaker numerous times; I am sure you could be happily settled if you had a mind for it."

Harriette looked at her pityingly. "Dearest, you know I am a determined spinster. I am quite content in it. I shall be useful to the family as a nursemaid to children" —here she shot a glance at Amelia— "if ever there are any. Or, I shall spare us the need to hire a governess or tutor. But *you*," and here she turned a smile of sainted patience upon Lettie, like a priest upon a sinner, "have been a wife. You were almost a mother. You are meant for marriage and children. I am not."

Lettie raised her eyes to the ceiling. "There is no reason on earth why you are less suited for marriage than I."

Amelia said, "Harriette, dear; Mr. Dellacort has made his intentions clear. He is interested in Miss Alden, and we must respect that."

"Besides which, he is a scoundrel," added Lettie.

Gently, Amelia said, "As for that, you might withhold judgment, my dear. You cannot know so soon, upon so short an acquaintance, what is in a man's heart. I've made inquiries and could discover only that Miss Alden's family seems to have rejected Mr. Dellacort in favour of Earl Brest. But, aside from avoiding 'the parson's mousetrap' longer than most men," she said, smiling, "his reputation is untarnished."

"What of the numerous broken hearts in his path?" Lettie asked with arch assurance. "Surely you have heard the same stories that I have!"

"I could not discern that he was intentional in their breaking."

"What do you mean?" Lettie looked up.

"The broken hearts are on account of young women who were foolish enough to imagine, not only themselves in love, but that their love was returned by him. When they discovered his conversation and polite attentions meant nothing more than conversation and polite attentions, they suffered declines. I daresay, I never believed in such declines. But was he at fault, truly? I wonder."

Lettie instantly remembered her own beating heart when Dellacort paid *her* his style of "polite attentions." He'd stolen a kiss. She imagined that he must have done so with these other ladies as well. He was, as she suspected, a scoundrel! "I believe he was at fault," she said.

"Now, now," said Amelia. "He is, perhaps, a bit forward in his manners for a man so pleasing in appearance and unmarried. But it does not follow, then, that he purposely trifles with the female heart."

"Oh, but he does!" Lettie cried.

Harriette rearranged herself on her seat. "I see what Amelia means. Some men are rogues intentionally, from an impudent or wicked nature. But others, like Mr. Dellacort, merely by default."

Lettie cut in bitterly. "Mr. Dellacort is a decided flirt! And he takes no pains to discourage a woman from setting her heart upon him."

Amelia searched Lettie's eyes. "That seems harsh, my dear. I found him charming. If I do not mistake me, you resent the man for his good looks."

Lettie wished she could tell Amelia about Dellacort's shocking conduct, how he had attempted a kiss! But Harriette must not know of it. Well-meaning Harriette would find in it the perfect reason why she must become Lettie's companion. The last thing Lettie needed was to have Harriette installed at Russel Street.

As if reading her thoughts, Harriette turned large, tan eyes upon her cousin. "If he is a decided flirt, what you need is a companion to safeguard you."

"Not at all," Lettie said quickly.

"But at least you must beware your heart, Lettie. If you are correct about him, his persistent bachelorhood must be intentional, and very like, dishonourable." Harriette had in mind the recent scandal in the papers purporting that many upper-class men were no strangers to the lightskirts on St. James's. Mr. Dellacort was perhaps among them.

Harriette wished to see her cousin securely married again, not only from fear of competition in the "poor relation" category, but from genuine affection. Nevertheless, she could not wish her upon a decided flirt. "If you must do business with him, especially considering his charms, beware your heart," she said again.

Lettie said, "I assure you; I have no other ambition concerning him but to keep him clear of my heart."

The following day, Lettie's misgivings about having agreed to work with Mr. Dellacort weighed heavily upon her. This very night she was to accompany him to an evening party and prove her skill at flirting with the earl. A skill she had no heart for.

When he sent word to expect him an hour early, she hurriedly called for warm water to wash, and then had Betsey put up her hair in gold fillets of the Roman style. She donned one of Amelia's formal gowns, a silk satin confection with puffed sleeves and embroidered side panels; and finished her ensemble with gold filigree earrings and white gloves. She felt as equal to the coming night as a woman who knows she is dressed modishly can be said to feel. Betsey took exception when Lettie added a lace fichu and tucked it into her bust, but Lettie insisted upon keeping it. She could not bear to risk another episode such as had happened when the earl admired her necklace. She considered herself a modern woman but with Lord Elston particularly, did not wish to appear *alluring*.

When Mr. Dellacort was announced, she was sitting in the library as though she had been ready for hours. It was her favourite sanctuary, and where she read the daily collect in the prayer book. Books made her happy. The prayer book made her happy and secure.

Dudley presented Mr. Dellacort at the door and bowed himself off. Nick entered and regarded her with keen eyes that seemed brimming with more than their usual intensity and machinations. His presence, being so vastly nice to look upon, evoked the usual discomfort about her heart, but she kept her countenance carefully bland.

"I've come to a decision," he said.

"Yes?" A wild hope that he was releasing her from the scheme filled her breast.

"I believe you are in need of instruction. In the art of flirtation."

She put her book down and turned to him with compressed lips. "Is this why you came early? To let me know you consider me a failure?"

"Not a failure. You only need instruction."

"And what makes you sure of this?"

"For one thing, because you haven't flirted with me, not once. And you no doubt fumbled your opportunity with Elston."

She let out a breath of exasperation. "You are insufferable. Must every woman flirt with you?"

"Women of all ages do. Married or not."

"Perhaps if you did not suffer women to flirt with you, your reputation would not be that of a rogue!"

He smirked. "Excuses. Because you are not equal to flirting?"

She glowered at him. "Why should I flirt with you when I told you outright, from our first meeting, I had no intention of doing so?" In an irritated tone she added, "Besides which, you have no way of knowing how I behaved with Elston or what its effect was."

"Its effect," he said, coming around to face her, "was that he could not wait to be rid of you. And with me you have not flirted, I daresay, because you have no skill at doing so."

"Or perhaps 'tis because I loathe you!"

He put on a patient little grin that was quite infuriating. Putting out both hands, he motioned for her to give him hers. She ignored him.

"You blush like a schoolgirl."

This evoked a glare, at which he smiled wider. "How adorable."

"You menace! What do you want?"

"I want you to come to your feet. Come." He took her hands and gently helped her to a standing position. They were only half a foot apart, and she was treated to a close look at the handsome countenance of the man she was struggling to keep safely from her heart. Smooth shaven, a neat mouth, magnetic, beautiful eyes—eyes that were clasped on hers— but a scoundrel through and through.

"Well?" she asked.

He looked intently at her. "Flirt with me."

"What!"

"Pretend I am Elston. How will you flirt with him?"

Lettie looked at Dellacort for a long minute, her face working through discomfort and resentment. The difficulty was that Mr. Dellacort, the devil, against all reason, was more interesting to her than Elston, and it was not just that he was the more handsome. Try as she might, she could not pretend this was the earl. It was impossible.

"Come, come, it isn't that difficult."

Still trying to wrap her head about the task, she gave up trying to replace the man before her with the image of Elston. She dreamt, for a moment, that Mr. Dellacort really wanted her to flirt with him, not Elston. And suddenly, it felt possible. He wanted to see flirting, did he? Well, she was a woman, after all. She gave him a coy smile, not one of her brilliant ones, but one with promise. She dropped her eyes demurely, and then looked up at him again, meeting his eyes steadily. In a soft voice she murmured, "You, sir, are looking uncommonly fine this evening."

He nodded and squeezed her hand. "That's it! Give me more."

Lettie bit her lip, thinking. Then, mastering her expression to one of innocence, said, "Have you noticed, sir? Is it not exceedingly hot in this room? I would adore a breath of air." She sniffed and then, peeking up at him sideways, added, "But of course I could not venture out alone."

He chuckled. "You little vixen! You *do* know how to flirt."

Before agreeing to Dellacort's scheme, it had never been Lettie's ambition to flirt in her life. She and Steven had been promised to each other by their parents from childhood; flirting had not been necessary. They were friends forever, it seemed, and fell in love easily and naturally. But she smiled now, and her and Dellacort's hands, still clasped, swung happily.

"If he does not get you alone and take you in his arms after that, the man is impervious."

Lettie's smile vanished. Pointedly she said, "Or perhaps he is more gentlemanlike than *some* men?"

He looked down at her. "Or perhaps he is a fool." Swiftly, he kissed her on the lips. It was a brief, momentary kiss, as unexpected but as pleasant as a flower in winter. A little smile escaped her for she took it as simple approval on his part. But his eyes were full of more than approval, and then he drew her up suddenly and kissed her heartily, his lips taking hers with firm assurance. For a horrifying moment Lettie enjoyed it, but she thought of dear Steven and all enjoyment ceased. Guilt and practicality must trump folly and sheer emotion, and how could she think it was anything more? *Besides, did he consider her in need of instruction in this? Why else would he kiss her?* She pulled herself from his arms and turned away. "I need no further instruction, thank you," she said.

He turned her around to face him again. "Let us say, I do." He leaned his head in for another kiss, but she drew back. "I hardly think so! And you are out of line, sir!"

"Dearest Lettie," he purred. "What harm is there in it?"

She wavered for perilous seconds, and in so doing realised that Dellacort brought out a fatal weakness in her, for she nearly succumbed! He was a temptation. Her attraction to him contradicted sense and propriety and went against her better reason. There was much harm in it!

"For a man, I suppose there is none. For a woman, it is quite a different matter, and you have forgot that I loathe you."

He smiled thinly and released her. "But you must admit, I came into your life at an opportune moment. You were in need; and the Cantrells done up." He paused. "I have delivered you from disgrace."

"You are God's instrument. Only He is my deliverer."

"God would have you flirting with gentlemen, then?"

"That is *your* part in it!" she cried with flashing eyes.

He smiled. "You enchant me when you fly into the boughs."

"Oh?" she spoke in an icy tone. "Am I as enchanting as Miss Alden? Or have you also forgot you are in love with her?"

He sighed and shook his head, and then motioned her to sit. "Allow me to explain."

She sat down stiffly and looked at him expectantly. But then a scratch at the door opened to reveal Dudley holding a tray with a letter.

Dudley moved as though a weight dangling invisibly ahead of him pulled him slowly forward, headfirst, so that the rest of him followed. In this peculiar, slow gait, he came and held out his tray. "Begging your pardon, ma'am," he droned in his slow way, "but you asked me to bring this note to your attention when Mr. Dellacort arrived."

"Oh, yes, thank you, Dudley, I quite forgot." As the butler left, Lettie opened the letter, exclaiming. "This came today from my solicitors! I hadn't had correspondence with them for quite some time." Looking up at him in amazement she cried, "They tell me multiple parties are interested in acquiring shares in the mine, and the other shareholders are bought out! They require instructions regarding my shares as soon as possible."

"*Multiple* parties?" he asked, with furrowed brows.

She looked back at the letter. "Yes. They wish to know whether I desire to part with my shares." Looking up, she explained, "It seems the others gave standing instructions to sell for any offer; which speaks for how worthless the shares are! Except for the Cantrells; I believe they retain theirs, as I do." She gave him a pained look. "But why all this sudden interest? I wonder what can account for it?"

"Whatever it is, do not sell a single share," Dellacort said, firmly. "You must retain your majority holdings to interest the earl."

She stared at him, her brows furrowing. "But the mine is worthless. If someone, or many people, wish to buy it, I stand to earn something where I thought all was hopeless."

"Until the mine is plumbed further, you have no way of knowing its value or that of its shares."

She blinked and pursed her lips, considering it. "The Cantrells own the largest number, second only to me. I am happy, of course, if they will get a return after losing so much." With a sigh she added, "It could not have come at a better time for them!"

She looked from him to the letter in her hands, and then back up. "Are you certain I should not sell? If the mine is indeed worthless...this is a singular opportunity that will be lost if I hesitate."

He leaned toward her. "But I know your heart. You would not rest easy if you take money for something that ultimately holds no value. Let these speculators, whoever they are, be content with what they've purchased. Your mine has redeemed itself through the recovered fortunes of your friends; and if it turns out that more diamonds are discovered, you will be a wealthy woman. If, in the end, it is defunct, your conscience will be clear; and as a future countess," he added, eyeing her keenly, "you will have no financial concerns."

She turned her face away. "I have agreed to flirt with his lordship. That is tribulation enough. But you must know, I have thought upon it and concluded I can never marry him, earl or not. I cannot marry merely for security. I will not be a future countess, even if he wishes it, which I doubt with all my heart!"

When she turned to peek up at him, he was gazing at her benignly. "There are not many like you, Lettie. You will only marry for love, then?"

She nodded. "That is why, if you recall, I have no plans on marrying at all."

"Come, you've been arranging weddings for other ladies for three years. Is it not high time for you to have one of your own?"

The image of herself before the altar with Steven flashed across her mind. In a rare moment of unguarded longing, Lettie felt she would like nothing better than to have her own wedding. Why, she would! But it must be with a man she loved from her heart. A man like Steven. There was no room for the earl in such an image. Certainly, too, there was no room for a Dellacort. Not that Dellacort would make her an offer. The sun would as soon collide with the moon. She replied in a sad tone, "Love cannot be forced."

"I agree," he said, softly, studying her. But he blinked and glanced at her letter. "If you will allow it, I will make your reply and save you the trouble."

She looked disconsolate. "But since I am not to be a countess, does that not change your advice to me? Should I not sell?"

"Not yet. Keep your majority."

She stared at Mr. Dellacort and wondered. There was no reason on earth why she should listen to him, why she ought not to take advantage of this opportunity. She could cash out the shares of a worthless venture and perhaps come out with enough to live in comfort. But here he was, the scoundrel, looking supremely confident, and he was older and wiser in these things, wasn't he? She thought of Steven. He would not have given up on the mine. If he had lived and the expedition failed, he would have authorized another. He'd have raised the capital to do so, somehow. He would have done so again and again, until there was no recourse but to admit failure. She nodded.

"Very well." She handed him the missive. "I vowed not to give you the least space in my heart when first we met, but now it seems I give you my fortunes." She took a deep breath. "I will trust you, sir." With a tragic expression she continued, "God help me, I will, though I cannot say why!"

Dellacort studied her with an unreadable countenance, and with eyes that were mild. In a soft tone he said, "Let me kiss you for that."

In a choked voice she cried, "Oh, I do detest you, you cold-hearted ruffian!" She turned away, her face rosy, her eyes closed. The rogue! Wanting to kiss her when he was requiring her to flirt with Elston and even encouraging her to marry the man! He was wicked, that's what; and she was too, for she wanted nothing more than to say, *Yes! Kiss me, you scoundrel!* But she did not. By a supreme force of will, she did not.

He came to his feet. "It is too soon for you to know whether you can care for Elston."

She turned back to look up at him.

"Perhaps after tonight, you will thank me for putting you in his path. In any case," he said, holding out a hand to help her up, "I will ensure you will not regret your decision with regard to your shares. Come. Make yourself ready to be off."

Standing before him now, she said, "But I am ready."

His eyes fell to the fichu over the bustline and he motioned at it. "Except for this unnecessary accoutrement."

Blushing, she moved back a step. "That is a fichu."

His mouth twitched. "For modesty?"

"Yes," she said, nodding innocently with raised brows.

He stifled a smile. "Remove it."

"Why?"

"You look matronly with it."

"And if I do? I am a widow. Surely I have the right to look matronly."

"For daydress, perhaps. Not tonight."

She stared. "I shan't remove it."

"I insist you remove it."

"But I shan't."

"Are you certain?"

"Utterly."

"Very well." In one quick move, he grasped the fichu from both her shoulders and drew it up until he'd pulled the offending item free. He put it on the side table and turned to find green eyes sparking at him.

"How dare you!"

"Oh, you're much better now."

"You might have torn my gown. It was pinned into place!"

He glanced down at her bustline. "But I didn't." Offering his arm he said, "Shall we?"

With her mouth set in a grim line, Lettie took her gloves from the table and drew them on but did not take his arm. They made their way through the house; at the door she strode ahead of him in injured silence. On the pavement she said, "You are insufferable! I loathe you, you know."

"I know it."

"I would never take part in your nasty scheme if I were not forced to it by necessity!"

"I understand."

Reluctantly she allowed him to hand her up the steps to his gleaming ebony coach.

"Tonight you will flirt with the earl and this time win him over."

She looked at him plaintively. "Insincere affection is neither seemly nor becoming. If I fail tonight, please agree that my part in your business will be at an end. I am a matchmaker, but you would have me undo a match. Lord Elston is perfectly content with Sophia, and you want me to upset their betrothal." Hurriedly she added, "I will of course require nothing further from you." She could not bring herself to say anything so vulgar as that she would require no further *payment* or *fee*.

With narrowed eyes he said, "Ready to throw in your cards so soon? I thought you were made of stouter material."

Bristling, she replied, "Stoutness is not what your scheme calls for. Dissembling and dishonesty is what you want."

"Is that what it takes for a woman to do what's in her own best interest?" He raised a brow at her.

She understood what he meant by "best interest." He meant marriage. *Is it not time for you to have a wedding of your own?* he'd asked.

Ah, she thought, if Nicholas Dellacort would choose to settle down *with her*—then, perhaps, she could countenance a wedding. *Dear Lord! What was she thinking?* Her promise to Steven rang in her head, that she would only fall in love with a *good* man. Was she falling in love with Dellacort? Could anyone call him good? All she said aloud, with a sad and wobbly smile, was, "I will flirt this last time, as best I can. That is all I can promise."

Chapter Ten

Nick told her during the drive about their host and hostess, Lord and Lady Repton, very good *ton;* and reminded her, before they crossed the entrance portal of the mansion on Grosvenor Square, that she must try her best with the earl this night. It caused a pain in her heart, for it meant he was happy to push her at another man. It made perfect sense that he should do so, of course; it was why he had engaged her help to begin with. But it chafed at her.

"I will try, but I am afraid it will not equal your idea of a best effort."

"You need merely be more agreeable than Sophia," he returned. "Find him fascinating and you will accomplish a thing she cannot do."

Lettie was not unused to upper class balls with sparkling, attired guests, but this one seemed especially opulent. Whether it was the collection of aristocrats showing off their jewels, or the sheer magnificence of the cavernous ballroom lit with enormous candelabrum and chandeliers, she had to admit that being on Nick's arm opened doors she did not usually cross. When they were announced, Nick said, stopping to search the room, "You will be asked about our relationship, no doubt."

"And what shall I tell them?"

"We are acquaintances." The words fell dull and flat on her ears, though she knew of course, he was perfectly right. They were only acquaintances, indeed, more like business partners even, than friends. And that was just how it should be. And yet, she felt low about it. She also felt the start of a headache.

Nick spied the earl and Sophia, for even across the room amidst a crush of black and white tailcoats and gowns, the earl's stark bright cravat stood out like a clownfish among minnows. To her embarrassment, the earl also sported what looked like Hussar boots over pantaloons rather than breeches and shoes like most gentlemen. "There they are. Come. When I wander off with Miss Alden, you must set to work on the earl."

"Must you be so vulgar?" she moaned. "I have convinced myself I am doing his lordship a service by freeing him from Miss Alden, and 'tis in that thought alone that I am able to proceed in this."

He looked down at her with amusement. "And I thought the bank notes made you proceed in it."

"I loathe the bank notes!"

"You also spend them."

This was sufficiently quelling so that she said not another word but smiled brightly for the earl when they joined him and Miss Alden on the far side of the room in a small circle of people. She did not feel like smiling and could only hope her greeting was convincing.

"Nick!" said Miss Alden with a coy smile of her own. Miss Alden was no stranger to the art of flirtation, Lettie saw.

"Miss Wetherham," said the earl, bowing, and with his eyes clapped onto hers like a magnet on iron. With surprise she thought, *Nick was right!* The earl had only needed time. His eyes revealed an interest in her that hadn't been there, previously. Which meant she hadn't needed any instruction in flirting after all.

Nick positioned himself beside Sophia, but his eyes, deep and dusky, met Lettie's, and he gave an almost imperceptible nod. He'd seen the earl's reaction. The game was on. In moments he maneuvered the foursome from the circle, and they wandered off, Nick beside his prize, and Lettie with Lord Elston.

"I understand how it is," the earl murmured, watching Nick lead Sophia ahead of them. Looking back helplessly at Lettie he seemed devoid of ideas as to conversation. Lettie looked longingly at the dance floor. It would be a refuge from the business. The earl followed her gaze. Tentatively, he asked, "Do you dance, Miss Wetherham?"

Taking the question for an invitation, she smiled. "I would love to dance, thank you, sir." The earl's face blanched. "I—I believe I can," he stammered. He bowed politely, offered his arm, and they stood up for a quadrille. Lettie discovered shortly that his remark "I believe I can," was overly optimistic. He seemed *almost* to know the steps, but often was one or two beats early or late. Worse, his boots were noisy, making any *faux pas* more noticeable. She was mortified to see a few people tittering when he started a move early or hesitated to complete a figure.

She tried not to look about for Mr. Dellacort but could not help stealing little glances now and then. It seemed to her that Lord Elston did the same, only he, she knew, was looking for

Sophia. After the dance, she accepted his arm and he led her in a promenade about the room. The music for another dance began, but she would not make the mistake of standing up with him again. There was no sign of the transgressors. "Shall we get some air?" he asked.

With the idea of being more agreeable than Sophia, she acquiesced, though with some trepidation. Getting 'some air' no doubt meant going off alone. Was the earl now intent upon flirting with her? He led her to the ground floor and asked a servant to show them to the gardens. A maid led them through wide corridors and a long, narrow hall lined with offices and other private rooms; and then left them at the door to the back. The earl passed the maid a coin. Then he and Lettie stepped into an inky night with an ineffectual sliver of moon. Bushes and trees were only vaguely visible. The chill in the air was just enough to make Lettie wish she'd brought a shawl.

A shiver gave her away. "You're cold," he said shortly, and put an arm about her. Lettie tried not to shrink back, though every instinct cried out to do so. It was highly impertinent, was it not, for him to circle her with his arm? And yet was this not exactly what she was supposed to do? As they walked further from the house, the night seemed darker. And then Lettie's heart betrayed her, for each step became more difficult as if weights encircled her ankles. Moreover, her head ached. Lettie never used to develop the headache. It seemed to spring up when she must pretend an interest in the earl. She did not want to rendezvous somewhere off alone with him, as though it were an assignation.

She was a failure, after all, at the art of flirtation; and she was a failure at the whole enterprise, at turning Lord Elston's head, for she did not wish to turn it.

"Perhaps we had best go back," she said, stopping to look up at him. "Miss Alden may be in search of you."

"Doubtful," he said, "but kind of you to suggest. You are always kind, Miss Wetherham." He turned to her, too close for her liking though she could hardly make out his face.

"It is rather too dark here, my lord," she said, turning to head back. He took her arm.

"I am happy for the dark. I am happy to be with *you* in the dark, Miss Wetherham. And I must say, it seems to me, you are equally happy to be with me?"

He drew her up to him, right there in the middle of the path, and into a kiss. The image of dear Steven, like a guardian angel, entered her brain. And somewhere in the distance, the sound of Miss Alden's fluid laugh reached them. Nick was near! A rush of warmth filled her heart. If only she could run to Dellacort. *If only he was not in love with Sophia.* And just like that, all thoughts of being agreeable flew from her mind. She pushed herself from the earl's arms and cried, "Oh, they're here in the gardens also!" She was saved. Nick, wonderful Nick, just in time.

"Not quite here," Lord Elston said in a low voice. And then his lips came down upon hers, crashing down, it seemed to Lettie, because she did not welcome them. How brazen he was, with Sophia so close by! She endured it only for seconds and again broke away and pushed off his arms. "Forgive me, my lord!" She turned, ready to flee to the house and safety, and not a moment too soon, for Nick and Sophia were suddenly arrived. They appeared out of the darkness like phantoms from a fog, only half visible in the weak light.

"Elston, is that you?" Miss Alden asked. "Searching for me, of course."

"I believe I was," said the earl.

"Let us to the house," interrupted Nick, "where we can see one another to speak." He kept a hand upon Sophia's which rested upon his arm, and the earl was once again forced to watch helplessly as they took the lead.

Miss Alden's fluid laugh continued to be heard ahead of them as Lettie and the earl trailed in somber silence. They could hear the gist of the conversation, too, all centering upon things Sophia and Nick had done together, leaving the earl to listen unhappily, she thought. The mystery of it all was why he should kiss her when he was obviously heartsick for Sophia. He seemed utterly disconsolate. Whatever had moved him to kiss her, it wasn't love or affection. Lettie was a failure. She was torn between joy at her failure—for she did not want the earl—and sorrow for Nick's sake. He'd paid good money for her help. And she'd failed him.

As they followed the couple, she thought she might at least make herself agreeable in a benign sort of way. He seemed intent upon Miss Alden and Nick, and so perhaps she could ease his sensibilities with a distraction. She asked if the marquess and marchioness were often in town, and did they hold house parties often? He answered by warming to the subject of his mother's guest lists—for it was his mother, he assured her, who took a philanthropic interest in the arts, and opened her house to the greatest stars of theatre, opera, and even literature. She was known for her salons, he continued, but with the idiosyncrasy of not allowing political discussions at her table.

"That is quite unlike most of our famous town hostesses," said Miss Wetherham, thinking of women like Countess Cowper, or the Duchess of Devonshire, said lately to be at death's door, but who for years had run a famous salon for the Whigs.

"Yes, she is entirely interested in the creative arts and its many expressions," he said, smiling gently as if it were all amusing. He walked more and more slowly as he spoke; and Lettie felt satisfied that he seemed to have forgotten about the two people ahead of them.

She asked if he kept his own establishment for the season, or did he stay at Park Place, the mansion of his parents? He admitted uncomfortably that he had used to keep a separate establishment but recently simplified his life—and his pocketbook, he said with a grin—by coming home to the nest and keeping only his valet and his particular coachman. His parents were only in town for three months of the year, more or less, and he saw no reason why he should not enjoy the family pile and save unnecessary expense.

Lettie was impressed. Despite the vast wealth Lord Elston's family was said to control, he, the young heir, had a practical head for economy. And then he changed the subject. They were approaching the stairs, just in time to see the last of Nick and Sophia as they disappeared at the top.

He paused at the bottom of the stairs. "Why are you called Miss Wetherham and not Mrs.?"

"The ladies prefer it. The patronesses of Almack's quite insisted upon it, though I cannot say why, other than they apparently find it more genteel."

He smiled. "Ah. Come." He motioned to a small antechamber, the door of which was open. "There are candles lit, and look," he said after popping his head in, "a small fire. No doubt this room is for guests awaiting their carriages. We can speak here. Do you mind if I monopolise you for a few minutes before we return to the crush?"

Lettie nodded reluctantly. She must be agreeable. He stepped aside, motioning for her to enter. They sat upon a small rounded settee facing the hearth. The candles revealed enough of the room to show it was well furnished, its walls heavy with paintings.

"In truth, it is not your mine that interests me, Miss Wetherham." The earl turned to her with a little smile. He reached and took her hand. A heavy pall fell upon Lettie, and the familiar ache in her head returned, for she dreaded what promised to come next. Even though the earl was in love with Miss Alden, he seemed determined to trifle with her. What was she to do?

Mr. Dellacort was faintly amused at how willingly Sophia allowed him to move her away from her betrothed and monopolize her company. It should have pleased him, for all he wished was to undo her betrothal. It should have pleased him, too, that Lettie and the earl had not yet reappeared.

For some reason, he was not pleased. Not with Sophia, and not with Lettie. He was itching to get home and reply to Lettie's solicitors. He'd tell them she had authorized him to do business on her behalf; they were not to sell a single share belonging to her at any price; and she begged to know the identity of the many parties endeavouring to buy. He knew already the name of one: himself. He had authorized a large purchase in order to have standing to explore the mine. Lettie had made it clear that she had no intention of authorizing an exploration, and so he'd done what was necessary. The shares were going for a song. He was now the second largest shareholder. But the identity of the other interested parties was a mystery.

Why he should trouble himself to take an interest in the mine, he wasn't certain. But if her husband had lost his life endeavouring to locate diamonds, he had to believe that the man had good reason to suppose he would find them. And if more were found, the mine would return his investment many times over. Nevertheless, it irked him that, no sooner had he decided to venture into the business, when other unknown speculators did too.

Sophia was fortunately engaged in conversation with her friend, Lady Sefton, which gave him time for ruminations. And then his eye fell upon Stewart. Stewart who loved to gossip. Stewart who knew that Nick had decided to buy shares.

Nick waved him over, and Stewart came like an eagle on the wing. "Nick! You amaze us more and more. Becoming a regular this season, an't you?"

"Temporarily."

"How goes your scheme?" he asked in an undertone, with a raised brow and a sideways glance at Miss Alden.

"As expected," he said shortly. "Tell me, by chance have you let it out that I bought shares in a diamond mine?"

Stewart looked up in surprise. "Should I have kept it under the hatches? Gad, Nick, you never said. Surely you know I'd never utter a word if you had told me not to."

"Who else knows?"

Stewart thought for a moment. "I spoke of it at a salon last week. Mentioned that I meant to buy shares on your recommendation."

"My recommendation?" Dellacort's tone was sharp.

"Well, that's what I took it for. If it's good enough for your blunt, I suppose it'd be good enough for mine."

"Go on."

Stewart rubbed his chin. "I was at Lady Effington's, I believe, when it came up." He fell silent, remembering, and then dropped his hand. "I daresay only the marquess paid me any mind."

"Which marquess?"

"Worthington."

"Elston's sire! Of course."

"Why?"

"The shares are in demand."

"Don't I know it! I couldn't buy a one!" He shook his head. "Someone got there ahead of us, eh?" He looked at Dellacort as if they were sharing a mutual grievance. "Bought out all the stock for sale, I daresay." He turned toward the crowd, his eyes scanning it. "I warrant the marquess will be crowing about it soon!"

Nick took in a breath. "Of all the men you had to whisper it to…"

Stewart turned to him apologetically. "Dash it all, didn't think he'd step on your toes again. Who knew the shares would sell out so quick?"

"What is this about shares selling out?" asked Miss Alden just then. Smiling, she said, "Have I caught you speaking of business?"

Lettie decided, since she had rejected the earl's advance, tried to run away when what she ought to have done was *make herself agreeable*—those were Dellacort's instructions—she must make amends. *Headache or no, she ought to have allowed that kiss.* One kiss was not so very terrible a thing, was it? A guilty pang went through her when she recalled that Nick had been able to steal a kiss from her with more success than Elston, and she had not developed the headache in response to him.

So she listened to the earl with open eyes instead of lowering them when he spoke. "Tell me, Miss Wetherham, you seem to be intimately acquainted with Mr. Dellacort. Why, if he is determined to regain Miss Alden's affections, did he not offer for her while he had opportunity?"

She pursed her lips. "My lord, Mr. Dellacort does not confide in me to that extent."

"Ah, but you do not deny he wishes to have her back?"

She flushed, for her answer had indeed seemed to confirm that. "Sir, I cannot speak for him. We are only acquaintances." Lettie did not feel at liberty to discuss Dellacort's intentions or lack of them.

He leaned his head in toward hers. "And what are your intentions, sweet lady?"

Lettie stared but was speechless. She was certainly in no position to discuss her intentions any more than Nick's. She dared not reveal the scheme. "I do not understand you," she replied finally.

"Let me show you mine, then," he said, and moved in for a kiss. Quickly Lettie sprang to her feet. "I daresay, now that you mention Mr. Dellacort, my lord, he must be wondering where I am off to." It was just like the moment in the garden when he'd tried to kiss her. Something in her simply rebelled. She did not know why. She had not meant to. Lord Elston was not odious. Indeed, except for his propensity for garish cravats and elabourate waistcoats, he seemed a sensible man. There was nothing elsewise particularly objectionable in him. But she was doomed to obey her heart, and her heart did not welcome his kiss. Though it would displease Mr. Dellacort and end her part in the business, she could not pretend it did not.

Chapter Eleven

When Lettie and the earl joined the rest of the company in the ballroom, Nick's tall head caught her eye. He chanced to look over at them just then and raised a brow as if to say, "Well? Are you being agreeable?" She swallowed and turned to the earl to make small talk, as if she had not just rejected his advances, first in the garden and then the little parlour.

The rest of the evening passed without incident, except Lettie found herself the object of the earl's gaze now and then in a way which unsettled her. He spent half of the next hour watching Miss Alden and Mr. Dellacort (who spent all of it in one another's company); and the other half engaged in conversation with Lettie, giving her searching looks here and there, as if trying to read her thoughts.

Shortly afterward, Dellacort came up to her and said he was ready to take her home, "Unless," he asked, "the earl has offered to escort you?"

"He has not."

"You should know then, Miss Alden will join us in my coach." Lettie could hardly believe the earl had not objected to the arrangement. If Nick had troubled himself to ask Lettie's opinion, she certainly would have. Miss Alden did not seem at all concerned with what society thought of her. She was known to be promised to Lord Elston but spent the majority of her time flirting with Dellacort. And now, to be leaving in his coach! It seemed positively indecent. She must speak to Mr. Dellacort and tell him he was in danger of ruining Sophia's reputation forever.

During the drive, Miss Alden spoke gaily and only to Nick as if Lettie were invisible. Lettie settled her gaze out the window and watched streets slowly pass, content to be ignored, and happy not to have to face Nick's scrutiny. The more she considered the evening, the more she felt certain she had closed the coffin on his scheme. She had not let Elston kiss her. It was monstrous of him to try upon so short an acquaintance, but Nick would not share that thought. He who had also brazenly kissed her upon even shorter acquaintance!

Both men were thoroughly improper. But a blush infused her face as she thought upon it, for there was one difference between the events, the two attempted kisses. She had been very surprised, shocked even, when Dellacort's mouth came down on hers. But for some inexplicable reason, she had allowed the kiss. She'd allowed it until dear Steven had appeared in her mind's eye. But even so, she remembered Dellacort's lips as being warm and pleasant.

When the earl's lips had surprised hers, though he did not accost her violently, she had instantly abhorred it and broken away. She could not account for why she had reacted differently to Dellacort. If anything, Lord Elston was the gentler soul; her reaction should have reflected that. But now the question which formed in her head hung there like a stark accusation. Why had she reacted differently to Dellacort? Worse, why, even now, did the memory of his lips upon hers fill her with an ache, a longing, to have it repeated? She studied him for a moment in the dim interior, lit only when they passed beneath streetlamps. He was monstrously good looking, but that was no reason to give him an inch of her heart. His smile was sweet, belying his true nature. And he seemed wholeheartedly interested in only Miss Alden. No, there was no reason on earth why she ought to prefer the man to Lord Elston. She knew only that she did.

As Betsey helped Lettie into a nightdress and mob cap about twenty minutes after Nick left her at home before going on with Miss Alden, a knock at her bedchamber door, followed by Dudley's voice, startled both ladies.

"Ma'am, Mr. Dellacort is below." These were the sole words.

Betsey looked amazed. "At this hour! Ay, miss, he mus' be daft!"

Lettie said, "He is bold and bothersome, but not daft." She pursed her lips, thinking. Had he escorted Miss Alden home so quickly? If so, he hadn't spent much time with her. She drew a sheet to her chin. "Dudley!"

The butler came bowing and shuffling into the room, keeping his eyes averted from where Lettie lay on her bed as if she were Minerva who could turn him to stone. "Yes, ma'am?" he asked, his eyes glued to the floor.

"Tell Mr. Dellacort to call upon me tomorrow at a decent hour."

Dudley ducked his head lower. "Yes, ma'am."

Lettie sighed and sank her head in the pillow. Whatever was wrong with that man, calling upon her at such a scandalous hour? It was unheard of. She dismissed Betsey and was about to blow out her candle when she heard footsteps approaching.

He'd sent Dudley back with a message? Was he not going to give her any peace? She sat up, waiting for the servant. In a moment a soft knock followed.

"Come in, come in!" she cried. Didn't he know she wanted only to be done with the business so she could get some rest?

The door opened and in walked Nicholas Dellacort. Lettie's eyes widened. She gasped and drew her sheets back to her chin.

"How dare you enter my bedchamber!"

He smiled disarmingly and took a step nearer. "If you had come to me, I need not have bothered."

"You are too bold, sir!"

"You said, "Come in! Come in!""

Her lips tightened and sparks flew from her eyes.

Nick smiled wider. "Unhappily for you, Lettie, your face is one of such amiability that when you fly into the boughs you succeed only in looking adorable, not formidable." He took a step closer.

"Halt!" she cried. "You evidently believe I am a helpless woman, unable to protect myself from this monstrous behaviour—"

"And aren't you?" he asked easily, taking another step nearer.

"I have—a-a butler!" she cried.

"Indeed. A remarkable specimen," he said, "as ancient as they come, and as able to defend you as a lamb against a lion."

"That may be so," she said, fuming. "But I do not doubt he is off to fetch a charley or a magistrate as we speak. I'll have you hauled to King's Bench!"

Just then they heard the unmistakable sound of footfalls shuffling off in the butler's slow pace. Dudley had not, it seemed, been engaged in fetching a charley or magistrate.

Dellacort's eyes filled with mirth. "Actually, I did not expect to find you abed so quickly."

"Why are you not at home in your own bed?"

"I must know what happened between you and the earl."

"And it cannot wait for the morrow?"

"It can, no doubt. But I cannot."

"You are the most insufferable man I have ever known."

"Thank you. What happened?"

"What do you mean? Why do you suppose anything happened?" Lettie felt the dread of having to tell him. How disagreeable that he had come.

He came and stood beside her bed. She pulled her sheets yet higher. His eyes bore into hers. "Did he attempt to kiss you?"

She drew in a breath. "Do you suppose all men are like you?"

He smirked. "I suppose that he tried, and if I mistake me not, you did not allow it."

She stared at him, wide-eyed.

He nodded. "As I thought. I can read your countenance as easily as a child's. Why did you stop him?"

Her eyes widened even more. "Why? Why?" She stared at him, for his question was the very one she'd been asking herself. She said only, "He was impertinent."

His voice hardened. "Your part was to make yourself agreeable. Your aim is to lure the man away from Sophia. Or have you forgot?"

"I have not. But that does not mean—"

"It does mean. You must let him kiss you."

She was speechless for only a moment. "He was *monstrous* to try it so soon! If he had good intentions, he would not have."

"He will do so again, given the opportunity. So long as you do your part and are agreeable to him. I have invited the earl and Sophia to a small dinner at my home tomorrow evening. Afterwards, I will ask him to see you home."

She let out a breath of exasperation. "No! No. I will...walk off with him somewhere in your house...but I will not be unchaperoned with him. If I allow him to behave improperly to me with a kiss, he may wish to do more."

"That wish has propelled many a man to the altar, Miss Wetherham."

"You are exceedingly vulgar, Mr. Dellacort."

"I am also right." He paused. "I have given him to understand the value of your mine may be far in excess of Sophia's middling dowry."

"But it may also be worthless."

"I only said it *may* have great value. His father is already convinced it does." He did not add that the marquess was convinced on the strength of discovering that he, Dellacort, had purchased shares in it. He looked down at her disapprovingly. "When you see him tomorrow evening, you will have opportunity to do better than tonight. You must do it. You know what's at stake."

Lettie felt utterly defeated. She wanted to insist she'd have nothing further to do with the business. She was unfit for it. The thought had occurred to her that if she ignored his advice and sold her shares, she wouldn't even need to earn the remaining five hundred pounds. But justice prevailed. She had agreed to the scheme; she had even signed her name to an agreement. And she had accepted his money.

"I shall do better." She sighed. "But what is a kiss to a man? It will not do the trick, sir. He will walk away and forget me as soon as he looks at Sophia. Men do not hang their hearts upon a kiss, not the way a woman does."

"But they do hang their hearts upon diamond mines." He studied her, not unkindly. "And do not think you are so easily forgettable as all that, Lettie." He paused and came a step closer. "Did you push him away at once?"

She looked away, blinking, and swallowed. "I did, rather." She could not meet his eyes and face the censure sure to be in them.

In a soft tone, he said, "That is not the reaction I recall receiving from you."

Color rose in her cheeks as she turned to cry, "Humph! Because of you, I was better prepared for such insolence!"

His eyes sparkled as he surveyed her silently a moment. "We'll talk more on it in future. Good night, Lettie."

She looked up to see him turn and leave the room, quietly shutting the door behind him. She sank back into the pillows and wondered why he had urgently needed to know what had passed between her and the earl. He must be more intent than ever upon winning back Miss Alden, she realised. Yet he'd evidently left her at the soonest possible moment in order to return to Lettie's house so quickly. She rolled over and groaned at the memory of him standing in her bedchamber. Most men wouldn't dream of making such an intrusion. What made him suppose he was above displaying gentlemanlike behaviour?

The scene was so outlandish and brazen it must never get out. Even Amelia must not hear of it.

Chapter Twelve

The following evening a carriage arrived at eight-thirty to bring Lettie to Dellacort's townhome for the dinner party. He'd promised to send it, for Lettie could not, of course, keep a carriage of her own, not for the past two years, just as she'd also had to give up the largest part of her staff and other comforts. As she climbed the steps of the coach aided by Nick's footman, she swallowed nervous energy that rose in her throat. She must set her mind to doing what she'd agreed to. If the earl approached her again, even with the impudence to steal a kiss, she was prepared to allow it. Nick had certainly made it clear she was expected to. And if she did her part at least that far, she could then remove herself from the business, having done all she was willing to do. If Dellacort did not agree that she'd earned the second half of the payment – another year's living expenses—there was nothing for it but to be thankful she had the first half.

There was more to her nerves than what lay ahead with Lord Elston, though. She would see Nick's home tonight— and, try as she might to deny it, she was eager to see it. In fact, she was eager, for some perverse reason, to see Mr. Dellacort, even though the memory of him in her bedchamber the previous evening should give her nothing but a disgust of him. *Oh, if only!* But from the moment of their first meeting, she found Nicholas Dellacort strangely fascinating, however much she disapproved of his character. And she did disapprove of him, of his reputation, his breezy indifference, and famous aversion to marriage. Surely that was enough to give a woman pause. But now she understood even more what the source of her unease had been.

She had sensed almost immediately that he could hold a peculiar power over her. There was something about him, something intrinsically attached to his face, voice, and eyes, that stifled her good sense, her better judgment, and rendered her powerless to resist him. This, she knew, was why his very first stolen kiss had not met with the same cold reception Lord Elston encountered. Twice, Nick had had stolen a kiss from her, and both times, it was only by sheer force of will that she stopped him. It was as though an invisible thread ran from her soul to Dellacort's, a thread that only grew stronger each time she saw him. Yet he showed not the least awareness of an attachment or attraction to her. Oh, he might steal a kiss here or there, but it meant nothing to him.

She was all eyes as the carriage proceeded down the wide, tree-lined Berkeley Square, and when she disembarked in front of an impressive Palladian style dwelling. Inside the house, she gave her name, and a footman led her to a large, heavy door, opened it, and announced, "Miss Wetherham, sir." Swallowing a fresh wave of trepidation, Lettie plastered a smile of false bravery on her face and crossed the threshold into the war room. She felt solitary and friendless, for who would smile to see her? Miss Alden treated her like a flea; the earl knew her to reject his advances; Dellacort saw her only as a means to an end.

It was a beautifully appointed parlour in the classical style, but everything was at war within her. Her foolish, foolish heart for wanting to see Nick; and her acceptance of the disagreeable task of having to attract Lord Elston. To her relief, only Nick was there, and he stood to greet her with a short bow and what could be called a smile. His head went back as she entered, and his eyes, it seemed to Lettie, brightened. But in his usual voice, he said, "My other guests are behind time. Should arrive any moment, I suppose." He motioned for her to come and have a seat on a sofa facing the hearth.

When she was seated, he studied her, leaning comfortably against the mantel. "You are a handsome woman, Lettie. I see no reason why you should not succeed with Elston. Indeed, when you confirmed that he had for a fact approached you the other night as I suspected, I realised you have it in your power to make short work of this."

She blinked, looking up at him in surprise. "I have no power over the earl."

"But he is drawn to you." A twinkle glistened briefly in the dark eyes.

She frowned. "He saw opportunity to take advantage of a fawning female. And I am forced to be fawning, or you shall say I am not doing my best." He did not disagree, so she continued, "Many a man might see such a creature as game to be preyed upon."

"Elston is no rake, nor a scoundrel. Word is, he appears a gentleman of honour. If he approaches you, it must be a genuine *tendré*. You should receive his attentions as such."

Lettie looked away with almost a shudder. Nick's eyes narrowed and he came and sat beside her. "Is there something you have not told me? Has he misbehaved in some abominable fashion?"

She turned restless, unhappy eyes to his. "Besides trying to steal impertinent kisses?" She hesitated, choosing her words, and sighed. "No. But I never knew myself, you see. I never knew I am incapable of sustained pretence in matters of...."

"Yes?"

"Well, matters of the heart, you might say."

Nick stared at her. He stared at her for a long moment. "Listen to me carefully, Lettie. Tonight, you will save a man from a lifelong sentence of misery. Men, you know, can be bamboozled as easily as a woman if they aren't careful. And Miss Alden has no affection for his lordship. Tonight, if you must, you will silence your heart and do what you can to break the chains of infatuation holding Lord Elston captive. If only for this one night, think not of yourself or your little troubles; consider only how the earl will feel if he marries a woman who despises him; she will spend his money happily; give him an heir perhaps, but no joy. She will not be faithful; she will mock him at every turn."

"How do you know?"

He eyed her soberly. "She begins to covet the title. But not for like of his lordship. She scorns him. She is full of scorn and mockery, every time I see her."

A sound in the corridor told them the others were approaching.

Nick grasped one of her gloved hands and squeezed it. He leaned toward her and whispered, "Put on your best smile; take pity on Elston, and save him from himself!" He kissed the side of her face unexpectedly, bringing a fine blush to her cheeks.

And then the door opened and they were announced. Dellacort rose to bow.

Miss Alden appeared, the earl trailing behind her like a puppy on a leash. She wore a high, feathered headdress above an elegant pale blue gown with white satin sleeves, trimmed in white ribbon. A gleaming, bejeweled necklace sparkled from her bosom. But the earl was the more interesting sight, sporting a cringe-worthy bright yellow cravat, a pointed collar, and a tailcoat, though expensive, that looked somehow ill fitting.

Lettie gave the earl a *long* smile. It was a smile meant to convey that she had thought upon her foolishness in shirking his advances and come to her senses. A smile that said she had seen the error of her ways and was now prepared to receive him with open arms. At the same time, she infused her eyes with all the approval and goodwill she could manage. If any smile could broadcast that she had changed with regard to him, this was the one to do it.

The earl stared at her in surprise. Then, with a little bow of the head, he acknowledged her. "If I may say so, Miss Wetherham," he said, coming back to his full height, "You do no injustice to our party."

To her surprise, Nick cut in. "No injustice? Is that your compliment to a beautiful woman?" He turned to Lettie and said, "You are a vision, Miss Wetherham; and then, turning to Sophia, added, "As is our lovely Miss Alden."

Sophia's look had been one of indignation, but now it softened.

Nick took Sophia into dinner, leaving Lettie on the arm of the earl. As they walked, Lord Elston said, "I hope I will have an opportunity to speak to you privately tonight, Miss Wetherham."

Lettie was not surprised, but her heart sank. With any luck, dinner would last a long time, and then there might follow no opportunity to be alone with him.

At the table, Nick sat beside Sophia, while Lettie and the earl sat across from them. Lord Elston had waved off the footman who approached to pull out Lettie's chair, and took hold of it himself to help her.

Dinner party etiquette required that one speak to the person at their side; never across the table. Lettie saw Nick meant to uphold this rule, though there were only four of them. This meant she would converse only with the earl. She wasn't surprised at the arrangement but was startled by the disappointment she felt at being deprived of Nick's conversation. She told herself she ought to be relieved. His idea of conversing was challenging, no, combative. The earl, on the contrary, was always mild and polite.

When Lord Elston caught her eye, held it, and smiled, she thought, *Ah, now he will try again with me.* This was what must happen to fulfill her bargain with Dellacort, but *oh, her wicked heart!* For she did not feel anything more than friendship for the earl and to flirt with him, to encourage him, seemed a great transgression. How shameless and dishonest she was! In truth, she was unfit for the task, and no amount of payment should have prevailed upon her better sense and made her accept the deal. The pangs in her head began.

Why, why, had Nick Dellacort ever come to her for help? Why had he not fought his own battle and left her alone? Why must he force her to behave in a way that did not suit her feelings, that could only give injury to the man who believed them genuine? And why, most of all, did Nick's countenance and voice fill her head at night when she sought sleep? It was no wonder she got the headache from it all.

While each course of the meal was served, she and Lord Elston spoke, but both, it seemed, were guilty of taking long glances across the table where Nick and Sophia were happily engaged in conversation. Now and then Nick glanced Lettie's way, sending her into guilty starts and new attempts to engage the earl if their conversation lapsed, or inquiring on his taste in a matter. She learned he was not fond of Prince George, and doubted he would ever make a good king; certainly not as strong as his father, George III. The king's family, indeed, filled the last two courses, and while she enjoyed royal scuttlebutt as much as anyone, the end of the meal could not have come soon enough.

Nick announced that the men would skip their customary port in order to accompany the ladies to the drawing room. Lettie went upon the earl's arm, though he looked hopefully at Sophia until Nick claimed her hand upon his own arm and led the way. They were met in the well-appointed room with a roaring fire and a tray of little glasses of sherry. Nick handed them round, then moved off with Sophia, speaking in low tones so she alone could hear him.

Lettie and Elston looked helplessly at one another. The earl was growing unhappier, she knew, and yet she could not ease his discomfort. Indeed, she must behave as if he were the object of her affection, and yet more and more she realised her utter failure to fulfill that assignment.

When it was clear Nick and Sophia had abandoned the room, his lordship seemed to come to some decision. He got up and paced the room.

"Shall we search them out?" Lettie asked, assuming this was his intent. When there was no immediate reply, she came uncertainly to her feet. The earl came back toward her with a troubled countenance. Lettie wondered frantically whether to reveal all to him, confess the wicked plot; tell him Miss Alden was a shrew, merely toying with him? That he would do well to be rid of her? Would it soften the blow to his heart? For it seemed utterly clear, despite what Nick said about the earl's attentions being genuine, that he was hopelessly in love with only Miss Alden.

No sooner than she thought these things, his lordship took her by the arms. "Your actions have me confused, Miss Wetherham, but I must believe your eyes."

"My lord!" she cried.

And then his lips were upon hers. Lettie had one more chance to do as Nick bade, to allow the kiss. She steeled her heart and tried to do exactly that. But dear Steven was back, springing into her brain like a hound upon a fox. He may as well have stood in the room watching. What he must think of her, allowing a man to kiss her when she cared nothing for him! Her resolve fled and her lips turned to stone.

She pushed herself away, and, free from his arms, cried, "I cannot!" The earl grasped her by the hand. She would have wrenched it back, but he cried, "I beg your pardon! Please. Do not run. I—I was testing you, if you must know. The other times and tonight."

"Testing me?" she asked, blinking at him. Dancing shadows from the hearth revealed spectacled eyes that were earnest and gentle.

"I know I appear as a simpleton, but I am not, Miss Wetherham. And I cannot ignore what my eyes plainly see. You, I believe, are in love with Mr. Dellacort."

"No such thing!" Her eyes were large in the dim light.

He raised a hand. "Please. Hear me out. I believe you are, but he appears to be interested only in my betrothed. Unfortunately for us both, she returns his interest. That leaves the two of us dangling rather uselessly in their wake like two planets without an orbit." He paused.

Lettie was speechless. And rather cross at his saying she was in love with Dellacort. She was aware of a fatal, foolish, attraction to the man, but she was not, of course, in *love* with him. Ridiculous notion! But an unmistakable air of relief settled upon her as it sunk in that she no longer had to continue the charade of feigning interest in Lord Elston. Even better, his heart would suffer no injury at her hands in the end, for he was not setting his hopes upon her.

She waited breathlessly. She'd been ready to reproach herself for ruining the scheme, but the earl hadn't been swallowing it anyway.

"My father has instructed that I must marry Miss Alden. He demands it."

"And must you comply?"

He hesitated. "I find it is what I wish, also. I realize I am no match for Dellacort…" His gentle voice and downcast look completely disarmed Lettie.

He continued, "If I lose her, the marquess cannot deny me the title—primogeniture and all that. But he can and will make my life miserable if she returns to Dellacort."

Lettie wished suddenly to be as helpful to him as possible. Even the richest of men, she saw, were saddled with burdens. But what could she do?

He tightened his hold on her hand. "I am relieved you have set no hopes upon me, Miss Wetherham, for I should not have liked to injure your sensibilities. In fact—" he hesitated, choosing his words. "I daresay, if I fail to win Miss Alden, I would welcome your amiable company."

Lettie only frowned sadly, for her "amiability" as he put it, was never entirely genuine. But she said nothing, not wishing to betray Dellacort. His scheme was failing in any case. The earl had no intention of losing Miss Alden.

His lordship's eyes pleaded with her. "Miss Wetherham—I have no right to ask this of you."

She waited, wondering.

"But if you would, dear Miss Wetherham, you hold the power to make Sophia jealous. Her heart is consumed with superiority. If I am seen to turn away from her to your direction, I believe it will be the very thing to turn her toward me. She is a creature of contradiction but wants most especially what she thinks she cannot have."

"You understand Miss Alden well, I perceive!"

"I believe so. May I depend upon your help? Will you allow me to—to—flirt with you? It must be very much in plain view of the company. I have been tortured with the fear that I may be leading you on, giving you false hopes, but now with that danger safely past, and since I have made my intentions plain,you will not be misled?"

"No, sir, not at all." Lettie hid her astonishment. He was asking her to do the very thing Mr. Dellacort had engaged her for! To flirt! Dellacort had hoped, of course, for a real attachment to form between them, and the earl wanted only the appearance of one. But surely this would be even easier to accomplish. Nick would see her doing her part; she would earn the remainder of the settlement. And there was no fear of having to lead on His Lordship.

Lettie's heart lightened, and she realised for the first time how very heavy it had been heretofore. She hadn't liked having to deceive the earl. The only difficulty was that, if jealousy did indeed send Sophia to his side, then Mr. Dellacort must lose her. Lettie was supposed to be helping *him* secure her. She quieted this pang of conscience with the thought that if Sophia was fickle enough to abandon Nick out of jealousy, then he would be well rid of her. Surely he would not want such a woman for a wife. Surely, that was the only reason she warmed to this twist of fate, not because it meant he would be free to turn his sights elsewhere. Certainly not in the hope that he might turn them to *her*. Dellacort was so sure of himself he didn't realize Sophia was a poor choice. Thus, Lettie assured herself she would be helping him by helping the earl.

She saw how it would all work out. Sophia would learn to appreciate the gentle earl, and even, in time, come to love him. Nick would see her faithlessness, look elsewhere for a lady love, and in the end, Lettie would go her way, a thousand pounds richer. Unfortunately, she saw no ending that could ensure the happiness of all, for only one man could win

Sophia; it was out of her hands. She was responsible only to do her best. All this time the earl waited for her reply. "I *will* allow it," she said to his waiting countenance.

His eyes glittered. "I'm deuced glad! Hoped you would." With a little smile, he lifted her hand and kissed it. "Thank you. And I have thought of a way to tangibly thank you, Miss Wetherham, for your help in my cause. I will buy shares in your diamond mine, if you will allow it. We are told none are available, but you could, you know, create more."

"Oh, dear man, I dare not." She was about to add, that she would not even think of doing so, certainly not before she got word from Africa as to the mine's value. She would not create new shares for a worthless venture. But just then harsh voices wafted through the door, Nick's authoritative voice above Miss Alden's. A surprising warmth filled Lettie. *Goodness, why was she so fond of him!* It was nothing like *love*, of course—the earl was utterly wrong about that—but she could not help thinking again, *if only he was not enraptured with Sophia.*

"Are we in agreement, then, Miss Wetherham?" Elston said in his quiet voice.

"Yes, my lord." She expected he would engage her in the sort of loud banter and laughter that Nick and Sophia often engaged in. Or perhaps he would shower her with marked attention.

Just at the doorway, Sophia exclaimed, "You are as incorrigible as ever, I see!"

And without further preamble, Lord Elston drew Lettie up to him and into a kiss. Her impulse, as usual, was to push away from this unexpected, unwelcome, intrusion. But she'd agreed to help his cause—she could not escape it. She swallowed her pride. She swallowed her instincts. The voices of the others fell silent, as Lettie let him kiss her.

"A-ahem." It was Nick's deep voice. The earl released her, and they were suddenly looking into the surprised countenances of Nick and Sophia, both staring at them in the dim light.

"Begging your pardon," Nick said affably, with a smile curling his lips.

"Ha!" Sophia said, coming further into the room. "I beg no pardon. I daresay you, Miss Wetherham, should." She had a hand on Nick's arm and put her other on one hip and stood frowning at them. In an arch tone she said, "Have you forgot this man is my fiancé?" She removed her hand from Nick's arm and went toward Lord Elston, who kept his countenance bland. Sophia put her hand upon his arm and cast a defiant glare at Lettie.

"It was nothing, my dear," Lord Elston said, turning to Sophia. "I am certain, at least, that it was nothing more than what you yourself might have engaged in just now with Mr. Dellacort."

"Nothing of the kind!" she cried.

His eyes bored into hers.

"I cannot conceive what you are implying, my lord."

Nick's look, suppressing a grin, seemed to belie her protest.

Lettie turned to him. "Mr. Dellacort, would you be so kind as to have a servant secure a hackney coach for my use? I fear that once again I have the headache." Fresh pangs had burst on her from the moment the earl kissed her. She was evidently hopeless when it came to kissing gentlemen she did not care for. Forcing herself to do it only sprung pains in her head, and they seemed to be getting stronger in time. If the flirtation went on much longer, she'd be lucky to come out alive.

Nick looked to the others. "In that case, shall we call it a night?"

As they walked the corridor to the stairs, she and Nick ahead of Sophia and Elston, Nick said, "No need for a hackney coach. I will convey you home." Lettie said nothing, though she was pleased. They spoke no other words, said cool good-byes to the others, and soon were seated facing each other in Nick's coach.

"Well done," he said, as the vehicle rolled away from the kerb. "After your recent failures, I hardly expected such rapid progress."

"I did not expect it myself," she said, feeling her face grow rosy. The earl had said he would flirt with her—not kiss her brazenly at the soonest moment when Sophia and Nick could witness it. Good thing it was short. The pangs in her head were already subsiding. Somehow, Nick did not exacerbate them. Even when he'd stolen kisses, she was astonished, but had allowed them longer without feeling repulsion or developing the headache.

It flummoxed her. She stared at him, wondering why.

Nick saw her studying him. "Yes?"

"I beg your pardon." She looked away as a wave of unease crossed her breast. She hadn't been entirely honest with his lordship, for she hadn't told him about Nick's scheme; and now she wasn't being honest with Dellacort. It made her feel cross, having to bear all of this dishonesty. Both men were using her to secure Sophia for themselves.

She had no just cause to complain; she had willingly entered into the scheme and was being handsomely rewarded by Nick. But something inside her was aching. As she studied once more the man across from her, the situation felt more and more intolerable. She hardly knew why.

And then she did.

Her agreement with Lord Elston rendered the one she had made with Mr. Dellacort null and void. Though she felt it was ultimately in his best interest, still it was a different game than what he had engaged her for. And then it struck her: she was like a double-crossing spy! How discommodious to be in this muddle! And how unspeakably unkind it was for Nick to engage her to help him win someone else, when—when what? What was she thinking? The earl's words rang in her mind: *You are in love with Dellacort.*

"There is something troubling you, Lettie," Dellacort said.

Torn from her reverie, her eyes flew to meet his, just as they passed beneath a streetlamp. She saw eyes that were peculiarly clear, penetrating and deep, like pools with moonlight glittering on their surface. She could get lost in such eyes. *But this was precisely what she must not do!* Pettishly she said, "You have called me Lettie for an age; but I do not recall granting you permission to use my name."

"Call me Nick," he offered, with a little smile.

"I prefer Miss Wetherham, if you please" she returned. "And I shall continue to call you Mr. Dellacort."

"As you wish," he said, studying her. "But what is troubling you? Did something happen with his lordship to put you out of countenance?"

She shifted uneasily. His tone was considerate, even caring. It seemed intimate coming from him who was usually either caustic or businesslike. She said haltingly, "I am ill-suited... to this arrangement. To this type of arrangement, that is."

"What type of arrangement is that?" he asked, as if he had no idea.

"As I have told you numerous times, one that must involve deception!" she said, wide-eyed.

"But you need this," he said. "Your situation is dire, otherwise."

"Precisely," she said, sitting back with a sigh. "I was constrained to help by necessity; but you must know I cannot conceive of maintaining this much longer."

He rubbed his chin, eyeing her thoughtfully. "The earl has come about. Once he realizes he prefers you, that should suffice. Give me two more opportunities to throw you together."

"Two more," she echoed, in a hollow tone. Her heart sank, for she knew that no amount of being thrown together with Lord Elston would accomplish Dellacort's hopes. There was no chance at all that she could win over the earl. The more she considered it, the more she wondered: if she knew Dellacort's cause to be already lost (and she did), could she accept another farthing from his hand in good conscience? Yet she must continue the scheme, for now she had told Lord Elston she would!

When they reached her home on Russell Square, he put out a hand to help her up. Lettie rose, stubbed her foot into his and stumbled—he tried to stop her, but she fell forward. Right onto his lap. Their eyes met. He smiled.

"I beg your pardon," she murmured, staring up at him. Treacherously, she felt as though she was exactly where she belonged—how mortifying! He must not know it. She started to rise. But Nick stopped her and moved his head down toward hers. Lettie knew what he was about. She knew he'd kiss her just for the diversion in it. She knew it meant nothing to him. She knew he was the furthest thing from the good man Steven told her she must fall in love with. But she did not move.

He hesitated, his lips hovering near hers as if waiting for her to repulse him as usual. This was strangely considerate of Nick. And then something overcame Lettie, something that terrified her, for it made her raise her mouth to his, and throw an arm about his neck. He drew her up to him in a tight embrace, and they kissed. Finally, she pressed against him to let her go. He did, staring at her with an unreadable expression. Lettie's eyes met his in agonized embarrassment, as if suddenly she came to her senses. She scrambled to her feet and hurried from the carriage, allowing Nick's waiting footman to help her down the steps. She'd said nothing in parting, was far too mortified to speak. And she dared not look back, though it felt like heavy magnets were willing her to turn and do so.

What had she done? Dellacort knew he could toy with her, now. He would give her no peace, she was certain.

Worse, she wasn't sure she wanted him to.

Chapter Thirteen

Mr. Dellacort was just leaving White's the following afternoon when he was nearly bowled into by Mr. Horace Cantrell, who, with head lowered, and muttering to himself, was on his way in. Mr. Cantrell had just got a letter from East Africa, a copy of the original which had gone to Lettie; a letter which had him rather dejected and on a rare impulse to splurge by refreshing himself in the gentleman's sanctuary.

"I say, beg your pardon!" he said, his head coming up swiftly to take in the sagacious countenance of Mr. Dellacort, who always looked to Horace as though there was nothing in creation which could cause the unflappable exterior of that good looking face to crack. "Oh, it's you, sir!" Horace cried, recognizing the benefactor of his cousin, Miss Wetherham. He was not aware of the particulars of what had transpired between Mr. Dellacort and his cousin; he had a vague idea that Lettie had agreed to make a match for someone connected to the man. That was what she did, and he had been generous to her by spades. This was all he knew.

Mr. Dellacort stopped in surprise, his mouth turning up in amusement at this disheveled fellow saying, "Oh, it's you, sir," as if they were chums.

"Yes, it's me," he said, affably. "Should I be someone else?"

"Oh, no, sir," said Horace, growing a little paler. "That is, I mean to say, well, thank you, sir, on behalf of my cousin."

Mr. Dellacort's brow rose. "And who would that be?"

"Oh! Horace Cantrell, sir, Miss Wetherham's cousin," he said, offering his hand. It was reluctantly accepted for a handshake. "My father was her uncle, you see, and…"

Mr. Dellacort's brow cleared. "Ah."

Horace glanced down at the letter in his other hand, reddened, and, after giving Mr. Dellacort the fastest and guiltiest look as of a criminal caught stealing from a bank, shoved it into his pocket.

"Bad news there?" asked Mr. Dellacort, with a nod at the waistcoat pocket into which the guilty note had vanished.

"Oh, bad news, what? Well, yes, you might say that, sir."

"Does it concern the mine?" Dellacort asked.

Horace stared at Mr. Dellacort for a long moment, as if he thought that by some extraordinary mental powers, Mr. Dellacort knew the letter was from the diamond mine, and worse, knew its contents. How on earth had he known? Was the man a mind reader? It seemed too fantastic to be true, but those had been his words. *Does it concern the mine?*

The news had taken months to reach them, delayed by more than the usual time it took for the trip by the carrier ship's getting becalmed at sea for weeks. But it had finally come, and the report was lowering. The team he'd commissioned nearly a year ago to find gems had as yet located none. It was a blow to a man who had recently lost a great deal of his fortune and was hoping for a recovery. Only last week, he'd chosen not to sell his shares when mysteriously there were speculators willing to buy. Like Lettie, Horace had chosen to wait. But the thought that Mr. Dellacort would learn the bad news and spread word of it, just when this interest in the mine had surfaced, was a grave danger.

With any luck, Horace and Lettie could dump their shares now before word got out. And what a blow it would be to Lettie, who needed the mine to produce now more than ever. But sell they must, he was certain, for surely this was the final verdict for the deuced mine. The question of how Dellacort could infer what that letter was concerned with, he did not stop to fathom. He knew only that he must not part with a hint of its news.

Horace adjusted his skewed hat and straightened his waistcoat. Pulling himself together he said, "The mine? Great heavens, no! Goodness, sir, haven't heard from the mine." He disappeared inside the club, feeling like a hare escaping a great bird of prey.

Mr. Dellacort turned thoughtfully to watch his retreat, and, though he'd been ready to go to his own home, instructed his coachman instead to head for Russell Square, to the home of Miss Wetherham. Something was up. Though he disliked that she would be discommoded by his call—he could not forget the look of mortification on her face when she fled his carriage—he must look into it.

Lettie had received a packet of letters tied with string from East Africa that morning, almost the same time Horace had got his. Somehow six letters had been lost or delayed and had now been delivered all at once. She untied the string with sudden interest, realizing as she did that her life might change considerably if good news was contained within. After reading the first letter, which was bad news, she opened six others, each a summary of the work for one month, dating back to when they'd started searching at Horace's behest. But they were all alike. No diamonds had been found.

She was both relieved and disappointed. Relieved because there had been no loss of life involved; and disappointed because of the results. She was not very surprised, however, for she expected as much. If diamonds were to be found, dear Steven would have found them. It would have provided an instant cure for her shabby genteel existence, but she had never placed hope in the chance of reviving the mine. Her thoughts returned to Dellacort.

And with that thought came shame. How could she have given herself to him in that kiss? They both knew he was in love with Miss Alden. What must he think of her now? It was too horrible for words. She was considering writing to him and telling him he must release her from the scheme, she was never cut out for it, she would find a way to repay him for his outlay if he liked (although he'd said it was hers whether she succeeded or failed in the business). She would have to inform the earl as well, of course. Propitiously enough, he had sent word that he would call upon her that very day. Perhaps he wished to discuss their strategy moving forward. Now she'd have to dash his hopes and tell him she could no longer participate in the scheme. What reason she could give, she did not know. That was a bridge to cross when he arrived.

She was sitting at her little escritoire, trying to conjure the right words for the letter to Dellacort, but finding no satisfactory way to start. Various attempts crossed her mind.

Dear Mr. Dellacort. I have been a fool. You are hereby warned never to see my face again. No, that would not do. She tried again. *Dear Mr. Dellacort. I apologize for my rash behaviour yesterday night. Please understand that I am subject to fits of lunacy...*

She heaved another sigh. And then she remembered she ought to write to Horace and Amelia. That was much easier to accomplish. She was in the midst of writing a note of commiseration for their shared remorse upon the mine's failure when Dudley, whom she had informed earlier must expect a gentleman to call, announced her guest had arrived.

Her heart sank. She glanced at the clock on the mantel. Lord Elston was an hour early. She was endeavouring to form an explanation to him when, to her great surprise—and horror—the door opened to reveal Nick. He strode in, gave a short bow, and cleared his throat.

"You!" Lettie cried with a little gasp as her cheeks filled with colour. She was still seated at the escritoire.

For once, he did not display a look of haughty amusement as if he were above the affairs of mere mortals. Instead, he studied her with a gentle look. "Your butler said you were expecting me?" This had been a surprise to him, since he'd come only as a result of a sudden decision after seeing Mr. Cantrell.

"I am expecting Lord Elston."

Nick shut the door behind him and came forward, his eyes on hers. "He is coming here?"

She nodded.

"The gentleman is most eager to see you." His eyes bore into hers. He did not sound pleased. Lettie shifted uncomfortably on her chair. Ought she to tell him what the earl had asked of her? He would discover that his cause was hopeless—Lettie would never elicit an offer from the earl or turn his head from Miss Alden. But she could hardly focus on it. Instead, her brain was reeling with the discomfort of having Nick here after what she'd done the prior evening.

Nick's gaze deepened. "Come sit with me, Lettie," he said softly.

Lettie rose, but in great agitation. Her hands came together and apart. And then words poured out from her. "Mr. Dellacort! Yesterday night—was a monstrous mistake! I don't know how to apologize to you. I have no words to express how deep my mortification is—." He strode toward her as she spoke, and she gripped the back of her chair for support, leaning away from him.

"Do you imagine I want an apology?" he asked when he reached her. He took light hold of her arms, but she slipped from his hands and moved hurriedly away.

"I insist upon apologizing! I cannot say what came over me. And you must know, I have mourned over it every waking moment."

He said, "I thought it might be a new beginning for us."

"No!" She could never allow that. Dear Steven would turn in his grave. What had happened was proof positive that Mr. Dellacort merely brought out the very worst in her. He was too sensuous by spades. What he wanted was a diversion, and she could never allow herself to be only that to a man. They stared at one another and the look of horror in Lettie's eyes could not be mistaken.

Nick's mouth firmed into a line, and his eyes narrowed. "I see I am still odious to you. Very well, give me your terms."

"Either we must end our business directly—"

"That is no option. You gave your word to try your best." He crossed his arms.

"Or—" she swallowed. "Or, we must proceed as if last night never happened."

His eyes hardened. "Done."

"Thank you." Lettie felt a little sinking inside, as if a candle were snuffed out, but knew she had no choice in the matter. She could not consent to an affair, particularly one in which her heart was traitorously inclined to be lost. "Is that what brought you to my parlour?"

"I nearly forgot. You've had word of the mine?"

She stared in surprise. "How did you know?"

"Your cousin, Mr. Cantrell."

"Then you must know already what the outcome is." They were still standing across from one another; Lettie did not invite him to sit.

"He did not elabourate."

"There are no diamonds."

"Of a certain?"

"Apparently."

He seemed thoughtful for a moment, and finally nodded. "In that case, I suggest you sell your shares."

She frowned. "Knowing their value, how can I?"

"Knowing their value, you must. I happen to know someone eager to buy into the venture. He has the means to send a thousand expeditions to keep searching if he wishes to." He was thinking of the marquess, Lord Elston's father. Dellacort accepted that the verdict was probably final, that the news of this failure omened only more failure. But he'd let the marquess buy up as many shares as he liked, in fact he hoped he bought them in droves. It would be perfect revenge for him to own a worthless mine in exchange for the dual injustices Nick had suffered at the aristocrat's hands.

Lettie had been deliberating. "In truth, the foreman said they would continue searching for perhaps another month, for that is how long Mr. Cantrell's investment would keep them going."

"Mr. Cantrell puts no stock in that."

"Nor do I. I received seven letters in all, and each one bore the same news. They send monthly updates, you see, though it takes months to reach us, and for some unaccountable reason, all the letters came at once." She paused. "I certainly have no thought of there being any change. If there were diamonds," she said a little wistfully, "dear Steven would have found them." Her eyes swiveled to his. "But to sell what I *know* is worthless…it seems to lack honour."

"There is no dishonour in cutting your losses," he said gently. "That is how these ventures work. Every speculator accepts his risk."

With those words, hope rose in her breast. For the past three years, she hadn't a prayer of earning anything from the mine. Selling her shares now would bring a much-needed infusion of capital to her affairs. And if she waited for yet more news from East Africa, the opportunity to sell might evaporate. She steepled her hands together beneath her chin and came to a decision. Nodding, she said, "You have acted once on my behalf. I grant permission, then." She swallowed. Then, with difficulty as if parting from a limb or a loved one, she said quaveringly, "You may sell out my portion entirely."

Lettie felt suddenly tragic. The diamond mine was dear Steven's dream. Letting it go was like ushering in another little death of sorts. She fell into a kind of sad reverie.

Watching her, Nick said softly, "'Tis for the best." He found the bellpull and used it. In a minute Dudley appeared. "Two glasses of claret," Nick said, still watching Lettie closely.

Dudley was not in the habit of taking orders from guests, and particularly for claret in the middle of the day for his mistress; but one look at Nick's face brooked any objections. Mr. Dellacort's air of assurance was formidable. "Yes, sir," he said, and shuffled out.

Lettie said, "We do not have much time. His Lordship will be calling shortly. Best not to find you here."

Nick smirked. "A little competition does a man good."

While they waited for the drinks, Lettie said, "I will write the letter to my solicitors for you to take with you." She heaved a sigh as she returned to the little escritoire. As she wrote, Nick picked up her prayer book. "Are you devout, Lettie?"

"Not nearly so much as I ought to be," she replied. "But I do, of course, read the prayer book." She glanced at him uncertainly, but the question, "Do you not?" froze on her tongue. She rather assumed he did not. Instead she added, "I often attend the Grosvenor Chapel. And I try to pray nightly." She paused, giving him an opportunity to inject his own practice of religion, but he put down the book and made his way toward her.

"In that case, since you find me so odious..." His eyes were nothing but serious. "I hope you will include me in your prayers."

Lettie stared sadly up at him thinking that she did not find him odious at all. And that was entirely the problem! But she replied gravely, "I will, of course." His eyes held hers, but she looked away hurriedly in fear that her heart was revealed in them and would betray her traitorous longing for him. She did not tell him that she did already include him in her prayers. Or that she asked earnestly to be rid of her foolish attraction for him. Her latest prayer was that, if she must love the man, could it be revealed to her in some manner that he was, despite his wanting revenge, a better man than he seemed? That he was worthy of the love of the wife of dear Steven, who told her she must love only a good man?

She did not expect that prayer to be answered. Nicholas Dellacort was simply not the man to give her heart to, nor the good man that dear Steven had in mind. She may as well have wished for a miracle.

What might have been spoken next had to wait, for Dudley returned with a tray, and Nick went and removed the two glasses. He motioned for the servant to leave and turned back to Lettie. "Do you know," he said, delivering her glass. "I have only just thought of it. You are quite unchaperoned."

Lettie took a sip, eyeing him over the rim of her glass. "I am not a helpless young debutante, Mr. Dellacort. Nevertheless, if you intend to make a habit of calling upon me, perhaps I will ask my cousin Harriette to stay with me as companion."

"I had in mind your seeing Elston here alone. Could you not have a servant with you?"

Lettie eyed him evenly. "I have none now. And that does not seem to distress you."

He smiled. "Call your maid before he arrives." He upended his glass, drank down the liquid, and put it on a table. He strode toward Lettie and reached out a hand."

"Oh, here is the letter," she said, folding it quickly. Shall I add my signet?

"That won't be necessary." She gave it to him, and he tucked it into a waistcoat pocket. Then he reached for her glass, making her laugh in surprise.

"Do you want more claret?"

"I want your claret." He took it. "I ordered it in the thought of easing your distress at selling the mine. But I have thought better of it. With Elston on his way, you must not be compromised by something stronger than what you're used to."

"And how do you know I am not used to it?" She asked, challengingly. He was right, but she bristled at his knowing it.

He downed the contents of the glass quickly. "I remember the effect of that small glass of sherry upon you the other night."

Lettie was amazed. She had been light-headed, but who would have supposed that he would recollect her reaction? He—he was *concerned* for her.

"Now," he said, moving toward the door. "Call a maid. Or do not stay long alone with his lordship." He stopped. Facing the door, he added in a subdued tone, "Unless he appears ready to offer for you. You must, of course, welcome his suit, for it will be the making of you." He turned to her with veiled eyes. "You deserve the best of fortune, Miss Wetherham."

A stab of guilt went through Lettie, for she knew the earl would never make her an offer. Nick's words cut her heart, too, because he had not called her Lettie, but 'Miss Wetherham.'

"I'll deliver your letter," he said, reaching for the door handle. But he paused again. "We must sell while the selling is good. Until tomorrow, then. Lord and Lady Gresham's levée. Send me word if you are—betrothed—or engaged by the earl for your transport. Otherwise, I will come for you."

Lettie shook her head. "The Cantrells are invited and will take me."

He bowed and was gone.

Lettie stared at the closed door. For a moment, her face went through a spasm as she tried to control her emotions. Nick had walked in like a lover but left as one spurned. There was no other way to handle a notorious flirt, of course. She'd done what she must to protect her honour. But she felt terribly depleted and put her head down upon one arm on the desk.

And burst into tears.

Chapter Fourteen

Nick felt particularly low after leaving Lettie. So instead of delivering her letter to the solicitors as promised, and instead of seeing his own man of business to rid himself of his stock as well, he went home. There was no sense trying to wring water from a stone; both their shares must be sold directly. But he had no heart for business just then; it could wait until the following morning.

Unbeknownst to him, Horace Cantrell had earlier revived his spirits so well at White's, finding himself among friends, that he lost his earlier caution regarding the morsel of truth that the mining venture was irretrievably failed. In fact, he lost all sense of secrecy regarding both his late financial disasters and began broadcasting them to whosoever would— whosoever cared to listen, that is. He did it as a man seeking redemption, as though he was guilty of vast indiscretions of poor judgment and must confess all; with every glass of madeira, his sins lay only heavier upon his head until he had expunged his soul by clear admissions of guilt. He never should have invested in that doomed mine. Too, he should have steered his cousin Miss Wetherham away as soon as his brother-in-law's death proved it was cursed! On and on he expounded to his circle of fellows, all sympathetic gentlemen, for they were the priests who must grant him forgiveness.

Losing a fortune in business was common enough. But Horace, moaning that he'd been deuced unlucky, hounded by the devil, and was now practically done up, managed to get the ear of a man sitting at a nearby table. Unfortunately for Nick, this listener to the miserable, self-pitying drunkard was the Marquess of Warthenshire.

Upon hearing that the Wetherham's mine was worthless, ("dashed and deuced worthless, a devil's trap," in Cantrell's words) he started up from his seat. Leaving his fellows in gaping wonderment, he hurried off, muttering and mumbling to himself. He could hardly get his coachman to drive hard and fast enough to his solicitors, Malcolm and Mothesby, in the city proper. Upon arrival, he revoked his interest in the deuced mine, effective immediately. Only last week, knowing Dellacort had invested in it, he'd wanted to outbuy that devil. Thank heavens he'd never been able to.

He left the offices of Malcolm and Mothesby smiling with the thought that Nicholas Dellacort would suffer losses.

Dellacort was the son of a beautiful woman. That beautiful woman had been the marquess's first love. He wouldn't allow her name to pass his lips. He'd never got over her rejection, no, not when she could have been his marchioness. She'd shown her unworthiness by choosing a commoner over him. That should have been punishment enough to satisfy his sense of justice, but the Dellacort family was landed and steeped in wealth, which made it only a thorn in his side.

He was always on the lookout for ways to get even. This one took no effort on his part at all. What could be more fitting?

Nick saw to the business the following day. To his remorse, it was a day too late. At the offices of Lettie's solicitors, he discovered they were in receipt of the marquess's revocation of offers on the stock. Only one possible buyer might be contacted, by name of Stewart Trafford. Nick grimaced and told them not to contact Stewart. He would not saddle his friend with worthless stock. But what truly dashed his spirits was that Lettie was now stuck with the lion's share of it—she'd missed her opportunity to sell, and it was his fault.

Her opportunity had come only because of Dellacort drumming it up by his investment; but he had told her point blank not to sell, knowing full well the marquess would have bought. He'd been hoping new diamonds would be found, in which case it would have secured Lettie's fortunes. But now he'd succeeded only in destroying her chance to make good on what she owned. His own loss in the venture mattered nothing to him, as he could easily afford it. But for Lettie it was a different matter.

He spoke at length with her solicitors, weighing different schemes and ideas, for he burned with the desire to make it up to her. They assured him it was no fault of his that the mine was unproductive; he need not take responsibility for it. But by the time he left, after receiving hearty handshakes, their best wishes for his success, and many a "God bless you," he felt he could face her. Still, as his coach pulled away from the offices, he stared sightlessly through the window. What he saw in his mind's eye instead of the London street busy with pedestrians and carriages, was that he must somehow ensure that the earl marry Lettie.

The realization brought with it a strange, cold feeling about his heart, but he'd steered her wrong, and she deserved the security the earl could provide. If she would think of him as a suitable prospect, he could make it up to her himself. But that, he knew, was impossible. She'd made it abundantly clear. And he could hardly blame her. He'd behaved abominably to her at times.

And yet...the memory of the night in the coach when she'd moved into his arms threatened to belie all that she said. He had felt sure, then, that she cared for him. When their eyes met, their lips so close, it had struck Nick that while he'd always been attracted to her, in truth he found her more than just attractive. She was delightful. Of high conscience, yes, to a fault, irritatingly honourable, but a little soldier to have endured it all so admirably.

The realization was so strong and sudden that it had stopped him in his tracks. He dared not kiss her, though he had been brazen enough to do so twice before. When Lettie threw an arm about his neck, Nick understood at that moment that she was what he wanted. He'd been a fool not to see it. Lettie was an extraordinary woman, surviving on her own, maintaining her good humour with dignity. And she'd never refrained from holding him accountable for his arrogance and impertinence.

What kind of fool was he, to encourage such a woman to dally with another man? What kind of fool, indeed, to pay her to do so, even when she found the matter distasteful? But now, perhaps, it had been for the best, for her best, that is. If the earl claimed her for himself, her future would be secure. He thought of Sophia with regret, for now he saw she no longer had a claim on his heart. And if she lost the earl as well, she would be without immediate prospects. But Sophia would survive and still live in comfort.

Lettie was the one who needed security.

Lettie was the one he must help to get it.

Nick stopped home to change before leaving for the levée. In truth, he was weary of social engagements. He'd never been one to flit from one entertainment to the next; normally, he'd happily forgo the honour of today's societal outing. But he must see it through. He would—but with a heavy heart. He should have been happy in that the earl was indeed turning to Lettie from Sophia—that had been his aim all along—but instead of pleasing him, it chafed.

As his valet fashioned his neckcloth into a neat style, he recalled the scene when he and Sophia had walked in upon Lord Elston and Lettie in an embrace. His heart twisted. Dash it, if he wasn't falling for her—and just when it was too late. The earl had come to appreciate her, and her best course was to marry him. She'd be a countess and later a marchioness. Even if she cared for him, the earl's offer was superior to his.

And just like that, Nick realised he was doing Sophia Alden a grave disservice. He did not love her. And he'd interfered in her betrothal. If marrying a nobleman was better for Lettie, then it must be better for Miss Alden also. He was a meddling fool.

"Are we sighing, sir?" asked Penwith, his faithful man, who was in front of him, still working on getting the neckcloth just so.

"Did I?" Nick asked. "I suppose I did."

"Is it a matter I may be of service in, sir?"

"No, Pen, I wish it were."

"Did we lose at the gaming table, sir?" It was evident Pen wished to know more of what weighed upon his master's heart, but Nick said only, "No, nothing like that."

A footman scratched at the door. "What is it?" Penwith asked, in that arching tone of the servant who knows his station is superior to most of the other peons in the household.

A footman opened the door and held out a note. "For the master, sir."

"Bring it here," said Nick, holding out a hand. He unfolded it, and, holding it up so as to see around Pen, he read quickly. He came to attention.

"Finish the blasted thing, I must be off!"

"Yes, sir!" The discerning Penwith could see that Mr. Dellacort had found sudden purpose. "Is it good news, sir?"

"She wants to see me," he said.

Penwith finished his work and gave a little pat to the snowy cravat, smiling.

Nick arrived at Lettie's house, trying not to appear as though he'd rushed from his own abode in a flurry of hope and excitement to see what she required. Her note was short and cryptic. "Please come for me. You must know!" The "you must know!" was underlined.

Coming for her meant he would take her to the levée, not the Cantrells. *But know what?* He asked himself as he waited for his groom to hitch the gig—and it seemed as though the man moved as quickly as Rip Van Winkle waking from hibernation, despite Nick's urging him on in irritated tones. *Know what?* He'd asked himself a thousand times since, as he sat in crawling traffic which seemed to progress like an overladen barge in a bracken river, when what he wanted was a smart clipper ship bounding across open sea.

Finally, he arrived, dressed sharply in fitted knee-breeches and white stockings, a tailored topcoat, snowy cravat, and black shoes. Hurrying past Dudley, who called out with a pained look, "The first parlour, sir!" Nick made his way there; and knocked.

"Come in!" Lettie was right near the door, standing in agitated torment of soul. She was ready for the levée in a beautiful sheer over-gown with a blue silk chemise beneath. The silk was embroidered at the hem, and the gown at the puffed sleeves and sash. Lettie's hair was tied up in layered Roman bands and her one remaining diamond sparkled from a gold chain about her neck, adorning her bosom. All this, Nick took in with one glance.

He rushed to her and took her hands. "What is it? What's happened?"

She stared up at him. "Forgive me! I should not have written such an abominably poor note. But the thing is," and here she hesitated. She drew her hands away and turned toward the circle of furniture. "Please, have a seat."

"Just out with it, if you please, Lettie," he said, though he followed her and obediently sat down.

She sat across from him, practically wringing her hands. "I no longer know what is best." He waited, striving not to lose patience.

"You see, here it is. What you saw the other night, when you walked in and the earl and I—well, you know."

"When we found you in an embrace?" He hoped to nudge her along.

"Yes. We—that is, the earl, well—you must know." She took a deep breath, met his gaze, and said, in a quavering voice, "'Tis all a ruse! Nothing will come of it."

Nick blinked. "Of course it's a ruse. I put you up to it."

"No, no, what I mean to say is, there was nothing in it on his lordship's part. He only wishes to rouse Miss Alden's jealousy."

Nick felt something unfamiliar, something akin to *joy* that the earl wasn't in love with her. For a second, his heart sang and something in his eyes danced. But then his gaze narrowed. "Are you certain?"

She nodded. "Yes. And I agreed to go along with him." She frowned. "It seemed reasonable; only you must realize, that if his scheme succeeds—and I believe it will—yours, sir, will not."

He took his first easy breath since receiving her note.

Lettie was still in the throes of sorrow and felt more explanation was in order. "I said nothing to you at first," she admitted with large eyes, "for I felt it did not signify, as he asked me to do the very thing you had engaged me for! To flirt with him. It seemed positively propitious that he asked the same thing of me that you had." Here she gave him a look of regret. "Only I came to see that the scheme will work in his favour, not yours. So I thought I must tell you. I am ready to give up my part in the business altogether if you—"

"You mustn't do that." His gaze was infused with a gentleness Lettie was not used to seeing in him.

Nick could think only of how he'd ruined her chance at independent wealth, which meant Lord Elston was still the best alternative for her future happiness. "Continue with the scheme. If Elston is happy to flirt with you, let him do it. Until they are wed, actually wed, all is not lost."

She seemed doubtful. "Today he intends upon hanging about me very much so that Miss Alden cannot overlook it." She heaved a sigh. "I daresay, if she would make her choice, we could all be free of this! But if you wish to secure her," and here she swallowed and gave him a very direct look. "You must offer for her!" She said this as if it was very brave to say outright, and for Lettie, it was, as she loathed the thought of Nick marrying Sophia.

She swallowed again and pressed a hand to her chest. Then, smoothing an imaginary wrinkle from her gown, added, "I asked you to come, chiefly, so that you can head off the earl's game." Here she looked up. "He claims that in her vanity and pride Sophia will suddenly find him more agreeable if she perceives that his loyalty is in danger." She shook her head. "But if you truly love her, then you must claim her."

He gave her a penetrating look. "Do you begin to have hopes of the earl?"

"No! Not in the least."

"But you wish to free him of Sophia."

"To prevent the grief of a loveless marriage, I suppose, but my thought was more for you, Nick, to ensure your happiness!"

Nick's eyes softened. Lettie seemed not to notice she'd used his Christian name, but it did not escape him. If only it signified. But he knew it did not erase her prior aversion to him. "Give no thought to me." In a brisker tone he continued, "Continue with the scheme. For all I know, the earl is not hoping to rouse Sophia's wrath but to ease you into a courtship."

Lettie's fine brows drew together. "He has no intention of courting me; or of losing Miss Alden, as I said." She paused, surveying him to gauge his reaction. "I'm afraid you do not understand Sophia as well as you thought. Did you not see her rush to his side when she found us together?"

"I see no reason for that to flummox you," Nick said, affably. "Leave Sophia to me. But surely this can only ease your qualms, as you no longer need fear injuring the earl with feigned affection. This ought to make the endeavour more agreeable to you.

"It is still a hoax," she replied. "And I can hardly stand to allow him to—" She stopped, not wishing to say she disliked the earl's kissing her.

"To allow his touch? His kiss?"

Her cheeks flushed. She hurriedly added, "What he asks has the appearance of being in keeping with what you asked; but his aim is exactly opposite. Does this not concern you?"

"Sophia is just as like to take a disgust of him as to suddenly prefer him."

"Mr. Dellacort, as a woman, I can assure you, she will fight to keep him!" She paused, looking at him earnestly. "I have no doubt she would sooner die than lose him to me, a poor widow, for that is her nature. I am afraid Lord Elston is correct in his estimation of her, and that you, sir, for all your intimate knowledge of Miss Alden, have been mistaken."

"You may have the right of it." He sat forward in thought. It did concern him, because now he considered that Lettie must win the earl, not Sophia. He rubbed his chin in thought. "I seem to have come at it from the wrong angle. I've been a gudgeon." He paused, considering, staring at her. "You are the matchmaker. What do you suggest?"

Lettie stared at him. Nick Dellacort was everything Sophia could want, she was sure. Too handsome for his own good, thick hair and brows, a hint of sideburns, smooth jaw with a faint shadow, neat mouth. He was arrogant but could be warm and caring when he chose. His wealth was vast; he lacked only a title, if that could be said to be lacking. "If you will not lose her, what you must do," she said slowly, with sad eyes and an aching heart, "is marry her yourself. That is my best advice."

Nick came to his feet. "Come. We'll go to the levée. And on the way, I shall tell you something about Lord Elston."

Chapter Fifteen

Side by side atop the board in his sporting gig, Nick explained to Lettie, after snapping the ribbons to start the horses, "Elston may say he wants to play upon Sophia's jealousy, but what he truly wants may be another thing entirely." He paused and looked over at her. "I believe he means to court you in earnest."

Her mouth opened to protest. "But—but—why would he assure me that his intentions were quite the opposite?"

"To obtain your cooperation. Your determination not to remarry has preceded you, coupled with your prior reluctance to receive his advances. But he now has *carte blanc* to flirt with you, for he managed to get your willing consent to do so."

Lettie slumped in her seat. "I do hope you are mistaken! Elsewise, this grows worse and worse!"

Her reaction braced him, but he said, "There is no tragedy in an earl wanting you for a wife."

This brought her back to earth. For a few minutes she'd been reeling, unnerved by the thought that she'd stepped into something of a trap. But the suggestion that the earl really wished to have Lettie as a wife made all her fears slink away like ashamed children caught being naughty.

"You cannot truly credit that. I am a poor widow, and he is in love with Sophia, I assure you. It is all just as I said; he wishes to flirt with me on her account."

Traffic had grown slower and slower as they approached the street of the affair, for the carriages of all the guests made a terrible deadlock. They moved forward only inches at a time it seemed, before having to stop again. Finally, Lettie could see the house where guests were disembarking, with footmen standing by to assist. More servants were lined up on either side of the entrance, forming a passage from the street, and holding back the working class curious, those intent upon glimpsing the aristocracy and rich upper class in their finery as they exited their coaches and entered the house.

Mr. Dellacort surveyed the crowd as they drew up to the front, and then returned his gaze to her. "Play along with it," he said. "Whatever his intentions, play along." He turned to her with a very determined look. "I give you my word, I shall release you after today, whatever happens."

Lettie was so surprised she did not at once reply. She felt delighted for a moment, but in a minute, while a footman helped her down, her feeling changed to one of suspicion. Soon Nick was there, offering his arm. She glanced up at him. "Whatever happens you will release me? Why am I convinced you are plotting what will happen?"

He chuckled and looked down at her appreciatively. "Little escapes you, Lettie. Here it is. I will maneuver it so he'll have no choice but to marry you."

She felt stunned. And something about her heart ached mightily that he so much wanted her to marry the earl that he would try to manipulate the matter. "Do not dare! I won't allow it!"

He spoke into her ear. "It will ensure your future security and happiness."

"Happiness? When neither I, nor the earl, desire the match?"

He did not answer, as they were ushered into a great room decorated in stunning neoclassical style and humming with the conversation of people talking in small circles. Immaculate footmen made the rounds carrying trays heavy with glasses and refreshments. Lettie returned the nods of some acquaintances but did not see the Cantrells and could hardly pay heed to the company elsewise. Her mind was still in a flummox. "We must speak more on this!" she hissed. With an effort to keep her voice low, she added icily, "I should have thought you understood me by now. I can never marry a man apart from real affection."

"If he compromised you, you could."

She stared at him. "You are more diabolical than I imagined."

"Indeed! A black-hearted cove. For I want what's best for you." He looked around for Elston and Sophia.

Her brows came together, and she glowered at him. "You care nothing for how your schemes affect other people, so long as you achieve *your* desired ends."

"That is partially true," he agreed, affably. "But not entirely."

"You will sacrifice *my* future happiness for your present victory, even though," she said, almost trembling with anger, "as I begin to suspect, you are not in love with Sophia at all! You are merely vexed by her family's abuse of you." This got his attention. His lips firmed into a line. "Come." He drew her back out of the grand apartment and followed a corridor, looking for a suitable spot to speak in privacy. The corridor turned; they came upon a large sculpture on a pedestal. He took her hand and drew her behind it.

"We are hiding like children," Lettie said.

"We must settle this." He stared into her eyes. "Whether I love Sophia or not was never a condition of our agreement, may I remind you?"

She pursed her lips, blinking at him. "But—but you must love her. Why else go through all this? Why engage my help at all?"

"You hit the mark. It was revenge of a sort. Coupled with what I believed at the time would better suit her."

"I cannot agree to help in this."

"You already did. You signed a contract." His eye was sharp, his tone merciless.

"You are *abominable*!"

A shadow crossed his eyes, but his tone and look were not harsh when he replied, "I am well aware of your verdict concerning my character. But if you recall, I said I would release you from any further dealings in this so long as you play along today." Their eyes were deadlocked.

"I will *not* allow you to maneuver me into a compromising position."

"Is that so?" A spark of his usual humour flickered from his gaze. "Are we not at this very moment in one? If anyone were to come along, this could be construed badly, do you not think?"

She looked about them at their little corner behind the statue as if seeing it for the first time, and her eyes widened. Making a move to leave, he caught her hand and stopped her.

"What I hope to accomplish for you with Elston is entirely for your future benefit. There is nothing abominable in it."

"I beg to differ!" Her brows knit together.

The indignation on her pretty face made him stifle a smile, which only aggravated her further. She continued in righteous indignation, "Everything you said about revenge, it was all a whisker! You *are* in love with Sophia, and you will sacrifice me at the altar, quite literally, to have her back. You wish to maneuver me into a compromising circumstance with his lordship to force our wedding so that Sophia will be free—you will get your prize!"

"That's not it, Lettie!" He grimaced. "You mistake the matter; but even if that were my plan, it is nothing more than what you originally agreed to, and for which I paid you handsomely."

Now she blinked back tears. "You are a heartless scoundrel."

"What on earth makes you say that now? Can you not see—" And here he turned her about, drawing her by her hand up against him. His eyes bored into hers. "I am not in love with Miss Alden."

"How good of you to make that clear, sir," someone spoke, icily. It was the fluid voice of Sophia. Nick and Lettie came apart guiltily, just in time to see Sophia and Lord Elston come around the bend, spy them behind the sculpture, and gape in astonishment.

"I thought I heard your voice," Sophia continued. "But little did I think to find you..." she stopped and ran her eyes up and down Lettie as if appraising an object to be discarded for charity. "Engaged."

"This isn't what it seems," said Lettie.

The earl stepped forward. "Of course not, of course not; you are old acquaintances." He held out an arm. "Will you join us, Miss Wetherham?"

It struck both Nick and Lettie just then that the earl was transformed. He was perfectly attired, approaching Nick's level of neat elegance, even his cravat a thing of snowy beauty to rival Dellacort's. Lettie smiled encouragingly at him. "You look marvelous, my lord."

His topcoat was tailored to perfection, his waistcoat a respectably soft gold; he wore neat, close fitting pantaloons and polished black shoes on his feet.

He thanked her, trying not to grin. When he had called upon her the day before, missing Dellacort only by minutes, it was to seek her advice in sartorial matters. Lettie had given him strict orders as to neckcloths—absolutely no more yellow or green—and told him he must stop at the tailor for an immediate alteration in his topcoat. She advised him to give up the boots for full dress social affairs, and, before he left, went over the dance steps to the quadrille with him. He now stood in a much better way to catch Miss Alden's eye, she felt.

But the others knew nothing of her tutelage. The earl nodded a secret thanks to her, which Lettie acknowledged with another smile.

Nick said, "Miss Alden, if you will, may I have a word with you?"

Sophia hesitated, eyeing him resentfully. Finally, she turned to the earl. "I'll be just a minute." Lettie stepped away from Nick and accepted Lord Elston's arm. Together, they turned in the direction of the party, she, with Nick's words ringing in her brain. *I am not in love with Miss Alden.* She glanced back, wondering if it were true—she could hardly credit it—and wondering what Nick could say to smooth things over with Sophia.

Sophia came up to Nick with a look of having been ill used. "What is your game, Nick, since you have admitted your disdain for me?"

Nick studied her a long second. "Your hopes are not dashed. You intend upon marrying Elston, do you not? You've intended it from the start."

She sniffed and tossed her head. "What is it to you? I have long ceased to wait upon *you* with hopes."

"What is *your* game, then, in giving every appearance that you favour me and are indifferent to him?"

She arched a brow and said, "I thought I might have an opportunity." She eyed him coldly. "To break your heart, if you must know, just as you broke mine!"

His lips firmed into a line. "I comprehend that you wanted an offer from me; but I never raised your hopes with a false word. You knew what I was."

She lifted her nose. "I did. But I convinced myself you would come about for me!"

His eyes softened, but he said, "Let me understand you. You wanted me to pursue you right up to your wedding in order to punish me."

"That's it."

"But you overplayed your hand."

Her brows furrowed. Sharply, she asked, "How is that?"

"Will you suffer remorse if Lord Elston marries Miss Wetherham instead of you?"

She stared at him indignantly. "I daresay you give your lady friend much credit! Do you really imagine a future marquess would marry a penniless widow?"

"I do imagine it. In fact, I believe he intends to. Will you suffer for it?"

Anger deepened in Sophia's lovely blue eyes while she stared at him, forming her answer. But there was something more in her gaze that Nick observed; something which made him say without waiting for her reply, "It does injure you."

She put her hands on her hips. "I cannot credit it. But if he were to choose her over me, I should only pity him."

"Even though you know I will not make an offer in his place?"

The determination in her gaze changed to resentment. She glowered at him. "You have been abominable to me!"

"I have. I'm sorry for it."

"*You* brought Miss Wetherham to the earl!"

"I did."

"What induced you to it since it was not love for me?"

He grimaced. "If you must know, it was chiefly to interfere with the marquess. He arranged the match, no offense to you, Sophia, on my account, to cross me. He has crossed me before with no reason I know of; but I determined he should not succeed in it this time." In a softer voice he added, "And I was indeed piqued at your turning away." Softer still he added, "I am not completely heartless."

A look of satisfaction swept across Sophia's features. "I am glad of that, though you are a rogue."

"To my remorse, I am."

She met his eyes and then came to herself. A look of determination returned. "Well, I daresay we are done here. Should we not locate the earl and Miss Wetherham? I will not allow this to end badly." She gave Nick a piercing look. "And perhaps now you can keep Miss Wetherham far from my betrothed, if you would."

They began walking toward to the public rooms. Nick said, "We may already be too late."

Sophia gasped. "You cannot mean--! What are you thinking? The earl will suffer breach of promise if he dares to—to—" Her eyes grew wide and she looked up at Nick with trepidation. "You do not truly suppose he would dare to—do anything rash?" She spoke as though the world had suddenly changed before her eyes. Even Elston's sudden tasteful clothing—the horrible thought hit her that he had donned it for a wedding—a Gretna Green wedding! And it was not to wed her, Sophia!

Nick frowned. "I had no notion you had your heart set on him. I encouraged Miss Wetherham to turn his head in the understanding that it would relieve you."

She turned on him but hastened her steps. "How little you comprehend! Of course my heart is set on him. What woman in her right mind would turn away from being a future marchioness?"

I know one who would, he thought. Nick's heart went out to Lettie.

"And—and, if you must know," Sophia said, despite their hurried pace. "I have grown rather fond of the clod. Did you note his manner of dress today?" She almost smiled. "A sudden, marked improvement in one area must signify there is hope in others."

Just before they gained the first room of guests, Nick stopped her with a touch on her hand. "Can you accept my apology for meddling in your affairs? For trying to turn his head?"

She looked deeply into his eyes. "I can and I do. I appreciated it at first, Nick. It meant that you did care something for me, I think, at one time."

"I did, of course." He leaned down and gave her a chaste kiss on the cheek. "And now, let us find our wayward partners!"

They entered the room with eyes alert, searching the scattered groups for Lord Elston and Lettie. They traversed each of the public areas and checked the verandas. After their first sweep of the rooms, they made a second, slower search.

Afterward, Sophia's countenance was shaken. "Good heavens, they've gone!" she said. "They've gone!" She gripped his arm with one hand. "Nick—you must *catch* them!"

Chapter Sixteen

Lettie and the earl headed down the corridor to give Nick and Sophia space to talk. Lettie walked slowly, not wanting to give them *much* space, nor increase the distance between Lord Elston and Sophia overmuch. As seconds ticked past, and she endeavoured to pay heed to the earl's conversation, ringing in her head instead, like a beacon in her brain, were Nick's words: *I am not in love with Miss Alden.*

If only it were true. But would it change anything? No, for he was still Dellacort the devil. He would trifle with her if she let him, but never offer his hand. If only she could say with equal fervor, *I am not in love with Mr. Dellacort!* But she could not.

The earl cleared his throat. "Miss Wetherham, now that I may speak plainly, I must say how very graul I am for your assistance yesterday."

Lettie smiled. "I am sure Miss Alden could not help but note the change in you?"

He nodded, but with a little frown. "She did. Yes, yes, she remarked upon it." He turned and gave her a searching look. "But I must confess; I have done a deal of thinking, and, in truth, it is not Miss Alden's approval that concerns me."

"What is your concern, sir?"

He stopped walking and stared at her. An uncomfortable foreboding came over Lettie, for she saw in his eyes something that unsettled her. Something that suggested—as fantastic as it must be—that Nick was right. The earl meant to court her, Lettie, not Miss Alden!

He said, "My dear, dear, Miss Wetherham, it must be plain to you. Despite what Mr. Dellacort said just now about not loving Sophia, their every word and action has told us the opposite."

Lettie agreed; she nodded sadly. Much as she could wish that Nick's heart was free, it seemed Lord Elston had the right of it. Even now, she imagined Nick speaking with Sophia in such a way that she would forgive him that rash statement; she would forgive him anything, as indeed Lettie would too— if only he asked it of her.

The earl took Lettie's hand and held it between his two, still looking at her with an earnestness that set her nerves on edge and an ache to her heart. He was a sweet man. She did not wish to injure him. But she did not love him.

"As you denied being in love with Mr. Dellacort, I wondered why the two of us should not make a go of it, eh? Rather than try to pull the rug from their hopes, or stand in the way, why do we not facilitate their happiness while ensuring our own?"

"I—I do not understand you, sir," she stammered. "You are betrothed by mutual agreement to Miss Alden. Your families are in favour of it."

He shook his head. "My father approves of you wholeheartedly, ma'am," he said, smiling.

Lettie blinked in astonishment. Why would the marquess approve of her? "A poor widow?" she asked.

"Not so poor as all that," he said with a chuckle, as if she'd been joking.

"Oh!" Her face cleared. "You haven't heard! The mine is worthless. I received word the other day—"

The earl looked quickly about them. "Shhhh, my dear! I don't give a fig about your mine, if you must know. My father is the one to look at such things. Please, say nothing of it. Come with me to Gretna Green. We'll be married by this time tomorrow, and the marquess shan't be able to say a word to stop it." He paused, looking fondly down at her. "I daresay I have never gone on an adventure, and this would be a dashing adventure, don't you know."

She removed her hand from between his and touched his arm lightly. Looking up to him with gentle eyes, she said, "That is very kind of you, except for one difficulty."

"What is it, my dear? I am sure we can overcome it!"

Suddenly a sound further down the corridor made them look up. The Marquess of Warthenshire, with a determined, eagle-like look, his head bent but his eyes on them, hurried their way. "Is that you? You troublesome whelp!" he barked at his son. "I hope you haven't muddled things up!"

With astonishing strength and speed, the earl grasped Lettie's hand and pulled her into an adjoining side corridor. It was darker here, but he hurried her along as though the devil were at his heels. Gasping, Lettie cried, "My lord! Your father saw us! You will only enrage him further if he must chase after us!"

"No worries, my dear," the earl said, with surprising calm. "I know this house like the back of my hand. The Fortescues are my relations. I played along these corridors as a child."

Still hurrying her along, he turned down one narrow corridor after another and, to Lettie's utter astonishment, finally descended the servants' stairs and walked her through the kitchens and then through the service entrance to the outdoors! The kitchen staff, the cook and maids, even the scullery maid carrying a pail, had frozen in position, first gaping, then offering belated curtseys. Lettie had to hold back a sudden fit of giggles, for it seemed like the veriest lark, like playing hide and go seek, as she'd done as a little girl.

When they were outside, panting to catch their breath, she said, "My lord. What now?" She said this to illustrate that he'd taken them from the company to no purpose.

"To my coach. I have it at the ready. Let us to Gretna directly!"

"To Gretna?" Lettie exclaimed. "Sir, I cannot!"

"We can stop for luggage, if that is your concern."

"No, my lord. 'Tisn't that."

The earl's face crumpled. "Then what, my dear Miss Wetherham? You know, of course, what my offer entails." He still held her hand and was leading them toward the street. She knew, yes, what marriage to an earl entailed. Nobility, respect, wealth. All very well and good. But she said sorrowfully, "You must understand. I have an impediment that cannot be overcome."

"Name it."

She shook her head, suddenly blinking back tears. "It concerns Mr. Dellacort—that rogue! He is a devil, a scoundrel, and everything I dislike and loathe!"

The earl smiled. "Yes, yes? I am glad of it."

"But—but—" Her face was a picture of agony. She did not want to say what was in her heart, to acknowledge it aloud— but it seemed suddenly paramount that she must, for if she did, the earl would understand why she could never do as he asked. "I *love* him! To my eternal sorrow! I did deny it, I know, for I despise myself for it, but I do love him, I love him with all my heart, the miscreant!"

The earl's face darkened. Frowning, he patted her hand. "You must give him up. Sophia will not lose him."

Lettie said, "But you see, I am a prisoner of my own making. I am doomed to follow my heart. I can only marry for love." She gave him a look of compassion. "You deserve a woman who loves you."

"You will grow to love me," he said softly.

At that moment, a door opened, and the marquesse's indignant voice could be heard coming from the house like a volcano rumbling before eruption. The earl grasped Lettie's hand and ran. "Come! We can speak more on this, Miss Wetherham. But I must not face the marquess!"

Lettie was in a flummox. How scandalous it must appear for them to be running! But the street had cleared of curious bystanders, for the elegant upper class had arrived and were out of sight. With only a few footmen watching curiously, then, they passed through the entrance gate and within minutes came to the earl's coach, an impressive chaise and four.

A servant put down the steps, and the earl held out a hand, smiling gently at Lettie. She hesitated. If she entered his coach, would she be agreeing to a Gretna wedding? The life of a countess and later, a marchioness, could only promise luxury and freedom from all the worries she'd shouldered since Steven's passing. But her feet remained firmly on the pavement, as though something undeniably strong held her there. She had every reason in the world to accept the earl's offer, but no reason, no logic, could overcome her heart.

It belonged to Dellacort.

"Come, Miss Wetherham," the earl said, coaxingly. "Or, Lettie. May I call you that?"

Lettie could not answer. She was seeing her life, her future, pass before her eyes. She and Nick would never be man and wife, for he would never desire it. She would go to her grave with the burden of unrequited love; living a shabby genteel existence. Hoping the Cantrells would recover their fortunes enough to take her in, if need be. She would be sad, and lonely, and poor. But, looking into Lord Elston's mild, smiling face, agreeable as he was, she knew she could never be his, no matter the cost. She could not live a lie. Dellacort had been right. She was obstinate! It would be her ruin, her shame. But she could not accompany Lord Elston to Gretna.

Footsteps approached behind them. The earl turned, dropped his hand, and his eyes hardened.

Lettie did not turn. It made no difference whether the marquess came upon them. But it was Sophia who rushed up to them crying, "Oh, thank heaven! We are not too late. You have not left us."

The earl looked at her cautiously and searchingly. In his quiet voice he said, "We are not gone because Miss Wetherham refused to come."

There was a long, uncomfortable silence until she asked, in a sober tone that equaled his, "You are determined, then, not to honour our betrothal?"

"I was under the distinct impression you did not wish to keep it." He glanced at Nick. "And, if I may say so, that your heart was set upon Mr. Dellacort."

Miss Alden said flatly, "It is not."

Lettie's heart rose. What had transpired between Sophia and Nick, she wondered, to bring about this sudden admission?

In a miserable tone, Sophia added, "I do apologize, Elston. I've behaved abominably."

The earl's face lightened. He seemed at a loss for words, but finally managed, "It would seem that I have also, by inviting Miss Wetherham to Gretna, just now."

Sophia blanched, but then swallowed and gained control of her features. "That is neither here nor there." She paused and pursed her lips. "Let us begin again, my lord." Her voice was soft and wheedling, very unlike the Sophia Lettie had known heretofore. She could hardly credit her ears. Sophia had made her choice, and it was Elston!

The earl stared at Sophia as if he'd just stumbled upon unexpected buried treasure. His eyes were full.

Lettie realised suddenly that Nick was beside her. With her heart in her throat, she turned and met his eyes. All the hopelessness and sorrow she felt due to loving him, a rogue, was in her gaze. She wished for a moment that she could wrap herself in his arms, lose herself there, lose all her cares and sorrows. He stepped toward her as if he read her thoughts but stopped short of touching her.

"Why did you not go?" he asked, softly. "You could have secured your future."

Before she could answer, the gravelly voice of the marquess rang out. "I've found you, you worthless sprig! Stay where you are!" And the Marquess of Warthenshire, looking out of breath and undone, came determinedly up to them with a glare in his eyes as if he'd found a cache of jewel thieves.

Turning a stony glance upon Lettie he said to his son, "You will have nothing to do with this widow!" In a disgusted tone he added, "The mine's worthless! That makes *her* worthless."

Nick stepped before the marquess in silent fury, his face like stone. He stared into eyes that narrowed with suspicion. "You will apologize to Miss Wetherham."

"I'll do no such thing, sir!" In a grim, gravelly voice.

"Then you'll meet me on the field."

Lettie gasped. Nick would risk a duel for her sake? The thought both elated and horrified her. Her heart, the portion not already melted, was now warring to cede itself entirely to being Nick's possession, however unpromising his intentions toward her.

The marquess clenched his jaw. With lowered brows and a scrunched-up nose, he said, "Meet you on the field? I will not! Fool headed, you are."

"Have you no sense of honour?" Nick hissed.

"I shan't risk my neck on account of a hussy!" he returned in a voice rising with anger.

At that, to Lettie's shock, to everyone's shock, Nick landed a quick right to the man's jaw, toppling him back and almost to the ground. Lord Elston and Sophia watched in fascinated silence but made no move to help him.

"Are you mad?" the marquess spat out, recovering himself. He rubbed a hand along his smarting face. "How dare you, sir!"

"Do not," Nick said, in a tight, acidic tone, "insult Miss Wetherham again."

Lettie's heart pounded wildly. She stared at Nick with an amazing thought, with the thought that he must care for her! He'd been on the level about not loving Sophia! She hadn't thought it possible.

An ugly leer crossed the marquess's face. Motioning at Nick he said to his son, "This—this son of a whore—"

Nick moved in a flash, taking the marquess by the lapels of his coat. "Are you determined to force me to close your trap?"

"Remove your hands from my person, or I shall have you hauled to prison!" the aristocrat bellowed.

Nick made no move to obey. "You have long held a grievance against me. What is the cause?"

The nobleman stared belligerently at Nick. Slowly, he grumbled, "I have my reasons."

The earl spoke up. "His fight is not against you sir, but your mother."

"Quiet, you cur!" the marquess cried.

With a look of incredulity, Nick said, "My mother? God rest her soul, she has been dead these ten years. What did she have to do with you?"

The marquess's mouth twitched in indecision. Finally, he said bitterly, "She ought not to have been your mother! She was betrothed to *me*!"

Nick's brows rose. He seemed ready to lay another facer on the man, but Lettie put a hand to his arm. He looked over—their eyes met—such meaning in that one look! Such heartfelt emotion conveyed in an instant! He dropped his hold on the marquess and covered her hand with one of his. Though it lasted only a few seconds, the look between them filled Lettie's breast with wild joy. But the image of Steven crossed her mind, a frowning Steven. He would not approve of Nick as a good man. Why, why, must she think of that, now? Misery engulfed her.

The marquess brushed off his coat. Looking up at Nick, he said in acid tones, "Your mother chose a blasted commoner—your father. Could've been a marchioness with me. Got what she deserved, I daresay! And now, so have you."

"Eh?" said Nick. "What are you referring to?"

The marquess turned to his son. "This is the man who tried to cheat us of shares in the diamond venture. When we thought it had *value*," he added, with an accusing look at Lettie as though she'd been single-handedly responsible for making it otherwise. His eyes spit fire. "But now, haply, the tables are turned. He owns *all* the shares, I am told." He stopped to give a grunt of a laugh. "Bought out the lot—not worth a farthing, now! Just what you deserve, sir."

Lettie again turned eyes of astonishment to Nick. He owned all the shares? If that were true, why then, he must have bought out *her* shares! Could he have bought them, knowing them to be worthless? Could any action declare a man's love more than that?

She said, "Is this true?"

Nick turned to her apologetically, as if he had something to atone for. "I couldn't let you suffer that loss."

Her eyes widened. "You bought out my shares?"

"I did."

"Knowing how worthless they are?"

He said nothing, but his eyes spoke volumes, and it was all Lettie could do to keep herself from running into his arms. Instead, she cried, "You are too good, sir!" And then it hit her, that she had just acknowledged him to be good. Nicholas

Dellacort was, indeed, a *good* man. Not perfect by a long stretch, and with sins to atone for, doubtless. But silently she appealed to God. *Tell Steven, Lord,* she prayed. *Tell him that Nick's a good man. He defended my honour. He bought worthless stock to save me from ruin. He loves me, he must love me, but pushed me at the earl so that I might enjoy the life of an aristocrat. Please, Lord, tell Steven.*

Meanwhile, the marquess turned eyes of stone to Lord Elston. "You will marry Miss Alden," he said flatly, and with such weight as though giving a royal decree.

Sophia had been listening with something akin to suspense upon her face, but now she let out a sigh of relief. "Of course, my lord," she said quickly. She circled an arm through the earl's. "Elston and I are happy to hold the ceremony as soon as possible."

His Lordship looked adoringly at Sophia and then turned to his father with a curt nod. "Yes, m'lord."

The Marquess gave a last, withering glare at Nick and Lettie, then turned on his heel and stalked away. The earl and Sophia started after him, but Lord Elston stopped when he came abreast of them. "Miss Wetherham, I wish you the very best in life, the very best future, and God's blessing be upon you."

"Thank you, my lord. I heartily wish you joy, the both of you!" She included Sophia in her gaze with a nod. To her surprise, the venom had vanished from the beauty's dark eyes. She merely returned the nod and looked away.

The earl turned to Nick. "Miss Wetherham's future, sir, is entirely in your hands," he said lightly, but his eyes held unspoken words. "*Entirely* in your hands, sir," he repeated, before walking off with Sophia.

Nick turned to Lettie with a look of having a thousand things to say at once. He tucked her hand upon his arm. "Come. We cannot speak here." He found a footman and told him to find his coach and *be smart about it.*

"We came in your gig!" Lettie reminded him.

"Of course." This was good news for the mews were full, and the street lined with ebony coaches of similar shape and size. But a gig would be easily spotted. He told the servant, who sent a man scurrying out to retrieve it.

While they waited, Lettie could scarcely stop stealing glances at Nick, and only by sheer force of will looked away so as not to stare. The case with him was not very different, and, in order not to look like two fools in love, they stood in tense silence, constrained to contain their bursting hearts until the gig was finally delivered and stopped in the street before the house.

He grabbed her hand and hurried her across the pavement. "Come!"

His impatience made her giggle. "Mr. Dellacort," she said, laughing. "Anyone watching would suppose that we were anything but well bred."

"They are welcome to suppose what they like," he replied, while lifting her by the waist up to the board. When he was seated beside her, he snapped the reins but said, looking into her eyes, "Good breeding is all very well, but I can hardly contain myself. I must settle something with you."

Lettie's breath caught in her throat. She felt ready to burst with happiness, for surely he must be ready to acknowledge his love for her, and then it must follow that he meant to be honourable in it. He would, he must, make her an offer. Surely he was prepared to change his ways and settle down.

He cleared his throat, his eyes on the road. "I beg your pardon for my lack of discretion. For speaking to you in a gig! But you refused to go with Elston…and his last words to me…both have given me hope." He stole a glance in her direction. "May I hope, Lettie?"

The question in his eyes, the soft, longing in his voice, filled her with joy. "If it is my affection you hope for, you needn't hope at all. We needn't hope for what we already have."

He was forced to give his attention to the road, but she caught the edge of his mouth in a smile. "I am in mind to take us direct to Scotland!" he said.

Lettie's eyes widened. "Scotland! Did you say, Scotland?"

"I did." He hazarded another look her way, a look filled with affection.

Her heart thumped.

He interpreted her silence as dissent. "You nearly left for Gretna with that lily liver!"

"I never would have! I can only marry a man I love, as you well know!"

"And so you'll marry me, Lettie."

She could not help but smile, and when he looked her way, he grinned back. But she said, "You have never wanted to marry!"

"You have never wanted to marry again." He turned back to the street and directed the team expertly around a sharp corner.

"But a 'wedding over the anvil' for the renowned Mr. Dellacort?" she asked, for that is how Gretna weddings were known. "Will that not appear scandalous to society?"

His mouth turned up in amusement. "I have never avoided the appearance of scandal." As they drew up to her house on Russell Square, he slowed the horses and then turned to her. "Say yes, Lettie, for heaven's sake!"

Lettie bit her lip and smiled. She nodded her head in assent.

"Excellent!" he cried, in a voice so hearty, of such satisfaction, it thrilled her.

A groom held the horses while Nick accompanied Lettie inside. It took an eternity to walk calmly past Dudley and reach the parlour, but when the door closed behind them, Nick swept her into his arms.

His kissed her with urgent abandon. For the first time, the very first time, Lettie was able to return his kiss with no shame, no remorse, not a whit of misgiving. She gave herself wholeheartedly to it, and in doing that, to Nick, loving him more and more. She felt undeservedly happy. The thought of dear Steven crossed her mind, but—miracle of miracles—he seemed to smile! Afterward, while in Nick's arms, she had not one additional thought of her dear departed husband.

Minutes sped by while they luxuriated in the meeting of heart and lips, but then he drew away. "Here is the plan. Pack quickly, while I, in the meantime, will hasten to Berkeley Square for my trunk and the chaise, which is well sprung, for the long drive." He paused, stroking the side of her face. "There is only one thing I fear you may regret?"

"Yes?"

"Miss Wetherham's wedding. Only a bystander or two in Scotland shall witness it."

She smiled gently. "*I* shall be a witness, and God Himself. Miss Wetherham's wedding shall be all it needs to be," she reached up to kiss him, "because she is marrying *you*."

Gretna Green, thought Dellacort ruefully, could not be reached soon enough.

Epilogue

One month later

The butler at the house in Berkeley Square informed Mr. Dellacort, sitting comfortably across from his wife in the morning room after breakfast—a lively breakfast in which they freely shared disagreements regarding the latest news but without the least hint of discord—that a note had arrived by a post boy.

"Give it to Mrs. Dellacort," Nick murmured, not ready to give up his morning paper. But he lifted his head to watch her while she opened it. Lettie's hair was up, with little curls dangling fashionably about the sides of her face. She wore a morning gown of printed cambric, a fichu over the bust for modesty—which somehow her husband had grown to appreciate and now insisted upon—and a thick shawl about her shoulders against the mild chill in the air. The fireplace was at Nick's back, and he made a mental note to give her that seat for now on.

She opened the message, then pursed her lips. "Oh, dear. It's from East Africa. More dismal news, I am certain." She looked up at him. "Ought we to read it now in the morning when it shall mar the day?"

"Dearest, we have no hopes of the mine. A bad report makes no difference to us and is only to be expected."

She scanned the contents. He watched with growing amusement for Lettie could not disguise her feelings from him anymore than an infant from its mother, and her face, as he watched, filled with amazement. She said, "Oh, my!" and put a hand upon her heart. And then read it aloud.

"Dear Mr. Dellacort,

We wish to inform you, sir, of the latest development concerning the Wetherham Venture Mine. Please be advised that we have of late unearthed what appears to be a vast store of unrefined diamonds." She stopped here and gaped in astonishment, her mouth opening to form a perfect little 'o'. Nick grinned.

"My word!" she said. "You had best read it yourself." She rose and handed him the letter and then returned to her seat. He picked up where she'd left off but instead of reading it, paraphrased. "The foreman says he need hardly tell us how gratified he is after so many fruitless months of endeavour....so on and so forth." He glanced at her.

"Go on, I'm all ears!"

He returned to the pages. "In light of this success, he takes it upon himself to hire the necessary manpower to extract the gems, with all due regard to watchmen and security, as is usually necessary in these cases." He looked up. "So on and so forth."

"There is more," Lettie said. "He must give his report regarding the safety of the crew."

Nick skimmed the pages. Details as to estimated timelines for extraction and refinement, as well as operating cost estimates, were given. Then, "Ah," he said. "Here is it. Our foreman is pleased to report that not a man has suffered injuries in the pursuit and discovery of said gems except the usual physical exhaustion accompanying such labours." He looked up with a little smile. "I take it this tidbit is included at your special request?"

She nodded. "Yes, I insisted upon it."

He returned to the letter. "He waits upon my pleasure to learn whether such information will continue to be necessary in future reports."

"Of course!" Lettie quipped. She stared at Nick with large eyes. "Can you believe it? Who would have thought this possible after so many failures? It seems you bought me out just when I might have been a rich woman." She tried to look forbidding but failed to hide the smile forming at the edges of her mouth.

"But you are a rich woman," he countered. "In fact, you are richer, as Mrs. Dellacort, than you would have been as Miss Wetherham, diamonds or not."

"How do you know?" Her eyes sparkled mischievously. "We have yet to see how 'vast' this discovery is."

He smiled. "I am not sorry at this news. Your cousin will be in the doldrums, however." Lettie winced. "Horace should never have sent Harriette to wheedle us into buying his shares! It was shamefully done, when he believed them worthless!"

Nick was nonplussed. "We agreed to do it in thanks for the years when they lent support when you needed it."

She sipped her tea. Putting the cup down delicately, she admitted, "Yes, I know. But still it was monstrously underhanded in him. Amelia would not have countenanced it, had she known."

"He will rue the day, now."

Lettie nodded. "We must be kind to them always, darling."

His eyes twinkled. "Come and sit on my lap and I will be as kind as you please."

She smiled, rose, and did as he bade.

"Now," he said, stroking the side of her face. "Tell me again how much you loathed me when we met, and why."

"But I've explained all that. 'Twas because I found you irresistible from the start! I did not truly loathe you; I despised myself for having a weakness for you."

"I never grow tired of hearing it."

"And I shall never grow tired..." she hesitated, putting both her hands around his head, digging her fingers into his thick hair... "of you."

The conversation ceased. And when Nick rose with Lettie in his arms and carried her through the house to their bedchamber, the servants cleared the dishes without so much as cracking a smile or a snide word. They adored their new mistress, were delighted for the master, and had grown quickly practiced at seeing nothing, nothing at all, when the master and mistress were "getting along."

For her part, Lettie had already learned that to protest, to ask Nick not to carry her in full view of the staff, was a fruitless endeavour. Moreover, in his arms was the place she most belonged and wished to be!

Still carrying her, Nick managed to latch the bedchamber door, and then turned, planting kisses on her face, toward the plush, four poster, mahogany bed.

IF YOU ENJOYED THIS BOOK
PLEASE tell other readers!

Please leave a review on Goodreads,
Bookbub, Barnes and Noble, Amazon, Facebook,
MeWe, or any social platform.

Don't do book reviews?
Just write what you most liked about the book in one
or two sentences, and it's enough!

On behalf of Linore Rose Burkard and Lilliput Press,

Thank you!

Ahead: Bonus Outtakes!

Other Historical Romance Novels
by Linore Rose Burkard

The Regency Trilogy

*Inspirational Regency Romance that will
delight you!
Before the Season Ends
The House in Grosvenor Square
The Country House Courtship*

Forever, Lately: A Regency Time Travel Romance

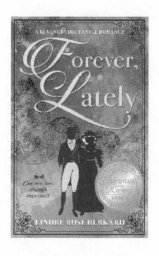

2019 Book of the Month Winner
2019 Book of the Year Finalist

Winner of the Readers' Favorite Award

"A writer of historical fiction travels back in time—
and into the world of her characters. An enjoyable and
dramatic era-spanning love story."
Kirkus Reviews

FREE SHORT STORY OFFER

"A Highly Sensitive Bride," is the quickest Regency tale you'll ever read, designed to give a lift to your day. It's short enough to read it in minutes.

Get it free to your inbox when you join Linore's mailing list at:

LinoreBurkard.com/newsletter

Three French Hens
A Romance Novella

Mademoiselle Christine D'Ornay and her family are exiles in England, seeking safety from the Revolution and *Madame La Guillotine.* At her first Assembly ball, Christine meets the dashing and elegant Lord Russell. But the lives of French aristocrats are cheap in an age of betrayal, and Jacobites are on the prowl. Can Christine and her family trust this new friend? Or is Lord Russell the enemy they fear most?

Available online only.

ABOUT THE AUTHOR

Linore Rose Burkard is a serious watcher of period films, a
Janeite, and hopeless romantic. An award-winning author best
known for Inspirational Regency Romance, her first book
(*Before the Season Ends*) opened the genre for the CBA.
Besides historical romance, Linore writes contemporary
suspense (The Pulse Effex Series, as L.R. Burkard),
contemporary romance, and romantic short stories. Linore has
a *magna cum laude* English Lit. degree from CUNY which
she earned while taking herself far too seriously. She now
resides in Ohio with her husband and family, where she turns
her youthful angst into character or humor-driven plots.

About the Bonus Material…

For the first time, I'm sharing scenes that didn't make the final cut for one reason or other. If you enjoyed Lettie and Nick, you might have fun with these. If you don't want the reading experience affected by alternate scenes, then just skip what follows.

Why are many scenes cut? Some are simply repetitious—they don't reveal anything *new* about a character or situation. New information is one test of whether a scene is necessary or not.

Others were written with a different ending in mind. As a plot develops, I often play around with various directions to take the characters. If I change my mind about which direction to take, scenes get cut to pave way for the change.

Same for character development. Sometimes I envision a character with certain traits, but further into the story, I decide that person is not what I first thought. (You might say, they decide for me!) Other times, I have to reassign their role in the story, and that necessitates changes to their character.

Finally, there are scenes which simply don't "pop"—they don't excite me enough to keep them. All in all, by the time my books are finished, I often have a second manuscript—all the outtakes—that is nearly as large as the final book!

I've never shared outtakes before. I've chosen some to include here, which I hope you find enjoyable!

Linore

OUTTAKES

[When Lettie decides to reform the earl's manner of dress]

The night before, Lettie could not sleep, mulling over and over her disastrous and mortifying behaviour to Nick in his coach. But she'd also kept thinking of her predicament of being called upon, first by Nick, and now the earl, both wishing her to secure Sophia for them. In the blink of an eye it had become clear to her that she did not want to help Nick's cause. It had no chance of success, first of all, since the earl had no interest in Lettie and was determined to keep Miss Alden. But now Lettie also did not want Miss Alden to have Nick!

Her only comfort in that regard was his reluctance to wed. If he did not make an offer to Sophia, she felt certain that lady would not turn from the earl and her future as a countess and marchioness, even though she loved Nick.

Nevertheless, for all their sakes, and to put an end to the business, Miss Alden must make her clear choice. Yet for that to happen, more was needed, Lettie felt, than mere jealousy. Indeed, to coax Miss Alden away from Dellacort, the earl himself must become more attractive. Finally, Lettie conceived an IDEA. It was the satisfying idea of reforming His Lordship's taste in cravats and waistcoats. Also, she must teach the man how to properly dance the quadrille.

This she told Nick. "I was going to school him in the art of sartorial excellence."

Nick frowned. "Why?"

"You must admit his manner of dress is…"

"Wanting?"

She pursed her lips. "He merely needs instruction."

"If the earl hasn't already had the benefit of tutors in the art of proper dress, then I don't know who has," he returned.

"He hasn't had the benefit of me," she said, matter of factly.

[In which Lettie proposes a different strategy]

She said, "One moment more, if you please, Mr. Dellacort."

He sat back down.

She swallowed. Her emotions were twisting inside. She was finding Nicholas Dellacort attractive and agreeable, and she hated it. "Are you making the most of your opportunities with Sophia? Surely you can ascertain if there is hope for you—"

"You wish to end the business, I see." He paused. "But it is not finished."

She swallowed again. "The thing is…sir…" She looked up at him plaintively. "I find that…that is, I would find it much more agreeable were I to pretend a flirtation with…you, rather than Lord Elston." There, she'd said the worst part of it. Hurriedly, she added, "And, if you think on it, Sophia has deduced by now that you care nothing for me. She is assured on that account. If, on the other hand, she were to think for a moment that there was a serious understanding…between you and I…she would harken back to your side in a heartbeat. The business would be ended, and far sooner than if I play the game Lord Elston's way."

When he remained silent, studying her, she added, "I believe she cares for you more than he. Her jealousy for him will pass swiftly, especially if a date is set, for she will be secure of him. Secure of all the advantages of such a marriage, and that would suffice her, for she cares nothing about winning his heart. But for you...it is another thing entirely. Her jealousy will grow greater the closer she gets to wedding another."

He stared at her, thinking. He looked out the coach window. Lettie's heart stuck in her throat. What on earth had compelled her to suggest such an outlandish thing? Yes, she would flirt with Nick Dellacort, she would happily flirt with the scoundrel, by Jove! It would mean nothing to him and in the end, her heart would be broken. But she could not carry on a flirtation with the earl, not if it meant kissing him again, and undoubtedly it would.

While she awaited his answer, she suddenly understood the source of the discomfort that had assailed her from the moment Nicholas Dellacort approached her at Almack's. Something inside her knew all along that he was a particularly dangerous gentleman. Dangerous for the simple reason that something about him was irresistible to her. Somewhere in her heart, she'd always known it. Thus, her misgivings about speaking to him. Her desire not to get involved with his scheme. Her anxiety since the moment he'd come into her life.

Finally, Nick smiled. "Lettie, you're a genius! I should have realised it myself. The moment I met you, I should have realised it. You are the very thing to drive Sophia mad."

[En route to the levée.]

The carriage jolted forward again so suddenly that Lettie, already leaning toward Mr. Dellacort in her ire, was propelled from her seat directly into his arms. He smiled down at her. "Are you alright?"

She moved to free herself from the pull of those magnetic dark eyes and strong arms. But Nick drew her up swiftly for a kiss, only this time she broke apart from him at once. She wriggled away and resumed her seat. "Why do you do that?"

He smiled. "Forgive me. I lost my head. You really are the perfect foil to Sophia."

She pursed her lips, looking away. "This caps it. I am not suited to the business. This night will be the end. If you do not deem my participation sufficient, I am prepared to forfeit any further remuneration."

"We'll talk of that later." His eye was full of mirth.

She looked bereft. "Everything is a mockery to you!" She crossed her arms.

"And you take everything too seriously."

"May I have your word that you will not try to maneuver me into a compromising situation with the earl?"

"I doubt there would be opportunity. The ball is packed. You will be surrounded by a crowd to protect you," he said teasingly. At that moment, a footman opened the door and let down the steps, and Lettie had no choice but to allow Nick to hand her down. She went in upon his arm, plastering a forced smile to hide the troubled countenance that more accurately reflected her feelings.

[In which Lettie goes on a rant]

"Well, I do not admire a dormouse. If a woman cannot speak her mind, she is oppressed, in my opinion. And I believe that a woman has as much right to make her own way in the world as any gentleman." She lifted her fork but stopped to add. "Having determination is a show of strength as much as obstinacy."

She took a bite of food and chewed, waiting for his response.

"You have strength of mind, I grant that. And I take it then, that you spoke your mind to Sophia? As you have always done with me."

Lettie nodded. "Yes, of course. I cannot help but do so. And if I am seen as obstinate, I maintain that it is merely because I guard my independence, as does many a man." She paused, and said pointedly, "You, sir, are a case in point. No one accuses you of obstinacy for avoiding matrimony. But in a woman, you must allow, it is severely frowned upon."

"In a woman, you must allow, it is precarious. Societal customs arise out of what is generally best. For some women, those who have no choice but to survive independently, it is seen as blameless—pitiable, but understandable. It is conceivable for wealthy women also. But In your case, young as you are, with no defect that should prevent a second marriage which would vastly increase your comfort, it is seen as foolish, or dare I say, obstinate."

Lettie's face flushed. "If I were a man, it would never be called obstinacy!"

"If a man has need of a wife, if he has young children, for example, but refuses to provide a step-mother, it would be."

Lettie took a mouthful of cold roast fowl and looked away in thought. Finally, she turned back and said, "If I had need of a husband, I could open my mind to it. I have not yet reached that certainty. 'Tisn't obstinacy but complacency that keeps me happily unmarried. And now, thanks to you, I may have two years of comfort ahead of me before I am ever compelled by need to think otherwise."

His eyes searched hers. "Compelled... Did you find marriage so difficult that you must be compelled to consider it again?"

Lettie swallowed and took a sip of her drink. Soberly she said, "I assure you, it was quite the opposite." Her tone was laced with such feeling that Dellacort said nothing more on the subject.

[A card game that ultimately did not take place.]

The game that proceeded was rather unnerving for Lettie, for there were stakes! She met Dellacort's eyes at the first mention of it. He nodded at her. She would have to go along with it. She wondered how he would respond if she lost a great sum.

"We'll play partners," Nick announced. "I have yet to see how Miss Wetherham gets on at this game."

"And you're willing to stake your bets upon her?" asked Lord Elston, as he watched Miss Alden dealing the cards. "You must have heard good things," he finished with a wink at Lettie.

"No, sir," answered Dellacort, "you must do that, as she is to be your partner in the game." With a little smile, he added, "I daresay if there is a loss you can best suffer it."

Lettie cried, "Oh dear! I believe I may play this game as well as anyone, but I pray you, gentlemen, let us keep the stakes low. Mrs. Cantrell will never forgive me if she learns that I squandered more than a few pounds."

Miss Alden raised eyes that glittered with disdain. "Would you rather sit out, Miss Wetherham?" She pursed her lips, as if, thought Lettie, to keep from smiling.

But Nick said, "No need for that. We'll keep the stakes as low as you please."

Miss Alden made a dismissive gesture, her brows raised in scorn. Lord Elston said, "Don't fret, Sophia, we'll play for whatever stakes you like. Tomorrow night."

"Tomorrow night! What is that to me now?"

"Only conceive how happy papa will be when he learns you haven't lost him another fortune," added Nick.

Miss Alden shared a secret smile with Nick. "I daresay," she murmured, and after that, let the subject drop.

[alternate levée]

A footman from the Cantrells arrived early the next day with a note from Amelia. She could not call that day but was certain to do so on the morrow. Lettie was not disturbed, as she would have one more day's events to tell her cousin by then. It also gave her time before the levée to consider how she might influence those events, to wit, to try again with the earl. She was sure she did not wish to try again, but Dellacort would know if she did not. And he would never pay the second part of her fee.

When he arrived in his gig, pulling up to the kerb, she emerged from the house. Dudley handed her up to the board where Nick sat with a little smile. As they started off he said, "I have it from Lady Merrillton that you are eagerly welcomed at dinner parties because of your wit." He stole at a glance at her before returning his eyes to the road, a glance that revealed surprise.

Lettie's lips pursed. "Do not be too astonished. I do extensive reading from travel books and newspapers. As I often say to Mrs. Cantrell, these provide the richest fodder for conversation, if one only pays attention."

"Travel books?" he asked.

"Details of foreign soils are endlessly fascinating."

The levée promised to include the brightest stars of society.... Lettie was glad, knowing she would likely be safely out of the spotlight with such luminaries to occupy the company. But she forgot that such guests would inevitably draw a crush, and it took them long minutes to enter the street where the event was held. Carriages lined the road for as long as she could see. Minutes ticked by as they waited to approach the house and for a groom to take the gig.

During the wait, Nick asked her to tell him about her life; how she came to be married; how long the marriage had been until the unfortunate passing of her husband, and other such things. Lettie spoke feelingly about her history. She'd been raised in a well-to-do home, was introduced to Steven Wetherham through Mr. Cantrell, her cousin. The men knew each other through their mutual interests in the mine. She and

Steven had been married only two years before his death; and her mother had died just before Lettie's wedding.

"So you are alone in the world, beside the Cantrells for family?"

"I have some distant relations, but we have not spoken or corresponded since before my mother's death."

He gave her an intent look. "Today's opportunity must be plumbed to the depth. Secure the earl, and you secure your future."

"You speak as if he were a hen to be caught and penned; I have no doubt this scheme will fail."

"Nevertheless, you must try your best."

When they were finally inside the house, Nick led her with startling intuition to an inner parlour where Miss Alden and the earl stood among a circle of acquaintances. Sophia spied them, smiled brightly at Nick, and came forward. The earl stood back like an obedient bespectacled puppy, watching with intent eyes.

"Nicholas!" cried Sophia, putting her arm through his free one.

"You remember Miss Wetherham?"

Miss Alden surveyed her. "Of course," she said, with cold politeness. "How do you do?" The earl stepped forward and bowed his greeting.

Nick said, "My lord, I have need to speak with Miss Alden. Would you do me the honour of taking care of Miss Wetherham in my absence?"

"Absence?" he asked. "Are you leaving?"

"There is a little park behind the house, if I mistake me not," said Nick, ignoring the question. "Miss Wetherham expressed an interest in seeing it. Would you be so kind?"

The earl looked uncertainly at Lettie who smiled weakly at him.

"I would be honoured," he said, offering her his arm.

Lettie allowed him to lead her from the crowded rooms, and they followed a footman who showed them the way to the garden. There were verandas overlooking the back garden, but no one occupied them. The earl and Lettie were silent as they walked. She was strangely without conversation, and he seemed equally so. Finally he said, taking them around a bend in the shrubbery, "Mr. Dellacort has hopes, still, of winning Miss Alden?"

"He does, my lord." Lettie felt only relief at the truth being out.

"And he also has hopes that I will turn from her to you with your winning smile and valuable diamond mine?"

So Lord Elston was no fool. "He does, sir." She almost chuckled. "It is rather obvious, is it not? Mr. Dellacort does not play his best game right now, I think."

"No," he agreed. "But he doesn't play alone. Sophia enjoys a bit of sport, herself."

Lettie said nothing. She saw it was true; she felt badly for the earl.

"And why, may I ask, are you willing to help him in these causes?" Lord Elston's intent gaze, behind the spectacles, searched her eyes.

"Are you so odious that I should not help him if I can? I am an unmarried woman, after all."

He stopped walking and turned to her. "I think it convenient for him that you are willing to step in." He took her by the arms. Miss Wetherham's pulse jumped. She could not tell if he was angry or not. He gently moved a stray curl away from her face. "But you are an unmarried woman, after all." And he bent his head to hers and kissed her.

This time, Lettie allowed it. This time, she didn't even mind. And yet, she felt no thrill at his touch, no hammering heartbeat or a desire for him to prolong the kiss. When he pulled away and again searched her face, he said, "But you do not care for me."

"I am sorry, my lord. I am willing to—I think."

He smiled. "Nonsense. We cannot choose where our affections lie. And though she is a termagant, I care for Miss Alden." He raised a brow as a thought must have occurred to him.

"Miss Wetherham—would it be too much to ask? Could you not try and turn Mr. Dellacort's head? I have watched him and Sophia on many occasions, and I cannot detect love between them."

She was about to object, to say that she was sure Nick loved Miss Alden, but he continued. "Oh, they share a certain enjoyment of the game, the thrill of the chase. But neither really wants the other." He looked blankly at her.

"Are you certain?" she asked. She would have to consider this, determine if it was true. How much her heart lightened at the mere thought of Nick not being in love with Sophia! But she could not share the earl's certainty on the matter. Dellacort was staking a thousand pounds and then some, on getting Miss Alden back.

He took her hand. "Miss Wetherham, if we were to appear as though we were truly enamored of each other—I believe it would be the thing to push the two of them out of their bluff."

Lord Elston had smiled, nodded, or chuckled at all the right moments, to be sure. But whenever Miss Alden spoke to Nick, or he to her, the earl's attention pivoted to catching every word of their conversation. It was unmistakable, Lettie decided, that he was strongly attached to Miss Alden. She saw no chance of success for Nick's scheme; and told him so.

Nick lit an interior lamp and studied her. "I agree," he said placidly, to her surprise. She felt relief—the masquerade was over. While she considered how to thank him for the opportunity, for the five hundred pounds he had given as well as covering her other debts, he said, "Elston isn't interested in having his head turned. He cares for her despite all her neglect of him; either that, or he is enamored of her dowry."

"I daresay, sir," Lettie said, trying to sound gentle, "all you needs must do is work on Miss Alden alone. She gave all her attentions to you this evening. Lord Elston may wish for the match, but it seems evident that she does not. Renew your suit with her. She will accept you."

He levelled his gaze upon hers while a little smile played at the edges of his mouth. "You are almost correct. We have been going about the business wrong, but it isn't a simple matter of renewing my interest. Miss Alden is playing a game, and I am merely another player, as is the earl."

"What is her game? And what do you intend to do, then?" she asked with a raised brow. She hadn't expected this sort of response. The carriage began slowing and she saw they had arrived, coming to a stop in front of her lodgings. Nick made no move to help her from the coach, but as she rose to leave, he said, "A moment longer, if you please." Lettie resumed her seat and looked at him expectantly.

"Miss Alden's game is to sit back while Elston and I fight for her. I have been operating on the assumption that Elston's heart was not set upon the match, but it appears to be so. For which reason, instead of hoping to pry him away, we must entice Sophia to make the break herself."

"She appears to favour you over him already. If you make an offer, will she not do her best to sway her parents in your favour? All you must do is make the offer."

Something crossed his eyes. "From the day Lord Elston appeared in their drawing room, Miss Alden's father informed me that no offer coming from me would be welcome or countenanced."

Lettie blinked. To think of Nick Dellacort being rejected! But she said, "In that case, should you not abandon the business? You do not strike me, (forgive me for saying so) as a man deeply in love. If your heart will not be much injured, should you not let her go? With Elston, she will be a marchioness one day."

"Did you see any evidence all night, any at all, that Sophia cares for Elston?"

Lettie hesitated. Miss Alden had flirted with Dellacort all evening, much to the earl's consternation. And when he did speak to Sophia, she replied off-handedly, almost as if she cared not for his opinion—or his sensibilities—whatsoever. "No."

"She does not want Elston."

"But sir, if she were so very opposed, would she not cry off?"

He smirked. "Ah, but you forget the importance of the game. Miss Alden, as I said, delights in playing. She is no doubt planning to cry off, but not before having her fun."

After a moment's thought she said, "I am surprised you wish to fight for her."

"I do not. Not in the sense that she desires me to, that is."

"Then what is your plan?" she asked.

"I play my own game, Miss Wetherham."

"What is your meaning, sir? And may I assume that my part is over, and I am done with the business?"

"You agreed to put in your best effort," he reminded her. "Henceforth, instead of trying to lure the earl from Sophia, we must turn our efforts to her. You and I will appear as a couple." Lettie felt a surprising rush of warmth to her heart. The memory of that stolen kiss suddenly filled her mind. Oh, dear.

"Sophie," he continued, "Will find it odious, confess her plan to cry off her betrothal, and proclaim her everlasting affection for me—which she will no doubt highly exaggerate. Once she determines to give up the earl publicly, her parents will be forced to accept it and give him up as well."

Lettie frowned. His suggestion would entail spending time in his company, posing as a couple. A part of her found the thought instantly appealing, as if she had tried on a perfectly fitted new glove. The rest of her was horrified. Dellacort was dangerous. She would be captive to thoughts of him, his manly beauty, piercing eyes, and depth of conversation—he was no prattler or empty-headed flatterer—while she would be exiled instantly from every thought of his no sooner than they parted. He would win his prize, while she was left to rue the loss of hers.

She said, "Surely if you only continue flirting with Sophia, the earl will come to his senses and drop her as a banker drops a counterfeit note. The counterfeit may be pretty, but the fraud in it must cause disgust. Lord Elston will seek the genuine article, a woman who appreciates and respects him."

"That will not do. The moment he entertains thoughts of looking away, Sophia will discern it, and mollify him. She will use every art known to a conniving woman, and we are back at the starting gate."

"But recollect, you said she does not wish for the match! All she need do is make herself odious to the man, and he will withdraw. Can you not instruct her to be yet more odious?"

"That is not how the game is played. She could easily do that but has not. She is in it for sport."

Lettie's eyes were troubled. "That is most ungenerous of her. Playing with a man's affections..."

"Indeed. But that is Sophia. Allow me to call upon you tomorrow night." He got out to hand her down from the coach. As she descended the two steps, his hand holding one of hers, he said, "The pretence of our relationship shan't continue long, if that is your fear. Sophia will need only one event, perhaps two, at which we not only appear together, but seem to be enamored of each other. She is a jealous cat; and will come round speedily."

They left the house and he handed her up into his two-wheeled gig. When he was seated beside her, he met her eyes. "The game is only begun. The stakes will go higher as we are seen to be in earnest as a couple; Sophia will second-guess her first conclusions."

Lettie looked steadily at Nick, until he said, "Yes?"

She cleared her throat. "Do not mistake me in what I must say. I am not relinquishing my part of the bargain." She paused and sniffed. "But why, if you are not in love with Sophia, are you willing to engage in this deception, particularly if the stakes must be raised, the lies go deeper? She has already seen us—seen that we must be upon intimate terms! And it failed to convince her. And why pay me a thousand pounds—even more, when you recollect the debts you satisfied on my account—and trouble yourself to such a degree if you love her not?"

He smirked. "Do you expect me to behave like a typical mealy-mouthed gentleman and slink off in humble acquiescence of Sophia's revenge? I assure you, it would disappoint her."

She shook her head. "What I should expect is that you will not trouble yourself to such lengths for a woman unless you wish to marry her."

"Does it make a difference to you what I wish? Are the terms of our agreement not to your liking?"

"I only meant that—very well, Mr. Dellacort. I suppose I shall have to say it outright. I believe you are in love with Miss Alden, and that it is regrettable—no, ill-devised—no, shameful of you to try and deceive her!" She blushed, instantly aware that she had no call to act as his conscience, particularly when he was paying for her compliance and help. Or that she was pushing him to make a declaration either way, for or against being in love with Sophia, primarily because she wished to know.

His mouth wavered in that maddening way he had, as if he were about to laugh but suppressing it. "Allow me to soothe your concerns. As you yourself have observed, Miss Alden is not deceived. As I told you before, she delights in the game."

"But how deep a game will you play?" she asked.

"As deep as it requires."

"And the poor earl is in the middle of it and knows it not."

He turned after handling a sharp right at the corner. In a matter of fact tone he said, "You could be his consolation prize. A man could do far worse."

Her lips hardened. "While I am posing as your love interest? I cannot play a harp and a flute at the same time, sir!"

His look became amused. "Whenever you lay aside the harp, you must pick up the flute, Miss Wetherham. And if any woman can do both, I think it is you."

"What makes you say that?" Lettie asked, flustered, and unsure whether she'd just been insulted. "Are you suggesting I am skilled at the art of deception?" Her heart felt as jostled and disturbed by his words as her body was from the rough cobbled street, making her hold to the board.

"Not deception," he said. "Your skill is in maintaining two things that are true simultaneously, despite being utterly at odds. You rely upon a business of matchmaking for your very existence, which means for all intents and purposes, you are in trade. This is true, despite your earlier remonstrances to me."

Lettie's eyes narrowed, but he held up a hand, his green-grey eyes raking through her carefully constructed appearance of respectability. "Simultaneously, you behave as a genteel, well-bred woman of the upper class, and are accepted as such. Acceptance in that class is its own proof, making it therefore also true that you must be respectable. Do you see what I mean? You deceive not, for every family understands (even if they pretend otherwise) that they are expected to compensate your efforts in some manner; and yet you are good ton, welcome in most any drawing room. I hear, in fact, you are popular at dinner parties for saving dull companies by telling anecdotes." He paused. "I call that skill, Miss Wetherham."

As he spoke, a slow blush had risen on Lettie's cheeks. Mr. Dellacort was doing it again—being far too direct and indiscreet. "Call it what you like," she said coldly, "I do it only out of necessity. And, if you consider the matter, the upper class are—are—hypocrites not to include people who earn their keep in a respectable manner, because, in a wider sense, they all do. Whether they are landowners, or investors, or speculators—every peer gets his income from something resembling trade!"

He nodded, a smile playing around his lips. "But not a trade they ply with their own hands, and that, unfortunately, is what makes all the difference." His brows came together as he surveyed her. "The upper class must have its boundaries, Lettie, or it would cease to be exclusive. And I meant no insult. Do not be cross. On the contrary, you have my highest regard for living out a balancing act that can only be precarious."

She turned her head away, suddenly blinking back tears. Dellacort completely comprehended her whole existence, it seemed. Why was it that his sympathy was more difficult to stomach than disdain? And he'd called her Lettie—had he noticed? Ought she to object?

"Come, I'll take us into Hyde Park. It is teeming with the elite at this hour. Those well-heeled hypocrites," he said playfully.

Lettie took a handkerchief to dab her eyes. She mustn't be seen crying with Nick.

One quick glance at his companion, dabbing delicately with a handkerchief at her eyes, assured Nick he'd hit a nerve. Ever since meeting Miss Wetherham, her directness in conversation and lack of nonsensical chit chat (which bored him to pieces in any case), had the effect of lulling him into thinking he could be equally transparent. Certainly, it relieved him of having to be at his best, his most gentlemanly. It was no excuse, of course. But their relationship was singular—he was paying her for a service. That, surely, also meant he did not have to tiptoe around her sensibilities as to a debutante fresh from the schoolroom.

But his conscience smarted. She was a woman, by Jove, an attractive woman, and susceptible to injury where he least expected it. He should move them past this unfortunate conversation. He cleared his throat. "If Miss Alden and the earl are not in the park, news of us will reach their ears soon enough. Probably no later than this evening."

He turned and smiled and looked back at the road, but Lettie stared at him. Mr. Dellacort was a rogue through and through, but he had a smile that would open the gates of heaven if smiles were sufficient to do it. She looked away, blinking. From the outset she knew that Dellacort could pose a danger to her heart. That danger had only increased. Drat his kisses! She must remember they were wholly meaningless.

Soon they drove through the wide open, black iron gates at the Cumberland entrance of the park, and shortly afterward enjoyed the sight of the richest clad people in London, promenading, sailing past in open equipages, or even on horseback. There wasn't a closed carriage in sight, which Lettie knew was because the point of being in Hyde park was to be seen.

Men's hats and women's bonnets, ostrich feathers and other plumes, lacy shawls, embroidered reticules, plush velvet spencers, afternoon dress of the most splendid variety, riding habits, jewellery and baubles, gowns and half boots, top-coats and military uniforms with epaulettes and tricornes, all went by in a dazzling display that Lettie, though not new to such a sight, felt she could not tire of. Lacking a carriage or a horse of her own, her ventures into the park were rare these days, made occasionally with Amelia in the Cantrells' equipage.

There was a difference today that could not be ignored: in Mr. Dellacort's company, the nods and greetings she received were offered with greater respect. Peers stopped to speak to Nick and bowed politely to Miss Wetherham. She'd never felt snubbed in the past but saw now that greater notice was indeed given her than previously. She thought wryly that she ought to be retroactively insulted for their past neglect. But no; it was all on account of Nick. Society loved a handsome devil, no doubt about it.

She accepted the attention thereafter with placid satisfaction, knowing it would vanish as soon as Mr. Dellacort turned back to Sophia. No matter. Many greetings were from true friends, for it was just as Dellacort had said. Lettie was a popular dinner guest for her ability to maintain the sort of bantering conversation much favoured among the wits. Without him, she was no outcast. She felt like one at times only because of her need to earn an income, a burden not shared by most ladies in her circles. To them, all one needs must do is marry well. Certainly, Amelia encouraged Lettie often enough to find another husband to end her financial difficulties.

But Steven's passing was too, too, heart-wrenching; for which reason she had never seriously considered marrying again. Subjecting herself to another devastation was far worse, to her mind, than having to live on precarious means, juggling costs and frugality with the need to be modish and respectable.

No, she was determined never to fall in love again. The very thought of dear Steven sent her into the doldrums. She cast aside all such dour ruminations, put on her brightest smile, and not a moment too soon. Earl Brest and Miss Alden went sailing past just then in a shining, jet-black high barouche with a coat of arms on the doors, led by magnificent high-steppers, their black coats gleaming in the afternoon light. Lettie ignored the lady's cold eyes and wore her smile until they'd passed.

Nick said, "Perfect. I couldn't have hoped for more."

[the feathered hat—an alternate idea to Nick's removing Lettie's fichu]

"Levées are every bit as formal as an evening ball, but even more diverting when it comes to dress, for one can wear more in the way of adornment and headdresses. For a ball, one must always consider how something will look when standing up to dance. At a levée, there is no such stricture."

Betsey nodded, wide-eyed, ingesting every word as greedily as a dry sponge finding water. While attending to Miss Wetherham as she prepared for an outing, she had questioned why her mistress wished to have her hair adorned in the manner of the French, not only with high, layered curls behind two tiers of ribbands, but with a delicate, curling ostrich feather that arched from the center of the first band, stretching out like a graceful angel's wing before her. A delicate strand of faux pearls along the ribbands completed the feminine, elegant look.

Secretly, Lettie wished to force Dellacort to keep his distance. If she had judged correctly, the feather's tip was just at his height. He could not sneak a furtive kiss upon her, for example, without brushing it aside, risking the ruin of her headdress. Knowing herself capable of an appalling lack of restraint when in his embrace, she considered an external prop necessary, weak as it was. She would also be careful not to enter any lonely verandas in moonlight, or anywhere else that left her open to his abuse. And abuse it was. It felt like the warmest caress of a lover, and therein was its devilish power, for he meant nothing by it. She was determined never to be agreeable to another instance of it. No, if it ruined the scheme, if it meant she would not get the second instalment of five hundred pounds—no matter.

Nick Dellacort's kisses were the new enemy.

Armed thus, she greeted him at the door ready to leave the house when he called. He eyed her quite noticeably, his eyes running from head to toe—stopping momentarily at the feather in his face—and then, moving past her with a strangely intent expression, proceeded inside. Lettie looked up at him questioningly.

"You look wonderfully pretty, Miss Wetherham," he said calmly, "but that feather must go."

"It shall not!" she cried. "I placed it carefully myself." She gingerly patted her headdress protectively.

He eyed the feather and in a swift move, plucked it from its ribband. "There. 'Tis done. You still look quite adorable."

With a gasp, she dove for the plume, but he ducked it behind him. Eye to eye, he said, "You must allow it was exactly in my way and might have left me with a poked eyeball."

"That, sir, was my sole intention!"

He raised a brow. "Was it?" And with that, the plume was abandoned, falling to the floor, as he pulled her into a tight embrace and kissed her passionately. Every ounce of Lettie's being filled with resentment. His touch was warm as ever, only his mouth more urgent than before. Not able to pull free, she kicked his shin, making him release her with a muffled oath.

He looked at her appraisingly. "Now was that fair?"

"You dare to ask that, when you know you are perfectly mad to expect otherwise."

"When you have heretofore been compliant, I did expect otherwise."

"Expect it no more! We have done with that. You must keep your distance." Her face was near scarlet.

His mouth hardened. "Privately, I will grant you that."

"Ha! Big of you," she said with a sneer. "You will grant me

the common courtesy of not attacking me like a bear! Your virtue is astounding."

His mouth twitched. "Publicly, until Sophia comes round, I will not keep my distance."

Suddenly she looked ready to cry. "You must think me so ill-bred!"

His eyes narrowed.

"What made you think you could take such liberties with me?"

His countenance softened. "I beg your pardon. You are perfectly right. I do not think ill of you, and I consider you perfectly well bred. The deficit is entirely my own. I mistook your, er, past reactions, and assumed you found me as agreeable as I did, you."

She let out a defeated breath. "I beg your pardon for that!"

"No, I didn't mean—" he began to say, but she continued, "I maintain that the surprise of being kissed by a man—after the years since I lost Steven—did somehow cause me to abandon proper caution. It reminded me of—" and here she could not continue, for her voice betrayed that she was on the edge of tears.

Mr. Dellacort sighed. "Of course it did. I am an ogre. Forgive me."

All this time Dudley had been standing in the doorway, frozen. He was torn between slinking away quietly to give his mistress privacy and staying to catch every word of this fascinating exchange. Nick noticed him now and scowled. "Do you wish to lose your situation?"

Dudley bowed and began backing away. "No sir, my apologies, sir! My apologies, ma'am!" He scurried off at three times his usual pace.

Lettie looked back and frowned, but turning to Nick said, "Are you his master? How dare you threaten my servant!"

He grinned. "I only meant to give him a fright, and I daresay he took it." His face sobered again. "Lettie, I do apologize. If ever a woman made me wish to behave well, it is you, right now. I will do my utmost not to offend your sensibilities again. Does that satisfy you?"

Looking down, she nodded. "Yes."

He took her chin and lifted her head. "Are we ready, then, for the levée?"

She shook his hand away, but said, "Yes. Hopefully, this will be the end of the business." There was both a ray of light with that hope, and a feeling of a door thudding closed. Whether Nick shared that hope, she could not tell. But for her peace of mind, Mr. Dellacort must be out of her life.

They rode in silence, giving her time to think. Somehow this very day she must ensure that Sophia believed in the strength of Lettie's tie to Nick, even as she must shepherd her own heart away from it. What a muddle she was in! If she succeeded, Nick would return to Sophia and her heart was safe—only it wasn't, for already she hated the thought of him doing so.

And if she did not succeed, she'd have to spend more time with Nick and get in deeper and deeper. Oh! Either way was like gravel in her throat. But better for their ploy to succeed so she could send him off now, before she fell truly in love.

She was facing the window, watching blindly as London streets went by, lost in thoughts. Glancing at Nick, she found his eyes upon her. She felt the blush rise in her cheeks as she hurriedly returned her gaze to the window.

She must not grant him the satisfaction of knowing her heart was compromised. She'd been very clear when they met, telling him she would not ever be the sort of doting female that hung upon his words; that he would not count her as one of his conquests, nor leave her a broken heart in the end. And yet it was happening. She'd been as gullible as anyone.

[a visit from Amelia]

Amelia called upon Lettie the following morning, all smiles and sunny disposition as always. When her gaze fell upon Lettie, however, her smile faltered.

"My dear gel! What is ailing you?" She came and sat beside her cousin, and took her hand.

"Nothing, dearest, I assure you," Lettie said.

Amelia studied her. "Nonsense. I can tell there is something. Has Mr. Dellacort behaved monstrously to you?"

"Oh, no, 'tisn't him!" cried Lettie. She sniffed. "He is his usual, diffident self. But he treats me respectfully." No sooner had the words left her mouth than she remembered how he had kissed her so abominably; and how he had barged into her sanctum, her bedchamber, unannounced and certainly uninvited.

"Well," she amended, "For the most part, he does."

"What has he done!" Amelia's eyes regarded her cautiously. "That rogue! Shall I have Horace demand an apology?"

"No, no," Lettie said. "'Tis nothing I cannot handle. He is …. arrogant, really, that's all it comes down to."

"How are you getting along with his lordship?" she asked, with a sideways smile.

"Oh, I must tell you. Lord Elston and I understand each other, now. And he has no intention of losing Miss Alden and asked me outright if I would allow a flirtation, for the sole purpose of making her jealous!"

"He asked that? And Dellacort wants you to flirt with him too? That seems to me to be providential, my girl. Kill two birds with one stone, and all that." She waved a hand in the air and smiled. Amelia had a very kind smile and almost made Lettie feel better.

But she shook her head. "I know I should see it that way. But the thing is, both men are determined to win Miss Alden, and only one of them can. And both are expecting me to help them do so."

Amelia nodded, and pursed her lips. "That is a conundrum."

Lettie nodded and continued, unhappily. "The thing is, Lord Elston kissed me, and—"

"He kissed you? The scoundrel!" Amelia could not help but to laugh, shaking her head. "Naughty man. Are you certain he is not… leaning in your direction?"

"No, nothing like that, I am certain."

In a low tone, she added, "If you must know, Mr. Dellacort also kissed me, but his kiss was entirely uncalled for."

Amelia simply stared at her, speechless.

"He kissed me only to be provoking, whereas Lord Elston kissed me to provoke someone else—Sophia."

"My, but you have been busy," Amelia said, biting back another grin.

"Do not make fun!" cried Lettie. "I have been quite lowered in my own estimation, on the one hand, and find I am elevated on the other, but not quite enough to equal the lowering."

"Whatever do you mean by that?" Amelia pulled off her gloves. "I am staying for a nuncheon with you; I must hear every bit of what's transpired with both men."

"What I mean," Lettie explained, holding out one hand toward her cousin, "is that..." She stared at Amelia uncertainly. "You will not share this with another soul?"

Amelia nodded promptly. "You have my word!"

"Not even Harriette?"

"Decidedly not Harriette!"

Lettie nodded, satisfied. "I mean that when Mr. Dellacort kissed me, though it was monstrously impertinent," and here she paused to look around to make sure no servant was within earshot, then whispered the rest. "I did not dislike it." She stared at her cousin with as much sorrow as if she'd just confessed to assassinating the king.

Amelia grinned, though she tried to hide it. "That is no crime, my love. He is uncommonly handsome."

"But I—I did not immediately stop him! There was something so strange about it—his touch on my lips—it felt familiar, almost like—" She stopped.

"Like dear Steven?" prodded Amelia, gently.

Lettie covered her mouth with one hand and her face scrunched up, but she nodded. "Oh, how wicked I am to think such a thing! Steven was the kindest, most amiable man to walk the earth! And Mr. Dellacort is a rogue, as you know, a black hearted scoundrel! How, how, can I have found him acceptable? I fear I must be wicked."

Amelia patted her arm. "Dearest, no, no, you mustn't think that."

"But you haven't heard all," Lettie moaned. "When Lord Elston kissed me—Lord Elston who is all gentlemanlike and easy—I felt an instant aversion. I disliked it exceedingly."

Amelia pictured His Lordship in her mind and saw nothing that should explain this other than his penchant for wearing loud colours. "Because he was impertinent, of course!"

"He was, yes, frightfully so. But so was Mr. Dellacort."

"Lord Elston must have been maulish, like a beast."

"I shoved him off with no difficulty."

Amelia, not one to give up easily, tried again. "His Lordship has some defect, something repulsive in his person that offended you," she declared with satisfaction. "Your reaction was perfectly sensible under the circumstances."

Lettie sighed and shook her head. "It wasn't that. He is not so handsome as Nick, but not bad in his way. There is nothing particularly wrong in him if one discounts his horrid cravats; and considering that I am charged with 'turning his head,' I should have been more welcoming." She looked tragically at her cousin. "I had only just agreed to help him rouse Miss Alden's jealousy." Hurriedly, she continued, "Of course I never conceived he meant to kiss me—I thought he would converse with me as though Sophia did not exist. I had to force myself not to run from his arms as though he were a member of the Grande Armée!"

Amelia patted her arm with sympathetic eyes. "Any decent woman would have felt the same. You are an honest creature and cannot lend yourself to false shows of affections."

"And yet I allowed Nick's kiss!! I even returned it, initially."

Even Amelia was bereft of further theories that would completely excuse this lapse in Lettie's virtue. Finally, she shrugged her head and said, "That is nothing at all. Mr. Dellacort has something about him that strikes a note in your breast, and it cannot be helped. We cannot dictate to our hearts how they must feel. We are subject to them; for better or worse, we allow our hearts to lead us, sometimes into the best path, but sometimes into folly. Partiality for Mr. Dellacort is a folly, but if it cannot be helped, you must be on your guard." She paused, regarding Lettie with earnest eyes. "He is a determined bachelor; I daresay his kisses are naught but a game to him, so do be wary, for I cannot countenance a man trifling with my dearest coz."

Amelia rose. As they walked arm in arm to the front hall, Lettie said, "Tonight, I must accompany Mr. Dellacort to a ball. Lord Elston will be there, and Miss Alden. And I will have to maintain this dastardly flirtation." She sighed deeply. "If only he and Sophia would set a wedding date! Then it would all be ended."

[Nick's anger at the Aldens]

Recalling the scene, the day he'd called upon Sophia only to find that his calls were no longer welcome, it still sent him into a silent rage. He'd been very generous to the Aldens. He'd sent his own head gardener and another man to reclaim the gardens surrounding their country seat after their man had proven inept, bungling the look of the place. He often sent gift baskets from London with other hard-to-find black market items, such as the finest teas, and sugar...

[This scene was discarded because by this point Nick has feelings for Lettie, but here we don't see any evidence of it. Remember the rule for a scene: if it doesn't propel the plot forward in some way, the story is probably stronger without it.]

Mr. Dellacort arrived precisely on time that evening at eight-thirty,

He stopped to survey Lettie and then bowed politely. "Charmed, Miss Wetherham," he said, looking as if he was impressed. "Methinks you are warming to the idea of winning the earl's affections?"

Lettie's face flushed prettily, but she said nothing. She hadn't decided whether to tell him about the earl's disclosure, though it weighed on her heart to reveal how the cards lay.

Seated in the carriage at the kerb, Mr. Dellacort made no move to signal the coachman to be off. Instead, he asked questions about her past. She told him quickly about the many weddings she had helped bring about; how she had an uncanny eye for a good match, and often attended the marriage ceremonies at special invitation of the grateful couples. She thought wistfully of the weddings she'd machinated; nary a tear from a doting mama had she seen, but Lettie was often on the verge of tears. Weddings did that to her. Much as she enjoyed matchmaking, enjoyed bringing two castaways together, she grew sad at the ceremonies.

In a matter of fact tone she said, "My weddings are never tragedies such as one sees in the aristocracy. I refuse to help foist a match upon an unwilling bride, you see; the weddings I propose must be agreeable to all parties. In some cases, I have even brought about love matches." She looked away. "I do not attend those ceremonies."

"You choose not to? When the love matches are likely the happiest occasions."

She stared at him, and a world of pain crossed her eyes. And then she seemed far away, looking into the past, no longer seeing him across from her, "They remind me too much of what I've lost."

"My dear woman," said Mr. Dellacort, leaning forward, "what you need more than anything in the world, is a wedding of your own. Another happy love match."

She shook her head. "There could never be another like the first."

"Tosh! I know a score of happily married couples who suffered heartbreak similar to yours but are now enjoying their second go at love at least as much, if not more, than their first."

Her lips tightened. "That may be true. For some people. I do not think it is possible for me."

"Tell me about your husband."

"Shall we not be late for the ball?"

"It will last all night."

"Very well." And in the next few minutes, she did just that, telling all about dear Steven, and what an honourable, gentlemanlike, upright man he was. She told how she'd met him as a child in the Cantrells' household, but grew to love him, though he was her elder by eleven years. Cousin Horace had at first violently opposed his suit; but the diamond mine began producing, so that soon Steven's wealth surpassed anything Lettie had claim to. The Cantrells even invested in the mine. Still they did not approve, until Lettie assured her cousins she would have no other. Finally, they gave their blessing.

"So he was your only love?"

"He was, of course. I was quite young when we met, and it never entered my head to look elsewhere. Dear Steven was everything I wanted." She looked out the window and swallowed a pang of sorrow that pierced her heart, even now, three years after losing him.

"What did you admire most in him?"

She regarded Mr. Dellacort curiously, for it seemed odd to her that he should ask. She considered for a moment and said, "His utter sincerity. In all his conversation and behaviour. He seldom even teased; he was gentle, and generous."

"A sense of humour, I hope?" Dellacort asked.

Lettie's memories of her hero faltered as this crack entered the picture. "Perhaps that could be said to be his lone failing. Life was too important to laugh at."

"A failing indeed," Dellacort said unkindly. "But a paragon of manhood elsewhere, if you add bravery to your list."

"Oh, but he was, too brave!" she cried. "He insisted upon searching the mine himself. If only—" But here she stopped.

"I beg your pardon," he said. "But tell me, how does the earl measure up to your hero?"

"Do you mock me?" she asked, blinking at him.

"Not at all."

She swallowed. Carefully she said, "The earl is a gentle soul, and earnest."

"I believe he is honourable as well," added Dellacort. "It seems to me you have found a worthy man, a man your dear Steven would approve of."

She eyed him disconsolately.

"You think otherwise?"

All the abhorrence of the situation that had been plaguing Lettie's sensibilities came to the surface. She could play this game no longer. While Nick's thoughtful gaze studied her, waiting for her reply, she grew desperate. Only the truth would extricate her, and if it meant forfeiting five hundred pounds, so be it.

"I must tell you," she said, with sad, plaintive eyes turned up to his. "You must know the truth—the earl's flirtation with me is merely a ruse."

"Of course it is; I put you up to it. I hoped, for your sake, that it might become more."

"You mistake the matter. There was nothing genuine in what you saw the other night. His Lordship wishes to make Sophia jealous, that is all it is."

Nick's brow went up. "Did he tell you that?"

"He did."

"So your kiss was solely for her benefit," he said, nodding.

"It was," she said, unhappily.

He surveyed her. Gently, he asked, "Are you disappointed in him? Did you, after all, hope to win him?"

Something in her green eyes turned to steel. "Not at all. I am helpless to manufacture affection for the sake of your scheme, or for a future benefit that could arise for me. I had only reached this conclusion, that I am supremely unfit for this task, for what you require of me, when the earl revealed his heart to me."

Nick said, "I see no difficulty here. He has enlisted your help in much the same fashion I did." He reached a hand back and thumped the wall of the carriage. In a moment, the coachman's voice was heard shouting to the horses, and the carriage rolled from the kerb.

[In which Lettie devises a different plan]

She said, "One moment more, if you please, Mr. Dellacort."

He sat back down.

She swallowed. Her emotions were twisting inside. She was finding Nicholas Dellacort attractive and agreeable, and she hated it. "Are you making the most of your opportunities with Sophia? Surely you can ascertain if there is hope for you—"

"You wish to end the business, I see." He paused. "But it is not finished."

She swallowed again. "The thing is…sir…" She looked up at him plaintively. "I find that…that is, I would find it much more agreeable were I to pretend a flirtation with…you, rather than Lord Elston." There, she'd said the worst part of it. Hurriedly, she added, "And, if you think on it, Sophia has deduced by now that you care nothing for me. She is assured on that account. If, on the other hand, she were to think for a moment that there was a serious understanding…between you and I…she would harken back to your side in a heartbeat. The business would be ended, and far sooner than if I play the game Lord Elston's way."

When he remained silent, studying her, she added, "I believe she cares for you more than he. Her jealousy for him will pass swiftly, especially if a date is set, for she will be secure of him. Secure of all the advantages of such a marriage, and that would suffice her, for she cares nothing about winning his heart. But for you…it is another thing entirely. Her jealousy will grow greater the closer she gets to wedding another."

He stared at her, thinking. He looked out the coach window. Lettie's heart stuck in her throat. What on earth had compelled her to suggest such an outlandish thing? Yes, she would flirt with Nick Dellacort, she would happily flirt with the scoundrel, by Jove! It would mean nothing to him and in the end, her heart would be broken. But she could not carry on a flirtation with the earl, not if it meant kissing him again, and undoubtedly it would.

While she awaited his answer, she suddenly understood the source of the discomfort that had assailed her from the moment Nicholas Dellacort approached her at Almack's. Something inside her knew all along that he was a particularly dangerous gentleman. Dangerous for the simple reason that something about him was irresistible to her. Somewhere in her heart, she'd always known it. Thus, her misgivings about speaking to him. Her desire not to get involved with his scheme. Her anxiety since the moment he'd come into her life.

Finally, Nick smiled. "Lettie, you're a genius! I should have realised it myself. The moment I met you, I should have realised it. You are the very thing to drive Sophia mad."

[an alternate path to a similar ending]

Nick's lips firmed into a line.

Seeing the frown on his features, Lettie said, "You asked for my advice as a matchmaker, and I believe you and Sophia make a better pair than her and the earl." But her face froze, for she was struck at just that moment with the thought that, no, this was wrong! At first glance it looked as though Sophia and Nick were the perfect pair, for they were so alike. Each headstrong, determined to have their way, handsome, and proud. But they were so alike that a marriage would sentence them to a lifetime of quarrels. As soon as their passion for pleasure waned, they would be face to face with a character that mirrored their own so minutely that endless clashes would ensue.

She saw it all in a flash.

"No, I beg your pardon! Nick, you mustn't marry her!" she cried in full earnestness.

His brows rose, but he wore a little smile. "You are adorable. But fear not, Lettie," he said softly, still with that little amused grin, "I have no intention of doing so at present. But tell me, what changed your mind?"

They had turned onto Park Place and were now in a queue of carriages, waiting while the occupants of those ahead were let off at the house. Between the few overhead lamplights, the carriage was dark, and she could barely make out Nick's face, though he sat not a foot away, across from her. When they inched beneath a lamp, the dim light revealed intense eyes.

"You and Sophia are too much alike. The both of you, headstrong, incorrigible, proud; determined to win at all costs in everything. If you marry her, you will subject yourself to a lifetime of locked horns, do you not see?"

His eyes twinkled. Lettie was exactly right. She had hit upon the reason why he had not offered for Sophia, but also the reason he could not yet call a truce. When the Aldens turned him coldly away in order to welcome Elston, they had dropped the proverbial gauntlet. He would not rest until he had thrown it back at them.

"Perhaps you are right," he said. "Or perhaps you underestimate me"

[shortly afterward, at the ball] Lettie glanced at the figures just lining up for the next dance. "You might ask me to stand up with you," she said, blinking up at him prettily.

"I seldom take to the floor," he replied. "Surely you noticed."

"I did notice," she countered, coming to her feet. "And that is why you must ask me." She met his eyes and smiled shyly. "Come, Nick," she said, coaxingly. "The gossips are all aflutter on account of our being seen together again this evening. Why should we not give them more fodder for the scandal broths? Won't it be a lark? Your standing up with the little matchmaker? They'll say I vanquished your persistent bachelorhood!" Her eyes sparkled with light and laughter.

And then he bowed lightly and took her hand and led her to the floor for a stately dance. Their eyes met whenever they were abreast of each other and as they dipped, or completed turns, or joined hands, or stepped around each other. At one point, when she and Nick shared a little smile, she felt a ridiculous sense of joy, but it was a stolen joy, like a child who finds sweets in the cupboard and eats them without permission.

A Short Glossary of Regency Terms

A

abigail: a lady's maid; any female maid (servant).
Ex. "I see you've hired a new abigail."

ape leader: an old maid; based on a strange myth that single women who never bore children would end up leading apes in hell.

ague: (Pronounced ah-gyoo) Originally, malaria and the chills that went with it. Later, any respiratory infection such as a cold, fever or chills.

assembly, assemblies: Large gatherings held in the evening for gentry or the aristocracy, usually including a ball and supper. Almack's in London was the ultimate Assembly in the early part of the 19th century. A handful of high-standing society hostesses had autocratic power of attendance as they alone could issue the highly prized vouchers, or tickets. . Competition to get in was fierce. The Duke of Wellington was once famously turned away—for being late.

B

ball: A large dance requiring full dress. Refreshments were available, and sometimes a supper. Public balls required tickets; private ones, an invitation.

Banbury tale: A story with no basis in fact; A rumour; Nonsense.

banns: Banns of marriage were a public announcement in a parish church that two people intended to get married. They had to be read three consecutive weeks in a row, and in the home church of both parties. After each reading, (and this was their purpose) the audience was asked to give knowledge of any legal impediment to the marriage. If there was none, after three weeks, the couple were legally able to wed. To bypass the banns, a couple could try to get a marriage license instead. Without banns or a license, the marriage would be illegal. (null)

beau monde, the: The aristocracy and the rich upper class. The fashionable elite. In practice, anyone accepted into their circle, ie., a celebrity or an "original.".

blunt: (slang) Cash; ready money.

C

Carlton House: Given to the Prince of Wales by George III upon reaching his majority, Carlton House was in a state of disrepair (for a royal, at any rate). The house consequently underwent enormous alterations and changes, and was the London palace for the Regent. He spent a great deal of time there but eventually came to favour the palace at Brighton—an even larger extravagance. The Brighton "Pavilion" is today a museum, but Carlton House, unfortunately, no longer exists.

chamber: A private room in a house, such as a bedroom, as opposed to the parlour or dining room.

chaperon: The servant, mother, or married female relative or family friend who supervised eligible young girls in public.

chemise: A woman's long undergarment which served as a slip beneath her gown. Also, a nightdress. (Previously, the chemise was called a 'shift'.)

chintz: Patterned cloth, usually floral, with a pleasant satiny "shine" for texture.

chit: A young girl.

cit: someone who earned a living in trade.

clubs: The great refuge of the middle and upper-class man in 18th and 19th century London. Originating as coffeehouses in the 17th century, clubs became more exclusive, acquiring prime real estate on Pall Mall and St. James's Street. Membership was often by invitation only. Among the more prominent were Boodle's, White's and Brooke's. Crockford's began to dominate in the very late Regency.

consumption: Pulmonary tuberculosis (TB)

corset: A precursor of the modern bra, usually meant to constrict the waist to a fashionable measurement, as well as support the high bust required for a Regency gown. It consisted of two parts, reinforced with whalebone that got hooked together in front and then laced up in the back. The garment could also be referred to as 'the stays.'

countess: The wife of an earl in England. When 'shires' were changed to 'counties,' an earl retained the Norman title of earl; his wife, however, became a countess.

cravat: (pronounced as kruh-vaht, with the accent on the second syllable). A loose cloth that was tied around the neck in a bow. Throughout the Regency, a fashionable gentleman might labour much over this one detail of his appearance, hoping to achieve a number of different, much-coveted effects.

curricle: Two-wheeled carriage that was popular in the early 1800s. It was pulled by two horses, and deemed rather sporty by the younger set.

curtsey: The acceptable mode of greeting or showing respect by a female. By mid-century the curtsey was less in evidence except for social inferiors like maids to their betters, or by any woman presented at court.

cut: An effective means of social discouragement that involved pretending not to know or see a person who was trying to be acknowledged. A woman might use this technique to discourage unwelcome attentions from a gentleman; but many others 'cut' people, too. Getting the 'cut direct' from a social superior was vastly humiliating.

D

Debrett's: A published guide to the peerage, often called simply, "the Society Book."

dowager: The name given to a widow of rank. i.e., If you were a duchess and your husband died, and your oldest son was married, his wife would become the duchess, and you would be dowager duchess.

draper (linen draper): Merchant who sold cloth.

drawing room: A formal parlour used in polite society to receive visitors who came to pay calls during the afternoon.

F

fichu: A fichu is a large, square kerchief women wore to fill in the low neckline of a bodice. It could be made of cotton, lace, or other fabric of a lady's choosing.

first floor: The second floor in the US. The English called the floor level on which one entered from the street the "ground floor." Entertaining was never done on the ground floor.

foolscap: A paper of certain dimensions, some varieties of which originally bore a watermark of a fool's cap and bells.

footman: A liveried male servant beneath the butler but above the boy or page. He had many duties ranging from errands to lamp-trimming to waiting table, or accompanying the lady of the house to carry packages when she shopped, or to deliver calling cards when making calls.

fortnight: Two weeks.

fustian!: "Nonsense!" "Don't be absurd!"

G

gaming: Gambling. Nothing to do with 'game' in the sense of hunting, or innocent playing of games.

gig: A one-horse carriage. Light, two-wheeled, and popular in the early century.

groom: The servant who looked after the horses.

Grosvenor Square: (pronounced "Grove-nuh") A part of Mayfair, considered the most fashionable square in London.

H

hack: A hack was a general-purpose riding horse, but the term might also refer to a "Hackney Coach" which was a coach-for-hire like a taxicab today.

have a pet: a tirade; a burst of temper. (To "freak out" in today's lingo.)

L

Ladies' Mile: A (horseback) riding road in Hyde Park for women.

lady's maid: The servant who cared for her mistress's wardrobe and grooming. A French lady's maid was preferred, and she was particularly valued if she could do hair in all the fashionable styles. A lady's maid was an "upper servant," and could not be fired by the housekeeper; she might also be better educated than the lower servants.

levée: A party or reception, usually formal for the upper-class, and held in the late afternoon rather than the evening.

lorgnette: Used by ladies, the lorgnette was eyeglasses (or a monocle), held to the eyes with a long handle, or could be worn on a chain around the neck. The monocle used by a man was called a "quizzing glass."

laudanum: A mixture of opium in a solution of alcohol, it was used for pain relief and as an anesthetic.

livery: A distinctive uniform worn by the male servants in a household. No two liveries, ideally, were exactly alike. Knowing the colour of the livery of someone could enable you to spot their carriage in a crowd. The uniform itself was an old-fashioned style, including such things as a frock coat,knee breeches, powdered wigs, and a waistcoat.

M

mama: Always pronounced by the English with the accent on the second syllable. Lower classes would say 'mum,' 'mam,' 'ma,' or 'mother.'

Mayfair: The ritziest residential area of London, in the West End, and only about a half mile square in size.

mews, the: Any lane or open area where a group of stables was situated. The townhouses of the rich often had a mews behind them, or close by, where they kept their horses and equipages when not in use.

modiste: (French) seamstress.

muslin: One of the finest cottons, muslin was semi-transparent and very popular for gowns; (beneath which a chemise would be worn).

O

on-dit: (French; literally, "It is said.") During the Regency it was slang for a bit of gossip.

P

Pall Mall: A fancy street in the West End of London, notable for housing some of the most fashionable men'sclubs. Carlton House faced Pall Mall.

pantaloons: Tight-fitting pants that were worn, beginning in the early 1800s, and which pushed breeches out of fashion except for formal occasions. They had a "stirrup" at the bottom to keep them in place.

parlour: The formal or best room in a modest home. Grand houses often had more than one; a "first" or "best," and a "second parlour."

peer: A nobleman, that is, a titled gentleman with the rank of either duke, marquis, (mar-kwiss), viscount (vy-count) or baron. The titles were hereditary, and the owners were entitled to a seat in the House of Lords.

pelisse: An outdoor garment for women, reaching to the ankle or mid-calf; and often hooded.

pianoforte: The piano. Genteel young women were practically required to learn the instrument.

pin money: A colloquialism for a woman's spending money. The allowance agreed upon in her marriage settlement, to be used on small household or personal (vanity) items.

R

regent: A person who reigns on behalf of a monarch who is incapable of filling the requirements of the crown. When George III's relapse of porphyria (most scholars agree this was his malady) rendered him incapable of meeting his duties, his son, the Prince of Wales, became the Prince Regent. The actual regency lasted from 1811-1820.

reticule: A fabric bag, gathered at the top and held by a ribbon or strap; a lady's purse. Reticules became necessary when the thin muslin dresses of the day made it impossible to carry any personal effects in a pocket without it seeming bulky or unsightly. The earliest reticules (apparently called 'ridicules,' as it seemed ridiculous to carry one's valuables outside of one's clothing) were, in effect, outside pockets.

rubber: In games like whist, a rubber was a set of three or more games. To win the rubber, one had to win two out of three or three out of five.

S

season: The London social season, in which the fashionable elite descended upon the city in droves. It coincided, not unnaturally, with the sitting of Parliament, though the height of the season was only March through June.

smelling salts (smelling bottle): A small vial filled with a compound that usually contained ammonia, to be used in case of fainting.

spencer: For women, a short jacket that reached only to the high "empire" waist. For men, an overcoat without tails, also on the short side.

squire: 19th century term of courtesy (like "esquire") for a member of the landed gentry.

standing up (at a ball or Assembly) To "stand up" was to accept an invitation to dance, or to dance. Presumably the term was used because some of the formal dances required instructions from the head couple, during which the rest of the company would stand and wait their turn; and because many dances required such waiting.

T

tendre: (French adj. *soft, tender;)* Regency slang for "a soft spot"; an attraction to.

ton, **the:** (pronounced 'tawn') High society; the elite; the "in" crowd; Those of rank, with royalty at the top. To be "good ton" meant acceptance with the upper crust, and opened most any door in fashionable society. Occasionally, those without fortune or pedigree could enter the *ton*—if they were an Original, for instance, having something either sensational or highly attractive about their person or reputation; or could amuse or entertain the rich to a high degree.

tulip: In Regency slang, an effeminate man or one who dressed in exuberant colours.

V

valet: The "gentleman's gentle- man." The male equivalent of a lady's maid, his job was to keep the wardrobe in good repair and order, help dressing his master, stand behind him at dinner if required, and accompany him on his travels.

Vauxhall: A famous pleasure garden, across the Thames from London, especially popular in the Georgian era.

W

wainscoting: Wainscot was a fancy, imported oak. The term 'wainscoting' came to mean any wooden panels that lined generally the top or bottom half of the walls in a room.

waistcoat: Vest.

Made in the USA
Middletown, DE
30 April 2021